Escape to Whispering Creek

Barbara M. Britton

T0282091

Escape to Whispering Creek
COPYRIGHT 2024 by Barbara M. Britton

Cover Art by *Nicola Martinez*
White Rose Publishing, a division of Pelican Ventures, LLC
www.pelicanbookgroup.com PO Box 1738 *Aztec, NM * 87410
White Rose Publishing Circle and Rosebud logo is a trademark of Pelican Ventures, LLC

Publishing History
First White Rose Edition, 2024
Paperback Edition ISBN 978-1-5223-0478-4
Published in the United States of America

Dedication

This book is dedicated to my dear late brother-in-law, Bob Gardner. Bob handled life, and the adversity of a debilitating illness, with grace and love. He held the hand of Jesus each day and told every caregiver, "I love my Jesus."

What People are Saying

...Barbara M. Britton has crafted a delightful novel with familiar characters. Emma and Wade take center stage in Escape to Whispering Creek...Britton has a gift for using figurative language that adds color and often a touch of humor. I thoroughly enjoyed reading this novel. ~**Kathleen Neely, multi-published author of contemporary Christian fiction**

Rarely is there a book that gives you a beautiful love story and a beautiful Christian message. "Escape to Whispering Creek" does both. Barbara M. Britton is a master storyteller. This book is a must-read and a keeper on your bookshelf. ~**Olivia Rae, award-winning author of the Sword and the Cross series**

If you smell the lingering scent of candles while you read Escape to Whispering Creek, it's no mistake. That's the lively prose and vivid imagery of Barbara M. Britton's sweet romance. Her similes pop and crackle, as do the witty dialog and chemistry between Wade and Emma. You'll find yourself rooting for them while wondering how it's ever going to work out in the web of job complications, danger, confusion, and self-doubt. Additionally, if you like a strong faith thread, you'll find it here. ~**Laura DeNooyer, author of All That Is Hidden**

1

Emma Uranova raced into a parking spot near the entrance to The Runyard Group. She had two minutes before she was officially late. There should be a law that the low tire pressure light cannot appear on a Friday or before noon. The interruption was a predictable hazard from a Wisconsin winter.

As she exited her car, a man waved from beside his gray luxury sedan. Mr. Van Wenkle, the mayor of a neighboring village, rushed toward the investment office. The man reminded her of a wind socket used for advertising: tall, thin, and constantly fluttering. The last thing she needed was a ticker tape of gossip this morning.

She grabbed her backpack, locked the door to her car, and carefully navigated January's ice and snow pods covering the asphalt.

"Morning, Mayor. You're up early on a Friday." She opened the door to the office, stomped clinging snow off of her boots, and switched on all the lights. The lingering sweet scent of a holly jolly candle she had burned the day before filled the suite. A small perk of having parents in the candle business.

"I hope Ron isn't running late." Mayor Van Wenkle followed her inside and headed to the display of K-cups. "I wanted to talk with him before meeting with my zoning committee."

Over the mayor's head, an elevated screen flashed images of villa floor plans and a golf course. Pictures of the Runyard

Group's future retirement community in Elm Brook, a nearby suburb. One day she'd be helping direct activities at the Greener Groves independent living complex. Hopefully soon.

"Ron should be arriving any minute." She hurried to stash her coat, gloves, and the backpack with her personal laptop in her office cubicle.

She stopped cold when her prickly cactus, Herbie, was the only item on her desk. Where was her office computer? Had Ron or his assistant taken it for repairs? She glanced over the short partition to the prestigious reception desk where Annette usually greeted investors. No computer graced the polished wood. Strange. Neither Ron nor Annette mentioned computer issues. A weird sensation as if she were jumping in a bouncy house overtook her body and made her doubt the sturdiness of her boots. She sprinted toward Ron's office and opened the door. His computer had vanished along with his books and pictures. The room had been stripped clean of objects. What was going on?

Her heartbeat reverberated in her ears. Had they been robbed? She power-walked toward the back door to check the lock. She gripped the brass handle and gave a shoulder shove to the door. Secure as always. No criminal had entered from the rear.

Doubling back, she strode over by the mayor who casually removed a Runyard Group mug from the coffee machine. Caffeine seemed to be his focus, not the stripped-down office.

"This is strange. The computers are gone. Wires, routers, everything." Her voice rose as her heart fluttered in her chest. Something wasn't right. "I think we've been robbed." She grabbed hold of her silver necklace and rubbed the tiny tortoise charm. Fingering the smooth metal gave her a sense of calm.

"Robbed?" The mayor gulped his coffee before scanning the office space. "If the place was cleaned out, why is the flat screen still here?" He gave a nonchalant flap of his hand in the direction of the front door. "I heard the bolt click when you opened the office. No one smashed the windows."

He made good points. "That's right." The business had been locked. Nothing else was missing besides the computers and Ron's effects. Her worry eased. No sense jumping to the lowest common denominator. "I'll ask Ron about it when he gets here." She checked her watch. A few minutes after eight. Her boss would arrive soon. Should she call him? Confirm about the computers and let him know the mayor waited? Ron may be leisurely running an errand before coming into the office. A polite nudge might hurry him along.

She retrieved her phone from her backpack and pulled up Ron in her contacts. An obnoxious tone screeched through the phone. "I'm sorry, but the number you have reached has been disconnected." She ended the call. Her boss was incommunicado. Why had he changed his number? A January chill settled over her shoulders. There had to be an explanation. She'd worked for Ron for six months, and he always remained accessible. His admin Annette would have his new number. She slumped into the office chair in her cubicle and dialed Annette.

"I'm sorry, but the number—"

Her finger trembled as she ended the call. She stared at her cactus. At one time you could see a rock at Herbie's base, but his greenness had engorged the stone. On the back of the rock, it read, *The Lord is my rock, my fortress, and my deliverer.* She had won the cactus in Sunday school over fourteen years ago when she was ten. She rubbed her temples. A slight caffeine headache settled in her forehead. *Lord, I think I need a deliverer.*

Embodying every ounce of her five-foot five-inch frame, she strolled toward the mayor. He glanced from the local magazine grabbing his attention and shifted in his comfy chair.

"You get a hold of Ron?" The mayor flipped a page, but his gaze swept to her face and hovered like a laser.

A bead of sweat fled her armpit and trickled down her side under her navy blue sweater. Time to confess she was a fish out of water, except her fish was already buried under ice in a busy marketplace.

"His line is disconnected." She swallowed, but saliva stuck in her throat. A sickening burnt toast taste filled her mouth "Annette's too."

The mayor threw the magazine on the carpet. He whipped out his phone and tapped on the screen like he played a mini-whack-a-mole game. The same screech declaring the number was no longer in service filtered into the room.

"I want to see my account." He jumped to his feet. "Now," he shouted.

Her parents never yelled at her. Ever. Shouting caused the air to lose oxygen. A motherism. From the scowl on the mayor's face, the oxygen level was free falling. She tapped her boot on the rug. Hadn't she warned him something was wrong five minutes ago?

"I'm so sorry." She cleared her throat. "I don't have a company computer. I can't get a hold of Ron or Annette. I can't do anything." She was rambling. Her lifelong default setting. "Something's terribly wrong." She rubbed the silver shell of her tortoise charm. If she kept this up, she'd have a flat coin by the end of the day.

"I'm calling the chief of police and my niece. She investigates scams for the local news." The mayor paced in front of the windows. Morning light illuminated his coiffed blond hair. He stopped and jabbed a finger at her. "Don't leave."

Good thing she wore black pants because right now they were absorbing the wetness in her palms. What had she done wrong except show up for work? Did she have to stay? Mr. Van Wenkle wasn't her boss. Though, if she left, the mayor could change his story and cast the blame on her.

The mayor's face turned a troubling shade of crimson as he whisper-screamed into his phone under the screen of geriatric villas. She could almost see an oxygen alert splayed on his forehead as he uttered words that might as well have been curses. "White-collar crime...scam...attorney general."

She perched in Annette's overstuffed black-leather chair, staring over the prominent desk at a surreal office space. Had Ron and Annette run off with the investors' money? Her money? She had given them a small nest egg from her late grandmother. How could they take her money knowing she would lose every cent? The poor mayor had over a hundred thousand reasons to hate her boss.

Red and blue flashing lights came into view. Two cruisers entered the parking lot. She rose and returned to her cubicle, fishing her key chain out of her backpack. She slid the office key from her ring. A metallic odor clung to her fingers. Whoever was responsible for the building now could lock the space when they were done.

She wrapped her arms around her middle. A strange ethereal sensation overtook her body like a melatonin-induced dream. Only it wasn't. She steadied herself by gripping the cubicle partition. Two police officers entered the office. *God give me wisdom.* The time had come to let the world know she wasn't a thief or a liar.

Too bad she didn't have her own police chief on speed

dial.

~*~

The police detective in front of her clicked his pen and set it on his pad of paper. "You don't remember anything else that could help us contact or locate Mr. Runyard?"

She shrugged and held her shoulders high hoping the officer would see her ignorance. "I've only been here six months. I was hired to run the senior community once it opened. I worked on policies. I didn't handle any of the money. We were all busy trying to break ground on the facility." So, she thought. Apparently knowing Ron and Annette were football fans and that they both liked salty black licorice wasn't pertinent information. She could give directions to the tanning booth Ron frequented, but his home address drew a blank. "Can I go? I'm in the dark as much as you." Pitch dark. Plus, she needed food and caffeine to stave off a massive headache.

Poor detective. Emma was only doing this interview as a courtesy to the mayor. She had waited three hours answering questions and had tried to console a few investors who had wandered in, but it was time to leave her former workspace. The mayor had been busy pounding a wasp nest with a stick. Too bad he hadn't gotten more pertinent information from Ron when they were playing eighteen holes of golf.

The detective glanced out the front windows where people from nearby businesses had gathered to hear the mayor rant. "Are you sure you can't remember anyone who had a beef with your boss?"

"Everyone loved Ron." If only they knew his personality was a façade. "In all my time here, we only had one visitor who got Ron upset. I was showing Ron my customer service software and didn't get an introduction." One person out of dozens didn't seem important. The visitor interrupted one of the rare times she'd discussed her personnel program with Ron. "Ron seemed startled by the guy's appearance. He even dropped my flash drive under his desk."

"Could you describe him? Give a name?" The officer looked hopeful.

She shook her head. "Not really. Ron ushered me out of his office and closed the door." Maybe it was nothing. Ron had a steady stream of customers. Or should she say victims.

The officer handed her a business card. "If you think of anything else that might help us get in touch with Runyard, please give us a call."

"Thank you." She accepted the card and cast one last glance at the scrolling images of the senior community that would never break ground. Her dream job lay shattered on the speckled carpeting.

She slipped on her coat, pulled the hood over her messy brunette bob, and slung her backpack over her shoulder. She grabbed one last cup of free K-cup coffee and clutched Herbie's container as she exited her former place of employment. The Ron Runyard Scam Group. A blast of frigid air tingled on her face. She needed the Lord to be a fortress right now and shield her from curious eyes as she bee-lined it for her car. Today, she called into question the choice of sunflower yellow for her Bug.

She balanced her belongings and hopped into her car. Her software flash drive lay in the cup holder. Good thing she didn't leave it in the office, or her custom senior citizen software would have vanished with her boss. Reaching for the backseat, she unzipped a small pocket on her backpack and placed the drive into a safe space. She put her coffee cup in the holder and wrapped her scarf around Herbie in the passenger seat. With a quick glance in the rearview mirror, she hit the gas pedal.

A black SUV pulled out of a parking space farther down the row. The vehicle matched every move she made from pulling out of the lot to turning on to a side street. Was she being trailed? This was insane! She sped toward the interstate to Milwaukee and made sure she didn't catch the attention of anymore police officers. The SUV followed her onto the ramp.

She gripped the cold steering wheel with trembling fingers. How was she going to lose the tail? The hospital complex flashed in her mind. Last year, shortly before she graduated college, her dad had suffered a heart attack. She knew the hospital grounds and could lose the suspicious vehicle among the numerous buildings and parking garages.

Exiting toward the hospital and medical college, she zigzagged through the massive complex and backed to a wall in an underground space near the specialty clinic. *Please Lord, don't have them find me.* She slid so her head couldn't be seen over the seat. How long did one wait to avoid a newsperson or stalker? Tears welled in her eyes. She wasn't a bad person. Her morning had turned into a Most Wanted show. Ron and Annette didn't seem like criminals. Were they really scammers? Con artists? Had she missed the signs? She blew out a long breath to slow her unsteady heart rate. How could she have known they were crooks if deceit was their specialty? They acted completely normal and trustworthy, and she had soaked it up.

A car horn broke her concentration. Her heart boomed in her chest. She peeked. Someone had come around the parking garage corner and drifted toward an oncoming vehicle. Drifting. Perfect word for her life at the moment. No job. No paycheck. No savings. Possibly being followed. What a mess.

She huddled for an eternity until her toes became dreamsicles. No black SUV with a license plate starting with

NI drove past her hideout. Straightening her crunched body, she started her car, drove out of the garage, and headed home toward Milwaukee, checking her mirrors constantly.

When she exited off of I-94 and approached her apartment complex, traffic slowed. Up ahead she glimpsed a news van. Not one, but two. A black SUV by the main building entrance caught her attention. Was it the same one that had followed her from work? "Lord, what is happening to me?" She prayed her Facebook picture wasn't plastered on television and that reporters weren't hounding her neighbors. Why did Ron have to ensnare the well-connected? Money, that's why. They had more than ten-thousand pennies to invest.

She swerved onto a side street and zigzagged down lesser traveled roads before finding an open parking spot on a street about a mile from her home. She placed her Beetle in park, and rested her head against the seat, staring at the beige ceiling. Fortunately, no one had chased her this time, but her nerves were a frazzled mess. She should cry, but for whom? Herself? The investors she thought of as friends, until now? If Ron had disappeared with the investment funds, elderly people wouldn't have a new retirement community. Her hopes of managing an independent living facility had disintegrated. None of this made sense. Why had God allowed this to happen?

Digging her phone out of her backpack, she called her mom. Her parents would be at the fashion mall, logging inventory and helping customers at Home ScentSations. She could hide out in the stockroom all day. Her mom answered on the third ring.

"Slow day at the office?" Her mom's cheery voice brought a momentary sense of relief.

"I wish." A flood of emotion crashed her seconds of normalcy. A sob threatened to burst forth, but she coughed it away. "Mom, Ron and Annette are gone."

"Really. Did they go away for the weekend? Leave you in charge?"

"No, gone, gone. I can't get a hold of them, and an investor thinks they absconded with all the money." Her hand flailed as badly as the mayor's. "The police came, reporters are at my apartment, someone followed me —"

"Where are you? Tell me you're okay?" Her mom's cheerfulness had died.

"I'm hiding out on a side street." Grabbing hold of her silver necklace, she rubbed the tiny tortoise charm. Her grandmother had given her the necklace on her fifteenth birthday. At least she still had the jewelry. Too bad her inheritance money was in jeopardy. "I don't know what to do or where to go. If I come by the store, I don't want to cause a scene with reporters showing up. Some of the investors have ties to the government, police, and local television stations." A flash on the top of her phone showed an incoming call. Samantha, her best friend was calling from Tennessee. "Sam's beeping in."

"That might be a sign. You loved spending Christmas…there." Her mom whispered the last word as if someone listened to their call. "And it's so close and warm."

A warm location near Wisconsin in January was impossible. Mom was spooked.

"Thank you for returning my call." Her mom babbled in a stern voice. "We have two-hundred defective candles that won't burn. The wick is melted into the wax. Go and do something about it."

Emma's throat hurt. "I love you, Mom. Tell Dad."

"I expect the full amount by the end of the day."

The contact ended.

A tear banked around Emma's nose and settled on her lip.

Salt sizzled on her tongue. "Please Lord, keep my mom and dad safe. They don't know You yet." She didn't want anyone harassing her parents.

She called Sam. God had provided a true friend in Sam and an eternal lifeline.

"Hey, I thought you were busy." Hearing Sam's voice eased Emma's panic.

"Fluff some pillows. I'm coming back to Whispering Creek." She glanced around to make sure the black SUV hadn't found her. "And this time, I'll need to buy underwear."

2

Wade Donoven attempted to de-claw his left hand. Tingles traveled across his palm. He'd lost count on his physical therapy reps. If he were honest, he'd receive a D for deficient. He swiveled in his black leather office chair and glanced at the clock on the wall. One minute after five on a Friday evening. He doubted a service call would come in this late to Donoven and Sons Electric. With the weekend beginning, Nashville would be plugged-in and ready to serenade patrons. No customer would be worried about changing a tricky fuse. Even if a call came into the office, he was useless. The doctor hadn't released him to drive on his healing right leg, and his left arm had a twitchy mind of its own. Darn auto accident.

He rotated and faced his abnormally tidy desk. Would he ever get back to normal? Be the mover and shaker business owner and not the tragic accident victim. *Soon. Please, God, soon.* How embarrassing at thirty-two to be temporarily living with his parents and relying on them to drive him around the city. The cost of shared-ride companies had consumed too much of the medical allowance from his insurance company. His parents would have to suffice as chauffeurs for now. Limiting the amount of money the insurance paid out was a top priority. He didn't want Donoven and Sons to be dropped because an uninsured motorist demolished their work van. Who was he kidding? The driver demolished him, too. Widening his palm, he fought the pull of his traitorous muscles to clamp his hand into a fist. Minimal nerve pain accompanied his success.

Francine appeared in the doorway to his office. "I'm heading out." His office manager tied the belt on her coat. "Mike should return soon. The Morgans decided to replace their panel." Sure, they did. Dad had a way of maximizing his service calls to save on repeat travel costs. Francine gripped her purse and forced a perky smile. "There's leftover subs in the mini fridge if you get hungry."

"Thanks. I appreciate it." He might check out the sandwiches later if his dad took too long finishing the wiring. His stomach rumbled at the thought. Eating was something he could do one-handed.

"I'll finish the work orders on Monday before I leave." She bit her lip. "You sure you'll be okay while I'm out for surgery?"

Whether he was or wasn't, he couldn't have Francine cancel her knee replacement. He'd handle her office duties until the doctor allowed him to go on service calls. He needed hand strength to grab a steering wheel and a flexible right foot to push a gas pedal. Maybe filing papers would rehab his stiff left hand. Even if a boat load of invoices buried his body, he wasn't going to let Francine worry about the business sinking in her absence.

He stood, balancing on his cane. "I'll be fine. Work is what the doctor ordered." No one needed to know the doctor prescribed light duty. Too much lighter and he'd dry up and blow away. "You just focus on getting rid of your pain and healing well."

"You've come a long way since the accident. By the time I return, you'll be good as new. We can race each other to the copier." She gave him one of her cheery, customer-engaging smiles and limped toward the main doors of the building. "Take care, Wade. Enjoy the weekend."

"You too, Fran." Good as new? He hoped so. He wouldn't be using a cane for support and rehabbing an arm if a distracted driver hadn't blown a light, slammed into his work van, and sent him careening into a utility pole. He'd been trying to surface from this nightmare for seven weeks. He didn't do useless well.

His stomach growled. Fran had planted the idea of food into his brain, and now it lodged in his psyche. A snack wouldn't spoil dinner. Fuse box work took time, and his dad didn't finish jobs as fast anymore.

Using the cane to absorb the weight his right leg couldn't, he hobbled through the hall and toward the reception area. The odor of onion permeated Fran's workspace. Had she checked the fridge before offering him leftovers? Just like Fran not to get his hopes up if another employee had grabbed the subs. He opened the mini fridge with his index finger and slowly grabbed a wrapped sandwich, forcing his fingers to stay in place around his meal. Shutting the door with his foot, he took a step toward Fran's desk. Even clean, the long countertop resembled a party store. Colorful Post-its stuck to her computer and small stuffed animals stared at her chair. Not very professional, but no one could match Fran's friendliness or keyboarding skills. Well, he'd come close to her words per minute before the crash.

He leaned against the long solid desk, hooked his cane on the countertop edge, and placed the sandwich a safe distance from Fran's work area. When he unwrapped the sub, an aroma of pepperoni and salami filled his senses. His mouth watered on cue. He wished Dad was here to enjoy the peppery spice. He hated that his dad had to pick up the slack in the business. Cole was coming into town for a few days to help with some projects, but he didn't trust his brother's dependability. With a new girlfriend and bid work out in

Sperry's Crossing, Cole acted like coming to Nashville was a hardship. Poor baby.

Halfway through the foot-long, he decided to save the rest for later. He re-wrapped the sandwich the best he could with his right hand and grabbed his cane. His left hand cradled the sub. He took a step toward the mini-fridge and another. The cane tip slipped on the smooth tile flooring. His support vanished. His right leg buckled. He reached to grab hold of the counter, but his claw of a left hand seized, maintaining a grip on the sandwich like it was a prized baseball. He cursed as his back hit the cold floor tiles and a bruising ache settled in his skull.

Only after staring at the fluorescent lights on the ceiling for a moment did he realize his claw oozed oil. Oil that had dripped on the floor. Spicy-scented oil.

"Should have gone with the mayo, Fran." He laughed because if he thought too hard about being taken down by sandwich dressing, he would cry. Cry at all the pain, the rehab, the hospital bills, and the feeling like a failure. He was a hindrance to himself. To his parents. To everyone who worked at Donoven and Sons. How could he run a company when it took twice as long to get things done? No, ten times as long. Some work he couldn't even do. *God, why did this happen to me? I am so done with it all.*

The door from the garage slammed.

"Wade, you here?" His dad's voice boomed in the empty office space.

Closing his eyes, a tear slipped out. *No Dad. I'm not. The real Wade Donoven isn't here.*

3

Emma turned onto the county road leading to her best friend Samantha's home. If Mr. Ted, the girls' former neighbor and grandfatherly mentor, hadn't died and left Sam his house in Tennessee, Emma would be hiding out in Wisconsin. Being far from the fallout of Runyard's crime, she had tranquility and a chance to think about the next steps in her life. And the next steps had better come quick because without a paycheck and with evaporated savings, she barely had any funds.

Her stomach gurgled and ached. She should blame the dollar hotdogs roasting at the quick mart. Rehashing how her ten-thousand-dollar inheritance from her grandmother disappeared into Runyard's secret offshore accounts, she readied to pull over and puke.

She slowed her Beetle and put on her turn signal. The bridge over the creek was up ahead on the left. Tall oaks and pines swayed gently in the nighttime shadows as if welcoming her back to Whispering Creek. Four weeks prior, she had celebrated Christmas here with Sam and her new boyfriend, Cole. The happiness and joy seemed like a decade ago. She prayed her bestie's home would provide a refuge and a foundation to find a part-time job.

Checking her rearview mirror, she made sure she hadn't been followed to her haven. No headlights glowed in the darkness this close to midnight. She wished she could shake the insecurity that someone was trailing her. South of Springfield, Illinois, she remembered to shut off the tracking on her phone and to power it down. She scanned every gas mart parking lot for a black SUV with Wisconsin plates. Swallowing the sour saliva in her mouth, she uttered a quick prayer to God. A truckload of prayers had been offered on her journey. She didn't want to bring trouble to her friend's porch steps. She'd do everything possible to keep Sam safe.

After crossing the bridge, she banked right toward Mr. Ted's house, now Sam's house. If anyone on this earth could make her feel safe it was her bestie. Emma wouldn't be praying to God if it wasn't for Sam. Her friend invited her to church, brought her to Sunday school, convinced her to try youth group, and whisked her to the pastor when Emma desired to follow Jesus. Too bad her own parents thought her relationship with God manifested as a personal mystical experience. She could sure use their prayer support right about now.

Light flooded from the living room window. She parked on the asphalt next to Sam's white SUV and quickly texted her mom that she had arrived without mentioning where. Stepping onto the drive, she stretched her arms toward the stars and eased the tension from her spine. A blanket of evergreens fragranced the air with the aroma of Christmas and country living. With her movements, a floodlight on the shed brightened the shadows. *Thank You, Lord, for safe travels.*

The front door swung open illuminating the planked porch and the walkway.

Sam jogged down the porch steps in her yoga pants, a Green Bay hoodie, and slippers. After rounding the back of the Bug, Sam wrapped her in a bear hug. "Em. I'm so glad you're here."

Emma gave her close-as-sisters friend a long squeeze. The unevenness of Sam's chest was a reminder of a battle with breast cancer and failed breast reconstruction. Sam had been positive and brave through her medical procedures. *Lord, help me be strong like Sam.*

"I'm glad to be here, too." Her voice came out breathy from their enthusiastic embrace. "It wasn't a bad drive until dark. I don't want to see any more headlights. Only a soft bed, fluffy pillow, and a bathroom."

"Well, I have all three." Sam hugged her one more time before pulling away. "I'll help get your things."

Emma hesitated before closing the car door. "I don't have much. I didn't run the gauntlet at my apartment to pack clothes. Reporters were stationed outside." Still in her sweater and slacks from work, the cool evening air goose pimpled her flesh. She had driven without the bulkiness of her winter coat. Was the shiver solely due to the cold? Tennessee was thirty degrees warmer than Milwaukee. She glanced at the shed. "Do you think my car will fit in there?"

Sam tucked hair behind her ear. "It should. I can leave the UTV outside. It's been mild." Sam's nose wrinkled. "You don't think the press will follow you down here, do you?"

"I hope not." Emma rubbed her stiff neck. She glanced at the stars above and silently asked the Lord for protection. She didn't want a circus on Sam's doorstep. "Though, I never thought I would be associated with an investment fraud scandal. If I had, I certainly wouldn't have bought a car that screams 'look at cute little me.'"

Sam laughed. The best sound of the day. "Your life screams 'look at cute little me.'"

"Only because my friend is a hottie."

"That's not true." Sam strode toward the shed. "Lopsided average beauty, maybe. I'll start the utility vehicle and park it by the trees. You can pull right in."

"We won't bother Gretta and Ernie, will we?" Sam's elderly neighbors lived down the lane.

Lit by the shed's lantern, Sam's expression radiated wide

awake energy. "Oh no. They'll be sound asleep. I told them you were coming." The shed door rose. "Cole and I go out for late night rides all the time, and they never hear us."

"Rain check for later. I didn't get to drive the UTV much when I was here in December. Your dad hogged the wheel." Emma hopped back in her car and started it. Must be nice to go for romantic rides in the hills with a boyfriend. She glanced at Herbie snug in the passenger seat. "It's just you and me, babe."

Once Sam pulled the UTV from the shed, Emma drove inside. Inquiring minds wouldn't spy the bright yellow paint sitting among all the greenery.

She squeezed out of the side of the Beetle, with her backpack and her coat tucked under her arm. After grabbing Herbie, she met Sam in the drive. The faint scent of gasoline marred the peaceful scenery.

"That's all you brought?" Sam's voice sounded like she finally understood the words mad dash. "We will definitely need to go shopping."

If Emma wasn't unemployed with a depleted bank account, a shopping day would have some appeal. She'd have to live off of her charge cards because a girl couldn't survive without extra pairs of underwear and comfortable leggings.

"I guess I missed the fugitive 101 class in college. I didn't have a to-go bag stashed in my car, only a few boxes of discontinued candles stuffed in my trunk." She yawned and followed Sam into her sanctuary of a home. "Today has been a nightmare." One she hoped never to experience again.

"Let me help you with your stuff. You must be exhausted." Sam grabbed Herbie. "I remember planting these in Sunday school. I don't know where mine ended up. Probably in the trash. I don't have a green thumb like you." Sam set Herbie in the center of the kitchen table. "Are you hungry, Em?"

"I've had enough fast food for the month." She plopped her backpack on a kitchen chair and placed her coat over the back. "But if you have hot water?" She unzipped the top compartment of her computer bag and held up a bag of chamomile tea. "My body still feels like I'm driving on the highway. I don't think I can sleep without this."

"I have my Emma box left from Christmas. My tea might be fresher." Sam winked and reached in the cabinet, drawing out an off-white box with lavender writing. She heated two mugs of water in the microwave and came and sat across from Emma with the brewing tea.

Emma took her cup and breathed in the warm vapor of tempered sweetness wafting from the mug. If she closed her eyes, she could almost believe she lounged in Milwaukee with her bestie.

Sam grasped Emma's hand like they were on a playground running to snag the teeter-totter. "I'm so sorry you lost your job. I wish you were visiting under happier circumstances. Everything was going so well when you were here last month."

Ignorantly well. Emma's throat tightened as her eyes tingled. "I can't believe my dream job is …poof…over. I had been working on a new software program to use at the senior community, and now there's no retirees to help and no computers to install it in. It's all gone. Like a mirage." At least she hadn't left her laptop or flash drive at work. That would have been a disaster.

She slipped her hand from Sam's warm fingers and tasted her tea. The heat almost burned her tongue. "I can't believe Ron and Annette were scammers, and I didn't even notice. Who has fake co-workers? I was the last one holding the office key while they had my savings in their pockets." She blew on the surface of her drink. "I feel like I'm on some streaming show. Undercover Dupe."

Sam leaned closer, her forearms resting on the tabletop. "You're one of the most intuitive people I know. Your boss was a professional criminal. He snagged a mayor in his trap, plus other older and wiser people. Don't beat yourself up." Sam's expression softened, yet confidence beamed from every soft line in her face. "God will get you through this. He'll get both of us through this."

Emma believed that truth. She attempted a smile through quivering lips. She didn't want to be a burden to her best friend. Having a place to stay was wonderful, but she wouldn't take any of Sam's money. Finding a job was number one on her to-do list, either a temporary job here or one back in Wisconsin. Although, her association with con artists in an investment scam might hurt her chances back home. Mayor Van Wenkle and his reporter niece were likely lighting up the airwaves in Milwaukee.

The Bible verse Psalm 18:2 nestled under Herbie's base flashed in her mind. *Lord, I need a rock, fortress, deliverer, and a job recruiter. Now that you slammed the door with the Runyard Group, could you please open a career window?*

She slumped in her chair and willed the tears in her eyes not to drip down her cheeks. "Thanks for letting me hide out here with you. I don't know what I would've done without your help."

"You are welcome to stay as long as you like. My life has been pretty boring when Cole's not around. Especially without you nearby." A tiny grin enlivened Sam's lips. "I've been working on getting my teaching license transferred and sending out resumes. I have an interview on Thursday for a first-grade position here. The sooner I get back in the classroom, the better. For my sanity."

"Kids love you. Schools will be clamoring to have you come teach. I'll pray your interview goes well." Emma encouraged her friend whose lifelong dream had been to instruct children. "And speaking of love." She attempted to waggle her eyebrows, but her coordination failed. "How's Cole doing?"

Sam tapped her fingernails against her mug. Wafts of calming tea traveled across the table. "Between the industrial park construction in Sperry's Crossing and helping his dad with electrical projects in Nashville, he doesn't have a lot of free time." A slight blush colored her friend's cheeks. "And he spends his free time with me."

"Guess I'm going to have to buy your neighbor some binoculars to keep an eye on you two." Emma winked as she imagined crusty old Ernie sitting on his porch.

"Em!" Sam's face turned a robust shade of fuchsia.

"I'm only kidding. Knowing Ernie, he has a set of binoculars." She grinned and stretched to release the exhaustion overtaking her body. Sam deserved every good thing to come her way after battling cancer, losing a breast, and losing their family friend to a heart attack. "Can Cole's brother help out now? Isn't he co-boss with their dad?"

"Wade hasn't fully recovered from his accident." Sam frowned. An uncommon sight. "Hopefully, he'll be able to jump back into the business. His leg and shoulder were badly hurt."

"Ouch. Poor guy. Shoulders can be tricky. My aunt's shoulder hasn't fully recovered from her fall and that was two years ago."

"Cole's mom has been trying to help Wade stay on top of his physical therapy. But...poor Linda. Wade is difficult at times." Sam sipped her tea. "Cole and I were going to drive to Nashville and see his parents after church on Sunday. We were planning to stay overnight so Cole could pull a shift on Monday, but now that you're here, Cole can go on his own."

"Don't change your plans on account of me." Her stomach clenched. She didn't want to burden Sam and make her miss her date. Besides, traveling to Nashville would place even more distance between her and Runyard's crime. If she had been followed here, no one would know she was leaving Whispering Creek or had a connection to Cole's family. "I'd love to visit Nashville and see Linda and Mike again if you and Cole don't mind. He has such sweet parents." She yawned. A yawn that had a little squeak to it. "I could use some fun. Guess I need some sleep, too."

Sam rose and grabbed the empty mugs. "That's great. I'll let Linda know you're coming. She always asks about you and tells me how much fun she had at Christmas."

"She sent me her stuffing recipe." Emma stood and arched her back. "I haven't tried it yet." Nor would she be whipping up a feast anytime soon. "How long are we staying?" With her dire finances, she needed to find a job soon.

"A day or two. Just enough time to stay on top of work orders and keep the customers happy." Sam rinsed their mugs and set them by the kitchen sink. Her eyes widened with a conspiratorial energy. "Hey, want to have a sleepover? It will be like when we were neighbors. You can share Ted's old room with me."

Thank You, Lord, that I have a friend who knows me so well.

"Whoo hoo. That's the best offer I've had all day. Good thing I'm still an edge hugger." She rounded the table and embraced Sam.

After having her life turned upside down this morning, or technically, yesterday morning, she didn't want to sleep alone. Her shoulders ached from death-gripping the steering wheel wondering if one of Ron's desperate victims would locate her and do her harm. She prayed for God to protect her family and their business. She didn't want any adversity to rub off on her parents.

"I'm so glad you came. I've missed you." Sam held on tight.

Closing her eyes, Emma allowed the comfort and security that only her friend could give to wrap around her unease. Sam and Mr. Ted had led her to Jesus. She needed her Lord now more than ever since a sink hole had opened under her footing. Being in Whispering Creek was an answered prayer. She needed faithful friends who could pray for her and give her wise counsel. Her parents meant well, but they weren't believers. They used their pristine Bible as a coaster.

Stepping out of the hug, Sam grabbed Emma's backpack and turned off the lights. "Tonight, we sleep and tomorrow…"

"We find underwear!" A simple task in a simple town was all Emma could wrap her head around. She lumbered toward a firm mattress and fluffy pillows. As she face-planted onto the bed, she mumbled, "Good night, Herbie."

~*~

Emma pushed her black cart to the cash register. After sleeping late, she and Sam grabbed lunch in nearby Sperry's Crossing and made a pit stop at the main store to buy clothes. Nude, black, and spotted underwear rested on top of jeans, long-sleeved tops, a sweater, and casual boots. She grabbed the panties and set them before the middle-aged cashier. Not even the soft cotton could calm her quickening pulse rate. How was she going to pay for her purchase with no money to her name?

The clerk unclipped the panties from their hangers and began ringing Emma's selections. "Did you find everything you needed?"

Not a job, peace of mind, or my savings. "Yes." Forcing a smile, she tried not to think about the interest rate on her credit card.

Two-hundred fourteen dollars and seventy-five cents flashed on the computer screen facing the customer side of the counter. It might as well have been two thousand dollars. She only had a few twenties to her name. Job hunting instantly kicked into high gear. If only employers were clamoring to hire a woman duped by con artists. How many jobs flew under the radar and paid in cash? A city might have more options than a small town.

"You can insert your card now." The clerk folded the clothes and stuffed them in a gray shopping bag. She cast a glance at the Saturday line of customers.

Emma shoved her card into the chip reader. She had done this mundane motion hundreds of times but never before had her fingers moistened the plastic. The firm financial road beneath her feet had disappeared.

Sam grasped the shopping bag. "You found a lot of nice things even though I would have loaned you some shirts. That red sweater really brings out the amber in your eyes. I wish they had a teal one in my size."

Little did Sam realize that red symbolized Emma's bank account.

"Yeah." Emma forced a smile to hide being destitute. "They have fantastic prices here." Sale prices. She needed more than one outfit with a road trip to Nashville and a visit with Cole's parents looming. Pretty soon, her get-out-of-town clothes would need a wash.

A soothing, melodic dinging brought Emma into reality.

"You can remove your card." At the push of a button, the cashier produced a receipt.

The burger Emma ate at lunch solidified in her gut as she received paper evidence to the fact that she paid with invisible money.

Lord, I need a job and fast. Preferably one with a reputable company where the boss doesn't abscond with everyone's savings.

Following Sam out of the store, she thanked God for one answered prayer. The much-needed petition for undergarments had been crossed off her list.

4

Wade sank into his parent's blue cloth couch and stretched his unsteady leg onto the coffee table. Cheering football fans enlivened the television screen. His Nashville team was one step closer to the Super Bowl with a win. He couldn't fathom a more perfect Sunday than relaxing after church in front of the TV with his favorite sports team.

His mom hurried into the living room, head tilted, trying to secure an earring. Her eyebrows arched as she scanned his jersey and athletic pants.

"If you're going to change before Cole and Sam arrive, you'd better get a move on. Sam is bringing Emma. The friend we met at Christmas."

Change? Move on? A shuffle was more like it with his injured leg. His mom's selective hearing must be getting worse. He'd stated earlier that he wasn't interested in going on a date and being a 'plus one' for Cole and his girlfriend. He wasn't the Nashville Welcome Wagon, nor was he in the mood for a matchmaking scheme. Cole could entertain Sam and her friend.

"There's no need to change. I'm not going. Besides we have a slight lead." He glanced at the score. "You'll have more fun without me."

His mom's mouth gaped. Her death stare had him slouching into the couch cushions for protection.

He'd seen a lot of that incriminating look lately, but he had never officially agreed to this outing. At thirty-two, he was a grown man. His silence wasn't an 'I'm in' to her plans, but a way to keep from saying something that he'd regret. His parents had taken care of him since the accident, but his independence was on the horizon.

"You like barbecue." Enunciating the dish wouldn't get him to change his mind. "Besides, Cole is driving all this way to help you and your father stay on top of service calls. The least you can do is eat dinner with him."

Prodigal son saves the day. Rescues his claw-handed, gimpy brother by keeping the family business afloat. Big whoop. He didn't need a front row seat to that movie.

Cheers erupted from the stands. Great. He'd missed the red zone catch. His shoulders tensed as he endured the hawk-eyed glare of his mom.

"Cole will understand." His brother would probably prefer it. Who wants to eat with a man needing a bib? Accidentally knocking over drinks. "I'll see Cole plenty at the office."

With her head shaking and her crossed arms, his mother was the poster girl for parental disappointment. Oh no, she brought out the nuclear option—glistening eyes. Couldn't she understand his aversion to awkward dining? Awkward for him and nobody else.

"It'll be fine, Mom." He repositioned his leg and focused on the fourth down conversion.

"I didn't make anything for you to eat. You'll have to order in." The last few words trailed after his mom as she stomped across the foyer and down the hall. A waft of her designer perfume stayed to heap more guilt on him.

Dad appeared from his home office and hooked a thumb in the direction his wife had fled. "What did you do? Your mother seems upset."

"Nothing." He squared his shoulders to weather another explosion. Dad hardly ever reprimanded him. They were business partners. Too bad the crash made him a burden at work and at home. His parents had taken him in and had been helping with his recovery. Fortunately, he inched closer to escaping physical therapy prison and moving back to his own place. "I couldn't be bribed with food to go out with y'all tonight."

"It's a family dinner." Displeasure bubbled under the surface of his dad's customer-pleasing voice. "And I'm paying."

"Then you should be happy with one less meal to pay for. And it's not a family dinner with Sam and her friend sitting across the table." His jaw clenched. The score increased by seven points. He'd missed the touchdown.

"Suit yourself. But if anything happens—"

"I'll be fine. Nothing is going to happen to me." No oil-slick floor waited to take him out again. He had to return to living on his own and in his own house sometime.

Dad ambled over to the end of the couch and stood like a judge about to pronounce a sentence.

"I can't come back to you on the floor again." His dad's statement broke apart in his throat as he squeezed the bridge of his nose. "I can't Wade. And I won't."

His dad's emotion threatened to crumble the determination to stay home. Hadn't he tried to live up to his dad's expectations? Now he was tarnishing them. How could he go and make a fool of himself, eating and drinking with an unpredictable claw? Oh, how he wished he could get back to calling the shots in his life and not be dependent on others.

The sing-song chimes of the doorbell filled the foyer before the door swung open.

"We're here." Cole's upbeat greeting frayed every damaged nerve in Wade's hand and sucker punched his gut. Little brother had arrived to receive the accolades that should have been reserved for the son who busted his hump the last few years to grow Donoven and Sons Electric. Cole had abandoned the business to chase his former girlfriend's music dreams. Now the prodigal arrived to fanfare.

"Come on in." His dad exuded happiness. Faker. The old man raced to hug Cole and shake hands with Cole's harem.

Mom raced from her bedroom and embraced Cole, Sam, and the mystery date who practically leapt into his mom's arms. The woman looked like she'd stepped out of an anime comic with her short dark hair and huge brown eyes. The girl could hypnotize you with one glimpse. He shivered. Not his type.

On cue, the group huggers turned in his direction. Pathetic brother on aisle one.

He grunted a "Hey," barely lifting his hand off the cushion. Hopefully, they would get the hint that he wasn't partaking in the festivities by his elevated leg and wrinkled workout clothes. His aftershave could be called eau de stale potato chip.

"Oh, football's on." Comic book girl proceeded to rush over to the couch. "It's a close game."

She hovered behind him, over his left shoulder. Couldn't she have stayed by the door? If he was rude and ignored her, he'd get an earful from his parents. A headache pulsed behind his temples, so he didn't need another lecture this evening. He shifted and made brief eye contact.

"I'm Emma." Her hand shot out as if she was catching a short five-yard pass. This girl was pushy too. "You must be Wade. I've heard a lot about you."

Cole and Sam had no business discussing his situation with strangers. Hadn't they heard about medical privacy? It wasn't his fault some guy sped through a red light and smashed into his work van. He shifted and shook her hand with his healthy one, deciding against a death grip. The girl would be gone momentarily, and he could get back to the game.

"Well, I haven't heard anything about you." The truth sprung from his mouth before he could censor himself. He'd use his pain as an excuse. His claw had begun to throb.

A disgruntled huff came from the vicinity of the foyer. His mom would give him a tongue lashing later about proper introductions.

"That might be a good thing." His almost-date barked out a laugh and leaned over the back of the couch. She fingered a silver necklace, rubbing it like a genie might appear. "I'm not popular with some people at the moment."

Her hundred-watt smile had him squinting as the stranger invaded his personal space. Couldn't he finish watching the game in peace? He didn't want to make conversation with a woman he'd never see again.

"Good to meet you then, Emma." He forced a grin hoping the measure was enough to please his mother.

"Wade, we're heading out." His dad's announcement garbled the game analysis.

Thank You, Lord. Seconds until solitude.

"Have fun." Wade stifled an elated grin.

Emma propped her hip on the back of the sofa. "You're not going with us?" She stared at his elevated leg like she was an orthopedist. "You're staying by yourself?"

Captain Obvious in a spiky wig.

"I don't want to be the fifth wheel." He'd be the sixth wheel, but who was counting except the matchmaking squad.

The couch squatter yawned and fanned a hand in front of her face. "You know, after driving to Tennessee, staying up late, and all the craziness of the past two days, I don't mind hanging out here with you. There's nothing like Sunday night football."

What did she say? He whipped around sending shock waves into his shoulder. 'No' boomed through his brain. He didn't need company, or this woman thinking this was a date, or worse, her thinking she was a babysitter.

His mother's smile hit him like a laser.

"If you're sure, Emma? Make yourself at home." His mom's tone bled sugar. "Our card's on file at the pizza place. Wade has the number in his phone."

"Glad you're feeling better, Wade." Sam waved as Cole tugged her toward the door.

Cole gave him a salute. "Have fun. Eat a slice for me."

"Wait." He rocked to grab his cane and came up short.

His family disappeared like they were dashing to the finish line of a 5K race.

This couldn't be happening. His loved ones were leaving him with a yappy Yankee.

Emma kicked off her shoes and curled into the chair next to the couch. Mom would have scolded him if he placed his feet on the cloth cushion.

"Do you like thin crust or thick?" Her cheerful tone seemed well-rested. "Can we get half the pizza without meat? I like extra cheese instead of sausage or pepperoni."

The opposing team's receiver danced in the end zone.

Could this day get any worse? So much for his solitude.

As fans cheered, a hot flash of pain traveled down his arm. He grabbed his phone with his healthy hand to place the pizza order while his other arm tingled. His claw had awakened, and so had Sam's friend.

5

Emma relaxed against the wingback chair and willed her eyelids to stay open for what felt like the hundredth time. Had it only been an hour since Sam and the Donovens left for dinner? She enjoyed watching football, but her hometown team wasn't playing so she didn't have an urgency to track the score. Her host, who was dressed as a lineman with the number seventy-eight on his jersey, had been ignoring her. Why did she stay? She should have gone with Sam and ordered a double espresso.

Wade rubbed his left arm and grimaced at the screen. Her heart went out to the Donoven family and what had happened to them in recent weeks. She had helped her mother keep Home ScentSations running after her dad's heart attack. Between college courses, supervising her dad's care, and pulling the occasional shift at the candle store, she didn't know how she stayed sane. She glanced at the ceiling. *Sorry God. You gave me the strength to keep going.*

The doorbell rang.

Her mouth pulled tight at the vision of crispy crust and tangy tomato sauce.

Wade glanced toward the foyer. His backside didn't move from the cushion indentation. Whatever happened to Southern hospitality?

"I'll get it." She wasn't in rehab. No sense letting Wade hobble with his cane and balance a box one-handed.

A young man verified the name on the order and handed her the pizza box. He hesitated. "Is there a tip?"

Money? Like cash? Like the finances she didn't have?

"Oh, we always pay cash for the tip." Wade didn't move except to increase the volume on the remote.

Ripping the clicker from his hand and bopping his brown bedhead played like a movie in her brain. She had been a waitress for a summer and knew the importance of tipping.

"I'll cover it." She swallowed the citrus taste in her mouth. Lord, multiply my few mites.

Setting the pizza on the coffee table in front of Wade, she rummaged in her backpack. A crumpled five-dollar bill and two ones were nearly all she had left to her name. Her face grew hot. How had she gotten into this mess with her savings depleted, no income, and no job prospects? Ron Runyard and his scam. Chasing thoughts of bankruptcy away, she handed the delivery guy the money and gave a smile as fake as Ron Runyard.

"Thank you, ma'am." The skip in the driver's step bolstered her sagging spirit. At least someone was having a good day.

By the time she focused her attention on the living room, Wade had the box open and a slice of pizza in his hand.

"Shall we pray? We can throw in a victory ask for your team." It was Sunday after all.

"I prayed to myself." Wade addressed the television screen with a mouth full of their dinner.

Was this what girls who had brothers dealt with during football season? Her dad watched Green Bay games. Only Green Bay games. And only to be able to converse with customers.

After scouting the kitchen for plates, napkins, and cans of soda, she returned to the living area and placed the dining ware and drinks in front of her host.

Wade nodded. He swept dark bangs out of his eyes. His

baby blues matched the color of his jersey. Wade had nice eyes. Too bad they were hidden under a V'd brow. "I should have thought about that. I didn't want to miss the last few seconds of the game." His apologetic tone smoothed the razor edges off of his gruff demeanor.

"Don't worry. I know you're into the game and didn't want company. But their kicker is never going to make a fifty-five yarder against the wind. He's too self-assured. Once your coach calls a timeout to ice him, he'll botch the kick." She grabbed a slice of pizza, placed it on a plate, and sat in her chair. In her peripheral vision, she could see Wade assessing her. She tamped down a grin. "I know this because I've seen it happen many times in Green Bay. Home of the Titletown Team." She reached for her can of soda. The fizz *tinked* off the can as she drank.

"You do, do you? Oh. Oh." He scooched forward and pointed at the screen. The football hit the goal post, cascaded sideways, and missed the end zone. "Yes! We win."

"See. Told ya." She bit into the cheese and savored the hint of salt, fat, and garlic.

He turned his attention toward her for more than a second. Exuberance enlivened his features, the ones hidden by a scowl most of the evening. He wasn't bad looking when he was happy. "You should have bet on the game."

Had he? She'd lost enough money without placing a bet. If her life had gone as planned, she would be home in Wisconsin instead of lounging in Linda's house with her recuperating son. In some sense, she felt a sort of déjà vu. She knew what it was like to have an ill family member and try to keep a business running. She wished there was a way she could be of more help to the Donovens.

The room grew quiet as they watched the post-game analysis.

Out of the corner of her eye, she saw Wade hold a plate in his right hand and cautiously lift another slice of pizza with his left hand. She tried to remember the injuries Sam had mentioned over Christmas and earlier the day before. Obviously, Wade's right leg had been broken since the cane hung near that side of him, but had his left arm been injured? Is that why Cole had to help with service calls?

A low rumble came from Wade's throat as if he was trying to hide a cough during a sermon. He flinched and arched his back.

Was he in distress? Staring wasn't polite, but she wanted to help him if she could. She knew a little about holistic medicine from her mom.

Euphemisms for curse words escaped Wade's lips. He grabbed the pizza slice from his left hand and flung it into the box. He secured his left wrist with his right hand and grimaced.

"Are you all right?" She jumped from her seat and hovered near the couch. Her heart boomed as she pushed up the sleeves of her red sweater. She didn't want to embarrass Wade, but if he needed help, she was ready to assist. Somehow.

"Do I look like I'm all right?" he snapped. "My hand is seizing." He closed his eyes and squeezed his wrist. Perspiration glowed above his lip.

Emma scanned the table and living area. Her body temperature rose to boiling. "Do you have medication?" Her parents hardly took aspirin.

He shook his head. "Doesn't work."

She remembered how her mother relieved pain. Her mom had massaged pressure points in Emma's hand to relieve headaches brought on by studying for final exams. Using essential oils and acupressure, her mom had made taking tests pain-free. Emma doubted that the Donovens had scented oils, but pizza grease might work. Maybe she could stop the seizing of Wade's hand.

Sitting down next to Wade, she grabbed the silver tortoise charm hanging around her neck and rubbed its shiny shell. *Lord, I could use some wisdom here.* What had she learned in Sunday school? Do unto others as you would have them do unto you.

Wade, hunched over tight as a ball of twine, didn't chastise her closeness.

"I might be able to help." She bit her lip and when Wade unfurled a tiny bit, she grasped his clawed hand and managed to get a thumb in the middle of the closed fingers. She began a circular massage.

Wade let out a muffled scream. "What are you doing?" His look of horror made it seem that her touch was worse than the pain. Hadn't he had a manicure or a pedicure? Nah, probably not.

"I'm helping relieve your spasms. Relax." She shifted her thumb beneath Wade's middle finger and stroked toward his ring finger. She prayed the acupressure worked.

"Stop!" The man breathed like he was in labor. He may have asked her to stop, but in his eyes, he was pleading for relief.

"Just give me five."

"Minutes?" His jaw nearly hit the sofa.

"No, rotations. I finished one." *Please, Lord, let this work.* She continued to massage his skin, applying more and more pressure. The aroma of a pizzeria wafted from her massage. "And two." Come on prayer and ancient medicine. "Three."

He blew out a long breath and slouched against the cushions. At least he wasn't rigid with fright anymore.

She applied a little more force. The claw opened wider.

"Four."

"I think it's working." Surprise riddled Wade's statement. For the first time all night, he looked at her like she was someone worth knowing. His trust was better than that double espresso.

Thank You, Lord. "How's the pain? I'm at five, but I'd like to try a point above the wrist."

"Keep going. My hand feels better. The shooting pain is down to a throb." He moved his arm ever so slightly. "I'm afraid it's going to cramp again later."

"With the blood flow improved, you should be fine for a while. I'm surprised your doctor or nurse didn't put you in some physical therapy. You injured this in your accident, right?" Was she prying into personal issues?

Wade turned his body toward her as she caressed above his wrist. Had she softened his demeanor with her pain relief tactics? His thigh wasn't soft where it bumped her knee. He could play on any offensive line with his broad shoulders and defined muscles.

"I broke my arm in the crash, but the doctor said this hand seizure may be coming from my shoulder. Nerve damage or something. My bruised shoulder healed fine. It doesn't bother me." He shrugged to prove his point.

She continued her circles toward the side of his elbow.

"How do you know that massage stuff?" He glanced at her fingers making their way up his forearm. He hadn't pulled away from her yet.

"My parents own a candle shop and several years ago my mom got into essential oils and aromatherapy. From there, she took a few massage classes and then studied acupressure. Let's just say my parents like alternative forms of medicine." Her parents didn't fit the suburban mold. In elementary school, she cringed when her dad wore leather pants and a flowing white shirt to a classroom play. The pirate jokes went on for weeks. Though, if her mom hadn't studied the pressure points, she wouldn't have been able to help Wade.

Wade's brows furrowed. "What kinds of medicine?"

Her body temperature spiked with his inquisitive blue-eyed stare. "Nothing illegal."

"I didn't mean…"

"Botanical supplements, vitamins, that type of stuff. What you'd find in a health food store." Was Wade blushing? Flushed was more like it. From the improved blood flow.

A noise sounded at the front door, and it opened.

The Donoven family and Sam entered.

Caught in the act. What would they think about her massaging Wade's arm? She scooted farther from Wade and clasped her hands in her lap. The warmth of his skin lingered on her fingertips.

Wade sat at attention on the sofa and rubbed his arm where she had caressed the pressure points.

Cole held a package high. "We brought your favorite ice cream, bro. Tin roof. There's vanilla swirl, too. Mom says she'll make hot fudge sauce." Cole traipsed toward the kitchen.

From the warmth she felt, her cheeks could rival strawberries and cream.

Linda hurried toward the couch. "Is something wrong with your arm?" Her nurse-o-meter hovered over "extreme concern."

"No. nothing. A spasm. That's all." Wade focused on the television, but the football talk had turned into an infomercial. "She, uh…"

He pointed in Emma's direction. Did he forget her name? He had ignored her when she arrived. Was she still invisible to him? She scooted further from Wade. So much for using her skills.

"Did Emma help you?" Sam came over and created a wall of Wisconsin-born women at the couch's end. "She knows a lot about massage techniques."

"Yeah, Emma." Wade's attention ping-ponged between his mom, Sam, and her. When his gaze found her, she quickly looked away. She hadn't been close to a handsome bachelor in a long while. The man's face was glowing enough for the both of them.

"Was it like yesterday?" Mike sauntered over and perused the screen.

Linda whirled on her husband. "What do mean? What happened yesterday?"

"It was nothing, Mom. My hand twitched." Wade grabbed his cane and pushed to a stand. "Where's my ice cream?" He headed after Cole.

"What do you mean twitched? That doesn't sound like nothing?" Linda crossed her arms. Mama bear wanted an explanation. "Isn't Francine's last day tomorrow?"

"Yes." A growl of an answer rumbled from Wade who had reached the kitchen.

"Are you going to be able to run the office if your hand is twitching?" Linda's voice strained. She shook her head and cast a glance at Sam.

How long had Linda been taking care of her son? More than six weeks, at least. Emma's heart filled with sympathetic pain. She recognized the weariness of caring too much and caring too long. She had pushed her own sanity limits when her father was ill. Linda looked and sounded exhausted.

Mike joined his wife and took her coat. "Maybe I should have called the temp agency. Francine does a lot of filing and handles the phone calls. She writes out some invoices. I thought his arm would be one hundred percent by now."

Sam nudged Emma's shoulder, and it wasn't about fudge

swirls. "This may be an answer to prayer?" she whispered. "You could use a job."

"You're looking for work?" Linda didn't need a hearing test. She was fluttering closer like a fairy godmother.

Mike slung his wife's coat over the back of the sofa. "Really. What line of work are you in?"

Sam's eyes rivaled the size of golf balls. Emma imagined her eyes did too.

"I, um, was an office manager."

A loud *clunk* could be heard in the kitchen.

"Dude." Cole's disgruntled shout carried into the living room. "You dropped the tin roof."

6

Wade stood out of view hovering to the side of the kitchen doorway. His parents were in a deep discussion with Sam and Emma. Why was his dad talking to Emma about her job experience? They didn't need to replace Francine while she recovered from surgery. He could manage the office work by himself. If he wasn't taking calls and scheduling service, what would he do all day? Didn't his family realize how far he had come to even be walking and using his arm? He'd done the company's yearly planning while he recuperated in bed. No one seemed to care about his hardships at the moment. His chest cinched tight as he remembered the injustice of his injuries.

Until the doctor released him to drive, there was no way he could make service calls. Hiring an extra employee would hit their bottom line. Salary costs circulated in his head as he leaned against the counter and hung his cane from the granite edge. Dad should at least consult his opinion. They were a two-man team, or at least they had been before the accident.

"It's not polite to eavesdrop." Cole handed him a bowl of tin roof. "Since Mom is talking to the girls, you get canned chocolate sauce instead of her homemade fudge."

The coolness of the ice cream scoops couldn't dampen the brush fire coursing through Wade's body. How could Cole act like nothing was wrong when he was to blame? Cole brought Emma to Nashville right before Francine's medical leave. Coincidence or calculated? With another person in the office, Wade would be relieved of most of his duties. He didn't need rescuing, especially by his brother.

"This is all your fault." Wade took a bite of dessert and flailed his spoon at his brother. "If you hadn't brought Emma here, Dad wouldn't be talking about hiring her. Why couldn't you come, do your job, and then go back to Whispering Creek? We don't need you and your friends meddling in our business."

Cole scowled and jabbed a finger his direction. "Keep it down. You're too loud. As always."

Little brother better be careful, or this kitchen would become a mixed martial arts arena. Wade still had a couple inches and thirty pounds on his brother.

"The construction is in Sperry's Crossing, and those friends," Cole mimicked Wade's accusatory tone, "are my girlfriend and her childhood friend. Sam drove me here after your accident. She even comforted Mom and Dad. Don't you dare say anything bad about her. You seemed pretty cozy with Emma when we walked in." Cole flapped a hand at the ice cream bowl. "You're even holding a dish with your left hand."

Wade glanced down. The claw acted normal after Emma's massage. Relief flickered through his body. Was full health finally within reach? He could still feel the sensation of her circles. But acupressure skills did not mean she was a good office manager.

"Let's be clear." Wade rolled his shoulders and broadened his chest. "She hopped on the couch and grabbed my hand before I could stop her. I didn't ask for physical therapy during the game." His little brother didn't realize how close he was to wearing tin roof.

"Well, apparently you need more therapy, not less." Cole buried the scoop deep into the ice cream container and left it. "Have you thought about what would happen if the doctor releases you to drive? Do you want Dad to pick up Fran's duties? He's been going on service calls and helping Fran with the filing and invoicing since your crash. Maybe he would like a break. He's not getting any younger." Cole scrubbed a hand over his jaw. "Open your eyes to what Mom and Dad have been through."

"That's ripe coming from you." Tiny runt. How dare he lecture Wade on anything after he left the family business to dabble in music with a gold digger. Cole knew nothing about the sacrifices Wade had made to keep up with service calls and staffing in his absence. He was on his way to a customer's house on a Sunday when the accident happened. His vision blurred as he glared at his brother.

"At least I woke up. I'm here in Nashville helping you and Dad out." Cole crossed his arms with an unimpressive swagger. "I'm out in Sperry's Crossing executing your bid while you're stuck being a —"

"Watch your language, bro." Wade stretched to his full height.

"Stink hole," Cole spat.

"I think you mean sink hole." Wade smirked at his brother's gaff.

"Oh, I know what I mean."

Cole removed the ice cream scoop. "You owe Emma an apology. All she did was try to be nice, and you sucked her into that sink hole of yours."

"I thought it was a stink hole." Who did his brother think he was demanding an apology? Tonight was game night, not entertain-a-stranger night.

"Whatever. If the hole fits." Cole's smirk irritated every nerve in Wade's body.

Dad rushed through the kitchen doorway.

"Lower your voices." With hands on his hips, he was in reprimand mode. "What is going on in here? Can't you serve dessert without getting into an argument? You're ruining a nice evening."

"A nice evening for whom?" Wade shoved ice cream into his mouth and bit down on the chocolate-coated peanuts. His molars almost turned the nuts into peanut butter. "You're not seriously thinking about hiring that girl to replace Fran, are you?"

"No one is replacing Francine." Dad whispered his answer with enough force to halt a challenge.

Wade ate another mouthful of dessert while Cole pulled more bowls out of the cupboard.

"But you do need help, son." His dad scrubbed a hand over his face. One that looked overly haggard. "And at this late date, this might be a way to help Emma and the company. I offered her a job."

If Wade had lived in California, he would have sworn an earthquake shook the floor. How could his father and business partner believe Wade couldn't handle office work? So, he had one fall. He was thirty-two and more than capable. He'd been running the company for eight years. A doctor's release would be coming soon. Hopefully, in a week or so. They had time to assess the office situation and hire someone else. His dad hadn't bothered to consult him about the matter.

He glanced between his dad and Cole. Both stared at him. Then, realization dawned like a kick to the gut.

"You planned this didn't you, bro?" He set his bowl on the counter. His hands trembled and not from a spasm. Darn if he didn't smell the faint hint of pizza grease. "You brought Emma here knowing Dad would grow soft and hire her. Nashville is my territory. Stick to Sperry's Crossing and the expansion west. We don't need you here."

Cole flinched. Good.

His brother fisted a handful of spoons.

"Get back in a driver's seat, and I won't have to step foot in Nashville." Cole turned to dish ice cream.

Wade grabbed hold of his cane and thrust it at Cole. He knew he was stoking embers, but he couldn't stop. He wasn't going to hog all of the hurt. "It's like you to run away again."

The clattering of spoons sounded on the granite. That jab struck a nerve. Wade grinned as Cole advanced closer.

"Boys!" Dad held out his arms. "Enough of this nonsense. I am co-owner of the company, and I will hire whomever I please. Do you hear me?"

Mom stormed through the doorway. Her flamethrower stare torched half of the kitchen.

"I am going to make three ice cream cones, and the girls and I are going for a quick walk around the block. When we return, whatever is going on in here will be over." Mom always had a way of making him feel like a school kid.

"I've got it under control, dear." Dad grabbed a box of cones out of the pantry, and scooped tin roof, handing Mom the domed ice cream cones.

Mom's foot tapped a rhythm as she wrapped napkins around the cones and fled with the girls' dessert. The front door opened and closed, leaving the house silent.

Cole glared at Wade. A tic pulsed in his brother's cheek. Cole needed to learn his place. He could help out in a pinch, but he didn't make company decisions.

Wade sat at the kitchen table. His dad joined him. Cole leaned against the refrigerator devouring his bowl of tin roof.

Once his dad ate some of his ice cream, Wade decided to ask about the mysterious Emma. He had a right to know who was working at the company.

"So, why is Emma unemployed? Why doesn't she have work in Wisconsin where she's from?" As far away from Nashville as possible.

Cole indicated for Dad to answer.

"Apparently," Dad swallowed some ice cream, "her former boss was a con artist. The investment operation was a scam. Her boss vanished in the middle of the night with everyone's money and left her holding the empty sack."

Really? Was his dad buying this story? Who was being scammed now?

Grabbing his cane, Wade rose and paced between the table and the doorway. "You want to hire someone who was dense enough to work for a shell corp?" He laughed instead of slamming his claw into the wall. "I can't watch her twenty-four seven. And where is she going to live? Sam's in Whispering Creek. That's over an hour and a half away. You can't commute from there."

Dad rested his elbows on the table and rubbed his hands together as if he had questions too. "Your mother thought she could live here with us."

Time warp. He had stumbled into a century where his parents had lost their minds.

"I am not working with that woman at the office and coming home with her at night." His body temperature had to be higher than when he had spiked a fever at the hospital.

"Maybe it's time you moved back to your own home." His dad looked at him with eyes deader than a popped football. "It's about time things got back to normal."

Except he wasn't normal. Not yet anyway. Had his dad forgotten about all the pain and suffering he had gone through? He had been driving a company van, working on a Sunday because Cole ditched his responsibilities. He'd show everyone that the co-CEO was back. Emma would be twiddling her thumbs at work. *Lord, don't give me any more setbacks.* His throat grew tight. "How long have you and Mom been planning to kick me out?"

"Come on, Wade." His dad's voice caught. "Have you ever thought that maybe God saw we had a need and sent us an angel?"

Angel? Hah! Opportunist? Pest? Scammer? "I have a lot of words floating through my brain to describe that girl, but angel isn't one of them."

Cole stopped Wade's shuffle and laid a hand on his shoulder. "Will you pray about it?"

Wade shrugged off his brother's touch and kept his balance. "I don't need church lessons from you." Wade had been praying a lot since the wreck, and God hadn't fully healed him. The last thing he needed was more aggravation. He'd been living a medical nightmare. Apparently, his family had short memories. "I'll give her a week. If she's a bust, she's gone." His brother wouldn't be able to blame him for not giving Emma a chance if she was incompetent.

"Emma will grow on you, bro."

Wade snorted. "Yeah, like gangrene on an amputation."

~*~

Emma rolled over in the queen-sized bed she shared with Sam. The Donovens had a house full. Wade and Cole were sleeping in their childhood rooms while she and Sam shared the guest room. Good thing the brothers weren't relegated to bunk beds or there might have been a brawl. What had she done to upset Wade? He had been somewhat polite while they ate pizza.

The red glow of the digital clock read 11:32 PM. An evening infused with adrenaline rushes had her wide awake and staring at her silver chain coiled on the nightstand.

"Can't sleep?" Sam whispered.

"It's hard to sleep when you've caused a family feud." She flipped to face her friend. "I don't know what I did to make Wade so upset."

"Wade's been a grump since the accident. Don't blame yourself." Sam scrunched her pillow. "What he went through is awful, but his family has been there for him every step of the way."

She had tried to help Wade, too, by using acupressure on his hand and not talking much during the game. He was quiet, but in a shy, mysterious sort of way. And he could probably bench press her whole body. She didn't even complain when he ate the biggest slice of plain cheese pizza. Causing Wade stress wasn't part of her plans. She didn't foresee an emotional eruption in the kitchen.

"Do you think I should work for the Donovens?" Emma tucked her long bangs behind her ear. "You know them better after dating Cole."

"That's a loaded baked potato question." Sam sat higher against the headboard. Her shoulder length hair splayed against the dark wood. "You will do a fantastic job. You've been around retail almost all of your life. Everyone I met at the Runyard Group sang your praises. It wasn't your fault that Ron ran off with everyone's money."

Emma placed a hand under her pillow and propped her head. "I know, but—"

"No buts. I'm right. You know it."

Grabbing her pillow, Emma lounged against the headboard next to Sam and snuggled the pillow like a plush bear.

"I know you're right." She blew out a breath. "Life feels so fuzzy lately. I liked my job, and I can't believe the senior community was a fairytale. I worked on software to keep up with the residents. Should I have seen something? Was I stupid? My future was all planned out and now it's upside down." Guess she had one thing in common with Wade.

"Ron was a professional crook." Sam unfurled Emma's fist and grasped her hand. "Don't beat yourself up."

"But I do." Pressure built behind her eyes.

Sam pulled her into a pillow-thick hug. "You can always come back to Whispering Creek with me. Free room and board. I'll even buy groceries. You know when Mr. Ted left me his house, he knew you'd be there too, eventually."

Mentioning their deceased elderly friend had Emma's tears flowing. Mr. Ted filled her head with wisdom from the Bible. He would tell her that God loved her. She knew that, but right now, she didn't understand His plan for her life.

Swiping tears from her cheeks, Emma dried her hands on the bed sheet. "I loved Mr. Ted, and I love spending time with you." Here came reality. "With an empty bank account, how can I turn down a job where all I have to do is give Linda an invoice, and she'll pay me in cash. Weekly. I don't have to give my social security number or fill out forms." She'd work out taxes later when she discovered if Ron's pay stubs were falsified. "The Donovens being flexible is like a God thing."

"With Wade in the mix?" Sam laughed. "All things are possible with God."

God had been Emma's rock for as long as she could remember. God's Word, Mr. Ted, and her pastor had guided her since her parents didn't know much about Jesus. Sam is the one who made sure she got to church every Sunday. With God's help, she could get through a week at Donoven and Sons Electric. Their office lady would return eventually. Temporary income was better than no income.

"You've talked me into it." Emma lay down with a bounce that jolted the mattress. I'll give it a week, and then I can reevaluate."

Sam slipped under the sheet and tugged on the comforter. "Reevaluate after tomorrow. You can ride back to Whispering

Creek with Cole and me if it doesn't work out. And remember, I'm only a text away."

Oh yeah, her phone bill was coming due. She needed cash flow.

"Pray for me extra hard."

"I always pray for you." Sam's voice sounded like it was fading away. "Your parents too."

Thank You, God, for friends like Sam.

Emma stared at the ceiling, debt mountains and office scenarios clouding her brain.

"Next time you visit, can you bring me Herbie and some candles from the trunk of my car."

"You mean my shed smells like Christmas," Sam mumbled.

"Better than Christmas."

Bunching her pillow, Emma prayed. *Sorry for being an ingrate, God. You provided a job for me. A place to work without Mayor Van Wenkle barging in and accusing me of a crime. You helped me survive one night in Nashville. Please help me survive seven more.*

7

How much time did a woman need to get ready in the morning? Wade leaned against the wall outside of the bathroom assigned to the girls. He'd been waiting a few minutes, but it seemed like an eternity with the previous night's events heavy on his mind. While everyone was enjoying his mom's breakfast buffet in the kitchen, he slipped away to find Emma. She must have pulled the short straw on bathroom usage because Sam was halfway through her sausage and egg casserole.

He hated to admit that Cole might have been right about their dad's stress level. Running the business and caring for an injured son and concerned wife had to be a monumental burden. The load would be lightening soon. Dad's co-partner was back, even if driving was still at least a week, maybe two, away. He vowed to make the situation with Emma the best it could be. For his dad's sake.

He flexed his hand instinctively as he remembered how Emma's rotations had helped ease his pain. He'd been cramp-free since her finger gymnastics. That was one of the reasons he had taken Cole's advice to apologize. His brother could ride off to Whispering Creek for all he cared, but he didn't want his parents, Sam, and Emma thinking he was callous and rude. Running a company had responsibilities attached. He didn't sound professional raising his voice and making accusations. During the night, the Holy Spirit had convicted him of the words he had said in anger. How much had everyone heard? Did it matter? The company needed help, and Emma was available.

Glancing at the hallway light, he uttered an arrow prayer. "Help me here, Lord. How do I apologize to Emma when I'm not exactly sure how much she heard?" He rubbed his clean-shaven jaw. "You know, life would be a whole lot easier if You healed me completely. Right now." He waited, his neck craned toward heaven, hoping for a miracle. "Still waiting, huh?"

As if God had misunderstood his time request, the bathroom door opened.

Emma's eyes widened for a second. "Oh, hey, good morning." She peeked down the hall.

"It's just me." He hooked his thumbs in the belt loops of his jeans. He didn't know what he was expecting her to wear, but she looked professional in black pants and a green turtleneck. "I wanted to apologize for last night."

Her nose crinkled as a quizzical expression flashed across her face. "You want to apologize for eating my cheese pizza?" Emma was wide awake and kidding him at seven in the morning. She had his heart beating faster than a chug of caffeine.

"For what you might have heard me say in the kitchen last night. I'm sorry if I hurt your feelings." The words came out heartfelt and polite. Better than he had rehearsed.

Her eyelashes fluttered. She had the biggest, most expressive brown eyes he had ever seen. If tears started flowing, he would be babbling apologies for hours.

"Oh." She sputtered and flapped a hand at him. "I know you run the business with Mike. It isn't easy when others make decisions for you. I get why you were upset."

She was right. He wouldn't have been caught off guard if his dad had consulted him about her hiring. Couldn't someone have clued him in about why Emma was in Tennessee? A text even? Would she confide in him during work? Did he want her to? "Well, if you were offended by anything I said, I apologize."

With the wave of her hand, she wafted a sweet, flowery scent in his direction. "Thank you, but we're good. I can understand if you're leery hiring someone with my background. I don't know if I'd hire someone with my work situation for my parents' candle shop." Her stomach rumbled its agreement. "If you don't mind, I'm going to follow that sausage aroma to the infamous kitchen." She brushed her bangs to the side of her forehead and gave him another upbeat smile. "See you in a few, boss."

Stupidest apology of my life.

As Emma hurried down the hall, he felt...odd. Like Emma was on his team. She voiced his frustration about not being consulted in work decisions as if they had talked about it over dinner. He liked how she was rational and not offended. He wouldn't mind hanging out and watching another game with Emma. Alarm bells buzzed in his brain. She was an employee now. Francine's replacement. Temporary replacement. Emma would be hightailing it north in a few weeks anyway.

He had to focus on getting his doctor's release and returning to the helm of Donoven and Sons Electric. If his dad needed a break or a vacation, he could take one while Wade handled the office. God and Emma had given him a much-needed dose of encouragement. He could envision being healthy and back in control of the family business. The sooner, the better.

~*~

Sitting in Mike's Suburban, Emma flipped the hood on her coat and secured her backpack over her shoulder. Rain pelted the asphalt outside of Donoven and Sons Electric. She would have to make a mad dash for the building. Wade opened her door and held an umbrella with his left hand.

His attitude toward her had pivoted since last night. She could get accustomed to Southern hospitality, especially from a tall bachelor in jeans and a navy-blue oxford bearing his name and a bright yellow thunderbolt. She tamped down those thoughts as her new boss escorted her gingerly toward their workplace. Her position was short term. She'd stay while Fran recovered from knee surgery and use the salary to pad her almost non-existent bank account.

The egg casserole Linda had made for breakfast festered like a cement pit in Emma's gut. What if scheduling electricians was more difficult than entertaining investors with coffee and conversation? Maybe it was harder, but Sam assured her that selling candles at Home ScentSations was the same as selling electrical parts. If only she knew the names of one or two of those specialty parts.

The Lord is my rock…

Holding the door open, Mike indicated for her to enter first. He wore a jacket with the same thunderbolt logo that was plastered in the upper corner of Wade's broad chest. The colorful logo caught her eye, but not the decor of the office.

The scent of stale food and old newspaper greeted her as she entered a waiting area. The place could sure use an air freshener or scented candle. She blinked as lights flickered on, noting where the switches were located.

"We don't get many customers in here." Mike motioned toward chairs, a magazine-topped table, and a mounted television screen. Too bad that blank screen wasn't looping golf courses and happy seniors. She could run Ron's real estate office from a gurney. "Occasionally, a vendor will stop by, or someone will walk in with a question. Most of our customers call. Fran can show you how to check inquiries from the website."

"I can show her." Wade gave an agreeable nod to his father. "I've been handling that duty lately."

Where was the grumpy yeller from the previous night? Wade's upbeat confidence bolstered her spirit. She averted her gaze. Had she been staring? At her half-boss? First day jitters.

"Over here is the front office where you'll be working." Thankfully, Mike continued the tour. He opened a door that led to a room visible to the main entrance by a glass window. She'd be able to see if anyone came into the building, was waiting in the lobby; and best of all, she could interact with people while being safe and secure. Not that anyone would locate her to ask questions about her former boss, but in case a reporter found her, they couldn't descend on her like a vulture with a camera mounted on its tail.

Fluorescent post-it notes covered the edges of the main computer screen. A plastic dancing flower sat at its base. Herbie would fit right in. Sam definitely needed to bring the cactus from Whispering Creek the next time she visited Nashville.

Across from the office counter, a door swung open. Cole held the door while a middle-aged redhead hobbled closer with a bejeweled cane.

"Good morning, Donovens." Francine was as vibrant as her color-coded notes. "Cole let me park in the garage so I wouldn't slip and fall before my big day." Fran's eyebrows rose as she cast a glance at Wade. "Who do we have here?" Her voice held a hint of innuendo.

Wade stood like a wooden carving next to the copier. "New employee."

How impersonal. So much for Southern charm.

"I'm Emma. A friend of Sam's. Cole's girlfriend." No sense letting rumors get started. Men in their early thirties were on the top of every matchmaker's list. She reached over the counter to Francine. "I'm going to be helping out for a short time with office work." That sounded better than insinuating that Wade needed help.

With a firm shake, Francine said, "Call me Fran. I'm so glad you'll be here in the office. Now, Wade can focus on getting back to service calls. He's been cooped up with me for too long." She grinned at Wade. "That doctor is going to be releasing you soon. I've been praying extra hard." Shuffling toward the computer, Fran plopped a brown purse on the counter. "Probably should get the coffee brewing. If you only master that task, you'll be appreciated. There are pre-measured packets under the machine." Fran pointed her cane at a cupboard.

"I'll do it." Wade opened the cupboard beneath the coffeemaker.

Where was helpful Wade when the pizza delivery guy came and took Emma's last dollar. She shouldn't complain. A good-natured boss topped a total grouch.

"Emma, you're in good hands with these two. We'll see you later." Mike and Cole headed toward some back offices, deep in conversation.

So far, Emma could manage turning on the lights and making coffee. Her muscles eased, untying a few knots. She sat in an empty chair by Fran and set her mind on understanding the electrical business.

Fran sat at the main computer and pointed out passwords and logins on the colorful post-it notes. She pulled up what looked like a work schedule.

"We have an employee out in Lockeland Springs today. Antonio is installing soffit lighting and dimmers." Fran pointed at the screen. "His schedule is full, so you won't see him until tomorrow morning."

Emma had no idea where Lockeland Springs was located. She barely knew the location of the small town of Whispering Creek let alone the city of Nashville. And what was a soffit and dimmers? Her heartbeat thudded in her ears. Could she learn to manage this office? She needed the money, but she wouldn't take it if she couldn't do the job.

Wade opened a drawer and removed a laptop. Was he going to check the website?

Mike and Cole returned and filled their coffee tumblers.

"We're heading out, ladies." Mike stopped in front of Fran's computer and leaned on the counter. "If this reno goes long and I don't see you, know that we are praying for a successful knee replacement."

"Thanks, Mike. Prayer chains have been activated all over the state." Fran patted Emma's hand. "I'll get this young lady familiarized with the office. She can always text me with questions, but I may be on pain meds. I'm sure Wade will be a big help." With a squeeze of Emma's hand, Fran whispered, "You'll do fine."

At the moment, Emma wasn't so sure, but she was fairly sure that reno meant renovation.

As Mike and Cole rushed out the door into the garage, Cole shouted, "I'd tell you to break a leg, Emma, but we have enough injuries in the office."

"Funny," she quipped. "Watch your step on the reno."

Wade laughed. "Good one."

Since meeting the elder Donoven brother, she'd never heard him laugh. Wade's deep chuckle made the room seem like a comedy club. She whirled in her chair. Had the ice sculpture of Wade Donoven developed a crack? Had he forgotten she was the office girl who-must-not-be-named?

His expression quickly sobered.

She longed for the quiet, calm office she managed before

Ron and Annette vanished.

Another employee jogged through the front entrance and came into the office from the waiting room. His shirt introduced him as Derek. Wavy long hair was swept into a man bun. She'd barter for some of that length and wave.

The phone rang. Fran picked it up and was talking to someone about bad breakers. Emma was fairly sure that wasn't surf talk.

"Hey Wade, I just saw your little brother." Mr. Man Bun craned his neck toward the parking lot. "Is he working with us again? In town?"

"Just today." Wade turned from his laptop. "Dad's working a two-man job. Can't wear the old guy out. Cole's still staying in Sperry's Crossing near the industrial site."

With all of the family dynamics she'd witnessed, she could see why Cole stayed away from the Nashville office.

"It'd be good to have Cole back." Derek scanned paperwork piled on the counter. "You new here?" He shot Emma a curious look.

"She's helping me run the office while Fran is gone." Wade rushed over by her chair without his cane. "Temporary hire."

"I'm Emma." She didn't need a man to talk for her. At twenty-four, she could introduce herself. Smiling, she side-eyed the information on Fran's screen.

"Nice to meet you." Derek pulled a work order from his pile of paper.

"Likewise." Short and sweet.

Derek studied the order. "This isn't the house in Shelby Hills with the big mutt. That dog nearly chewed my backside. The owner couldn't control it."

Wade squinted at the address. "Not sure. Let me check the incident cards." He flipped through notecards in a long metal box.

Shifting his weight to his good leg, Wade brushed her shoulder. One thing about Wade, he was solid. Had he played football in high school? Her face grew warm. She concentrated on Fran and reminded herself that she needed to survive her first day and not focus on Wade's muscles.

Fran ended her call. "If the customer isn't in the card file, then we don't have a record of any incident." Her fingers typed at the computer. "What's the name?"

"Bedford." Derek's jovial demeanor disappeared.

"Nope." Fran scanned the computer screen. "I don't see anything noted. The last call was a kitchen GFI."

Derek secured a strand of wavy hair behind his ear. "I would have sworn this was the address."

Emma straightened in her seat. Didn't Donoven and Sons have an entry field in their customer database to store important customer information? She'd developed software to keep track of the interests of residents at Runyard's senior living community. His fake senior community. Should she mention her program? She bit her lip. Donoven and Sons had their own system. No sense changing their system on her first day.

"That beast was a menace." Derek shut a few pens in his metal tray. "Wish I knew. Maybe I'll call from the truck to see if the lady could put any pets in a bedroom or something." Concern sprinkled with a granule of fear crossed Derek's face.

Lord, should I speak up? She sensed a laser beam coming from her backpack right where her flash drive was located. Surely, her People Peeps software could wait until she and Wade had the office running smoothly.

She pointed to the metal tray Derek held. "If you do meet that nasty dog, please make a note on one of the copies. We don't want you or anyone else getting hurt." Score one for the new gal. A little empathy went a long way.

"I second that advice." Fran popped a mint into her mouth. "Safety first."

"Yeah, dude." Wade joined in the love fest. "We don't want to be down another man."

What time warp had she stepped into with Wade? She stopped herself from gazing into the blue eyes of her boss while he stood sentry behind her chair.

"I'll definitely call the customer before getting out of the van." Derek organized his paperwork. "Nice meeting you, Emma." He waved and left through the garage.

Wade returned to his laptop. He added comments while Fran showed her how to schedule service appointments, fill out work orders, and how to invoice the job when it was completed.

Emma's temples throbbed after two hours of listening to procedures and electrical terminology. She possessed pages of notes containing Fran's wisdom. Once she got the hang of scheduling, the job wouldn't be too bad.

Stiffness in her writing hand had her assessing Wade's left hand. He typed on the laptop like a video gamer.

She arched her back and shot a short thank-You prayer to God. The morning had flown by, and her linebacker boss hadn't screamed at her like she was a renegade referee. Only God could have orchestrated this outcome.

Fran excused herself to use the bathroom.

Emma scooted her chair closer to the phone.

The phone rang as if it had been waiting for her solo flight.

Interacting with customers was high on her skill set. She breathed deep and answered. "Donoven and Sons Electric." She used a professional, yet perky voice and smiled at the receiver.

"Fran! That crazy dog mauled my hand. I'm at emergency."

8

"I'm so sorry, Derek. This is Emma." She gripped the phone tighter. An emergency couldn't be happening two hours into her new job. Who could have anticipated that an animal attack would be one of her first calls? Her heart rate sped and hampered her hearing. She needed to listen to Derek and process what he was saying. She had a job to do and do well. "Are you all right? How bad is the bite?"

"They're taking me for stitches." Derek sounded like a hysterical ten year old.

She waved Wade over to the desk and wrote on a notepad…. Derek. Dog bite. Her handwriting was a squiggly mess.

Wade's head tilted backward as he jammed his cane into the tile. His cheeks bloated bigger than a chipmunk's.

"I gotta go." Derek's tone needed a hug and a warm blanket. "They're updating my tetanus shot."

"Wait. Don't hang up." Not knowing the area, she needed to verify the location of the emergency room. "Where are you?" Some of Derek's panic had seeped into her words. "We'll come right there."

Wade reached for the phone, but Derek rambled too fast for her to relinquish the receiver.

She scribbled the name of the hospital as the line went dead. Her feet itched to race out of the building, but her mind cautioned her to slow down and make a plan.

"I wanted to talk with him." Wade scowled.

"He had to get off the phone. They were treating him."

She kept her voice void of emotion. She had grown up in retail, possessed a degree in business administration, and had managed a real estate office. Ron Runyard may have thought her foolish, but she was no fool. Customer relations ran in her bloodstream, and she would earn her pay. She could handle traumatized employees even if it wasn't on Fran's to-do list. "You should go to the emergency room. The wound sounds bad."

Fran limped back in with her contagious smile. "I heard the phone. How was your first solo run?"

"Awful." Wade shrugged into his company jacket.

Exceedingly awful. Good thing she knew her new boss was thinking about the dog attack, or she might be looking for a new job. She touched her silver tortoise charm and gave it a few strokes. Her grandmother had called Emma tough as a tortoise shell when she bestowed the gift. She'd need some of that strength with all the life changes coming her way.

Frowning, Fran eased into her desk chair. "What's up?"

Wade rocked forward on his cane. "That dog Derek was talking about earlier bit him in the hand. He's at the ER. I should go see him." He flexed his fingers. "I'll call a ride service."

"No, you won't." Emma bounced out of her seat and grabbed her backpack and coat. "I'll drive you. There's strength in pairs." They had Fran in the office for the rest of the day to run interference.

"Good idea." Fran rose and balanced with a hand on the counter. "You can talk with our claims agent while Emma drives. Derek may need a ride home." She reached and removed a key from a hook near the desk. "Here's the keys to the brand new van. Courtesy of our insurance and Wade's accident." She gave Wade a sympathetic head tilt. "You two can break it in. It's out in the lot by the garage."

Emma accepted the keys and met Wade's gaze. He looked like he needed another bowl of tin roof ice cream as he passed her in route to the door. "Does Derek have any immediate family close by that we can call?"

"He's single, and his folks live in Georgia." Wade rubbed his temples like a workman's comp headache raged. His left hand trembled. Was his hand going to seize? Was he having flashbacks to his accident?

Lord, watch over Derek and Wade. Let me be of help in this terrible situation.

Turning abruptly, Wade halted. "We should pray."

They agreed on something. Had he sensed her arrow prayer shooting toward the heavens? She stood between Wade and Fran and clasped her hands.

Fran bent at the waist, head down, in front of her computer.

"Father, please watch over Derek." Wade's voice frayed like her nerves. "Calm his fears and ease his pain. May the doctors and nurses skillfully treat his injury. Give him a full recovery. We ask all of this in Jesus' name. Amen."

A chorus of amens followed Wade's prayer.

Emma's eyes tingled. How many prayers for healing had Wade prayed for himself during the weeks he was in the hospital and during his rehab? Hundreds? She would send petitions for Wade and Derek to God. She had judged Wade as a grump, but how would she act if her recovery had stalled and everyone around her enjoyed life as normal? She'd probably be grumpier than Wade.

Fran opened a drawer and pulled out a file. A tab told her it was Derek's personnel folder. "You'll need this." Fran also typed on the keyboard. "I'm noting this dog attack on the customer file as we speak. I'll update the incident cards and call Derek's afternoon appointment. Did he drive the van to emergency or call an ambulance?"

"We don't know." Wade shot Emma a glance as he held the door open to the garage. His expression wasn't condescending or judging her actions. He resembled a friend in need of support and guidance.

Emma bit her lip. If they had People Peeps, they could have seen specifics about Derek's interactions at the house and if anyone else had qualms about the dog. She had designed a brightly colored warning box in her software and ample space to time stamp past experiences. You could even drop in a photo of the pet. She'd mention the software when things settled down. When managing the office was a breeze.

"Let's fire up that van," she said in the parking lot.

Wade must have needed to say another prayer because a look of horror flashed across his face.

"You've never driven a van in Nashville traffic."

Did he think she grew up in the sticks? Milwaukee counted as a large city. "It isn't even noon." She jingled the key chain. "Come on. I'll do what I always do. Pray angels on my bumpers."

"We're going to need a legion." He rushed toward an official lightning-bolt-insignia van.

Wade Donoven had a sense of humor? She grinned. "I'll take all the help I can get. What else can go wrong on my first day?"

"You're right." A flicker of a smile buoyed his attitude. "Let me text Derek that we're on our way."

She hopped in the driver's seat and breathed in the new vehicle smell of pristine plastic. The scent calmed her nerves. She could do this. Go visit a friend in need. With a new friend. Who happened to be her temporary boss.

From the passenger seat, Wade plugged in the address on the dashboard GPS. He pointed in the direction of the main road. "Take a right out of the lot."

His commanding voice and settled demeanor gave her the confidence to drive in a strange city and tackle a workman's compensation case.

She pulled out into traffic and glanced into her side mirror. A black SUV pulled from the curb and merged into her lane. It couldn't be the same SUV that followed her in Milwaukee. Several people owned black cars. Linda drove one. Sam's mom drove one. Annette drove one. But Annette had disappeared with Ron. A chill washed over her arms underneath her turtleneck. She adjusted her rearview to see if the SUV continued to follow. The mysterious car didn't have a front license plate.

"Hey, watch!" Wade's minor irritation broke through her delusions.

An alarm sounded as 'brake' flashed on the console above the steering wheel. Her heart bounced into her throat. She jammed on the brakes.

Wade jerked forward with a grunt.

"Sorry." She checked the rearview. The black SUV turned onto a side street. Ten pounds of angst lifted from her shoulders.

She thanked God she hadn't crashed Wade's new van on her first day at work.

"Are you sure you're okay to drive?" Wade's anxious bright blue eyes made her besieged heart do a flutter. A few of his gruff edges tumbled off.

"Yeah. My bad." She bestowed a reassuring smile. "I should have checked the mirror before we left." And my surroundings for the paparazzi.

"I've been jumpy since my accident." He rested his head against the seat. "I prefer people to drive like a granny."

"Understood." Poor guy. She probably almost gave him a

panic attack. "Granny driving coming up."

When the signal changed, she eased on the gas and prayed for green lights all the way to the hospital. She had worried about the SUV for nothing. Nobody would think to look for her in Nashville. *Right, Lord?*

~*~

Wade closed his eyes. The van waited at a red light. They had three miles to travel on this stop and go road. Emma hadn't triggered another brake warning since leaving the parking lot. Small victories mattered. Especially to his nerves. How much more tragedy could his family handle? Donoven and Sons was already down one man and depending on the severity of Derek's injury, now two guys might not be making service calls. Cole had been concerned about their dad's stress level before the dog attack. A workman's compensation claim wouldn't lighten the strain. He'd make sure to handle the brunt of the paperwork, so his dad didn't overload.

Lord, I don't know how much more my family can take. Why is all this happening to us? I can't take much more. Please heal Derek swiftly. And I'm asking again for full healing for myself. How long is my recovery going to take? If I could drive, I could work double time and handle service calls. Just a thought. In Jesus' name. Amen.

The van traveled through a major intersection. He tensed and dutifully checked left then right for drivers blowing the signal. He didn't want to get T-boned ever again. He needed to get better. Had to get better. If only Jesus was listening to his prayers.

"I'm so sorry all this is happening with Derek." Emma shot him a compassionate glance before returning her attention to traffic. "Unfortunately, I know what it's like to try and keep a business going when you have an emergency. It happened to me a few years back. With my dad."

What did she mean? His emotional energy circled the drain. Listening to her babble wasn't on his schedule. He feigned interest. Maybe she wouldn't share much. "Do you have many dog bites in a candle store?" His comment bordered on being rude, but his words garnered a laugh from his driver.

"Good one." Her smile remained. "You never know. It could happen with so many service animals." She adjusted her hands on the steering wheel. The ten and two positions met at midnight. "Actually, my dad had a heart attack while I was in college." She leaned toward the windshield.

A cool stream of adrenaline streaked through his veins. Didn't she realize that if the air bag deployed, it would slam against her chest? He had faded bruises to prove the power on impact. He cleared his throat. "Could you sit back. Maybe a little."

"Uh, sure. We don't need me banged up." She glanced at his cane. "Anyway, I don't know how I kept going to classes while managing Home ScentSations. My mom had to take care of my dad, so I worked nights and closed down the shop."

A dose of conviction weighed on his conscience distracting him from his own problems and her driving skills. "I'm sorry to hear about that."

Her eyebrows raised as she cast another glance in his direction. "We should set up a quarter jar for the word *sorry*."

He laughed at the silliness of her suggestion. Her joke overflowed with painful truth. "How'd you get through it all?"

"The simple answer?" She braked for a stoplight. "God. I prayed to Him constantly. My church family prayed and brought meals to my parents. Friends helped out where they could. Sam was amazing."

He'd heard that adjective attached to Sam's name

previously. His brother had reconnected with the family since he started dating Sam. Church was part of Cole's life again as well. It had always been part of Wade's life. That was one reason he couldn't understand why God was slow to fully heal him. "Sam seems nice."

"When I closed the store at night and inventoried boxes, Sam cleaned my apartment and did my wash. It's incredible how much brighter life looks when your bathroom is clean, and you have laundered underwear. Oops. TMI." Her big brown eyes grew wider.

She had the most expressive eyes he had ever seen. Their brilliance hit him like a floodlight. Scrubbing a hand over his jaw, he hid his grin. He could relate to being dependent on others. His parents had seen to his needs during his recovery. He hadn't thought much about clean boxer briefs.

The GPS warned of a right turn in eight-hundred feet.

"How's your dad doing now?" Getting back to pre-accident normal was Wade's constant prayer.

Emma changed lanes. "Physically, he's fine, but spiritually." Her mouth pulled to the side. "He hasn't asked Jesus into his heart. Not even after being healed. I pray for him every day. My mom, too. They won't even open the Bible I gave them. It's been a long road, and I'm still walking it."

"I'm sor—"

"Boy, do we need that jar." She smiled even though what she shared had been riddled with sadness.

He sympathized with her burden. He'd pray daily for his parents if they didn't know Jesus as their Lord.

"You know how God answers prayers?" She side-eyed him, commanding a beat of silence. "Yes. No. And wait."

And wait some more.

"Wisdom from my old Sunday school teacher." Biting her lip, she slowed for a stoplight.

At thirty-two years of age, he wasn't old, and he'd never taught kids the Bible, but he had heard that truth. "I remembered that wisdom during my recovery. Guess I'm in the waiting period." Which had lingered far too long. He had a business to run and an insurance deductible to recoup. What if he never got back to one hundred percent? How would the company function then?

The hospital's towering complex came into view as the GPS announced they were approaching their destination. Emma followed the arrows toward the emergency department. A car reversed out of its spot near the main entrance.

Emma stopped and tapped her fingers on the steering wheel. "If it makes you feel any better, I've been praying for you since December."

He stared at his leg where his cane rested against his jeans. She'd prayed for him, and he hadn't bothered to utter one petition about her employment woes. He hadn't even thanked God for the office help. The Holy Spirit thumped his skull. "Thank you." He cleared his throat.

"You're welcome. It's the least and the best that I can do."

She pulled into the parking spot and turned off the engine.

A similar van was parked diagonal across two spots near the emergency doors. Derek had driven himself to the ER. Derek may be doing better than Wade feared if he could drive. A ray of hopefulness cut through the dread of going into another medical facility.

Emma grasped the door handle. "Today, I've been praying for Derek's healing and that it comes quickly."

"I think we both need a fast yes to that prayer." He gathered the insurance papers from the office.

She gazed at him all serious and calm like he imagined a

soldier looked before he parachuted out of a plane. "Ready, boss?"

Her two simple words would have rankled his nerves hours before. Now, her short sentence became a rallying cry from a teammate. He'd misjudged Emma and had been kind of a jerk. After their conversation, he had a better understanding why God might have placed her on his team. She knew firsthand what it was like to have your work-life balance go totally off the rails. She'd also been praying for him for almost two months. He'd say a few prayers for her to get her life back on track.

"Ready."

He opened his door and steadied himself for what awaited in the ER. He was pretty sure he wasn't ready for weeks with whirlwind Emma.

~*~

A splattering of raindrops pelted Wade as he hobbled toward the emergency entrance, cane in hand. At least it was raining and not snowing. He was tired of gloomy weather and the gloom in his life. Emma walked by his side, holding an umbrella. He was the boss and co-owner of the family business and his sense of duty and empathy for his employees called for him to support Derek. Soon he'd get back to the life he had before the crash even if it meant limping into the future.

The glass doors opened and bathed his body with a warm blast of stale air. A faint aroma of disinfectant had images of hospital rooms filling his brain. He gripped his cane tighter. He wasn't going backward, only forward, away from doctors and sterile exam rooms. This wasn't about him.

A young receptionist in cat-themed scrubs opened an acrylic-glass window. "May I help you?"

Wade licked his lips. The events of the morning jumbled on his tongue. "One of my employees, a Derek Sullivan, was attacked by a dog. He drove here. I see our van in the lot." He pointed to the insignia on his jacket. "I'd like to see him if I could." He indicated Emma. "She's our new office manager." Hopefully all the pertinent paperwork was in the folder Fran had given him because Emma was in training.

The young lady scanned the computer screen. "I'll call back for permission to see if one of you can visit him." She dialed the phone. "Do you have his insurance information. It's incomplete."

"Right here." He held the file folder so she could see it. His damp palm had caused a wave in the paper.

As the receptionist talked on the phone, Emma tugged on the straps of her backpack. "I'll wait out here by the snack machine. I can call Fran and let her know that we arrived and that Derek's van is here."

He appreciated the help. His parents complained about the cell reception when he was hospitalized. Walls in the treatment areas tended to be Wi-Fi killers.

"Find out who Fran has notified." His poor dad didn't need distractions while working a two-man job.

Emma scanned the waiting room. "Will do." She gave him one of those smiles that said she didn't envy the task ahead of him. "I'll be praying for you."

"Thanks." God was being bombarded lately with petitions labeled "Donoven Family."

After getting consent from Derek, the receptionist buzzed him through the doors. He passed glass rooms with curtains blocking the view inside. A chill swept over his flesh. Hospitals did amazing work, but it was never pain-free.

A nurse in black scrubs with a pink stethoscope approached. Her uniform contrasted with the bright fluorescent lighting overhead. "Here to see Mr. Sullivan?"

"You're good." He tried to crack a grin.

She smiled. "It's the logo." She squinted at his name. "Wade." Her expression sobered. "Mr. Sullivan is in room four. He was going into shock when he arrived, so we gave him medication to calm him down. Don't worry. He signed his life away while he was with it."

Black scrubs, whose nametag read Maddie, ushered him down the hallway past a large desk area. "The hand lacerations were deep. We've called a hand surgeon. She should arrive shortly."

Great. Derek wouldn't be at work tomorrow, and the hand surgery bills wouldn't be cheap. With all the talk about hands, his left one throbbed. He needed another round of Emma's acupressure. "Will they do the surgery here? Or at another hospital?"

Maddie stopped in front of room four. "Right here and the patient will need someone to drive him home." She surveyed his cane. Had his gait rivaled an old man's?

Employees at Donoven and Sons couldn't stitch a wound, but they could drive Derek home. Now that Emma was on board, they had extra help. He hated to give Cole credit for pushing the idea to hire her, but Wade had signed off on the official hiring.

"The company's got it covered. We take care of our workers." He blinked at the garish canned fixtures in the ceiling.

Lord, help me be a comfort to Derek. You know how much I hate hospitals. May Derek be stitched and released soon.

Maddie opened a sliding door and whirled the curtain open. She skirted around the bed to an IV machine.

Derek lay on the bed. His man bun had exploded all over the pillowcase. Eyes closed, he sported an IV in one hand and had the other hand perched on a cloth covered riser. Blood-red lines marred his palm.

Wade understood why hospitals liked white linens, but the scarlet-colored lacerations looked horrific against the sheet. The top of Wade's hand itched as if Derek's IV poked his vein. He swallowed saliva that tasted like vomit.

"Hey, Derek." Fake happiness dulled his greeting.

Derek's eyes fluttered open. "Wade. My man." A goofy smile brightened Derek's face. "You came. Flew right over."

The only one flying right now rested in the hospital bed.

"We came after you called Emma. How are you doing?"

"Emma." Derek sank deeper into the pillows and let out a gust of air. "She's so nice. And pretty. She's a real keeper."

Wade shifted his weight. "She sure is." He needed to comfort Derek and find out about the incident, not sing Emma's praises. He paid Emma to manage the office and thinking about the way she looked wasn't professional. "The nurse says they're sending over a surgeon."

Maddie cut behind Wade and wrote vitals on a whiteboard.

Rolling his head side to side, Derek sighed. "I almost made it. Heading to the van when that dog burst past its owner. I hopped in the van. When I went to close the door…it latched onto my hand."

"You did everything right." He kicked himself that the office had no record of that dog. He should have paid more attention to Derek's concerns even though Fran and Emma searched for information.

Nurse Maddie crossed her arms and leaned against the counter by the sink. "We notified animal control due to the injury. The animal has to be watched for illness." Her penetrating stare clenched his gut.

He hadn't even thought of rabies. *Please Lord, protect*

Derek.

"Good idea." He nodded at Maddie. "I don't want anyone else to get hurt."

Maddie checked her watch and headed toward the sliding door. "The surgeon should be here momentarily."

The sooner this day ended, the better. "Thank you for taking care of Derek."

"My pleasure." Maddie swung the curtain closed.

"She's so nice." Derek scanned the checkerboard ceiling as if he counted leaping unicorns.

Wade relaxed knowing that all females today in Derek's estimation were nice and worthy of praise. He didn't care to hear anymore gushing over Emma. He and Derek needed to respect employee boundaries.

Wade shuffled over toward the IV monitor and pulled up a chair by the side of the bed.

"Is there anyone I can call for you? Your mom or dad, or someone local?"

"Hmmm." Derek's eyes closed.

Maddie peeked around the curtain and fluttered a pink piece of paper. "Mr. Sullivan's emergency contact called back. She's leaving work and coming on over. We tried to reach her since the patient was in shock when he arrived."

Wade stood. A blessing had occurred among the trials. He could have taken Derek home to Donoven central, but with Emma staying at his parents' house, that may have caused more issues. "Who'd you call?"

"A neighbor." Maddie glanced at the note. "Says she lives next door. Kelly's her name."

"I'll stay until she arrives and make sure Derek's okay."

"Suit yourself." The nurse inspected Derek's hand.

A middle-aged woman in a white coat entered. She relocated the glasses from her head to her nose and studied

Derek's lacerations. "Looks like I found the right patient."

After introductions and an explanation of the procedure, Wade headed toward the sliding door.

"Hey, man," Derek said. "Could you pray real quick?"

"Sure, I'd be happy to." His heartbeat raced as sweat beaded on his lip. Derek didn't realize some of Wade's prayers were falling on deaf ears. God seemed to be sending them through the shredder.

The surgeon shifted away from the bed. Wade rested his right hand on Derek's leg.

"Dear Lord, please take care of Derek. Watch over the surgeon and bless her abilities. Heal my friend fast and well. And please protect others from the dog. In Jesus' name. Amen."

"Thanks, dude."

Wade gave a thumbs-up sign and excused himself to the waiting area. His stomach rumbled as he retraced his steps down the tiled hallway. Why did hospitals have to look so stark? Relief flowed through his veins as he hit the electronic door switch.

The throb in his leg and the events of the morning made him want to dive into his own bed. One without rails.

He strode carefully into an empty waiting area. Where was Emma?

"Are you looking for the short brunette in the green shirt?" the receptionist asked through the window.

He swiveled on his cane. "Yeah."

"She went to the cafeteria to get you lunch." Her gaze found the wall clock. "She should be back soon."

"Thanks." He smiled as Derek's words echoed through his brain. *She's so nice.* He rubbed his chin. He actually agreed. His temporary office manager was supportive and on the ball, but they weren't becoming best friends or anything more.

Their relationship was solely business.

9

Later that afternoon, Emma leaned forward in her office chair and stared at the computer screen. Fran showed where to enter a part number. Who knew there were so many electrical gadgets. A plastic dancing flower underneath the screen mocked Emma's inexperience with electrical lingo like strip fixtures and recess cans. When Fran left the office and Sam brought Herbie to Nashville, that dancing flower was going in a drawer.

Pain shot between her temples. Could she learn this new business? Her shadowing time had been cut short by Derek's injury. Did she know enough to handle the office on her own with Wade's oversight? He would have to cut her some slack since the scheduling was a mess. Unfortunately, Wade didn't seem as patient as Fran. The woman's voice soothed angst like hot chocolate with tiny marshmallows and a cinnamon sprinkle.

"I know this is a lot to take in." Fran squeezed Emma's wrist and swiveled in her computer chair. "You've only been here a few hours and had to take care of an emergency. Don't be afraid to call me if you have questions." She winked. "But only after the pain killers wear off."

Emma smiled. Fran had been steadfast and encouraging on this crazy day. Too bad a work catastrophe marred Fran's send-off to surgery. "Thank you. I'll remember that."

Fran cocked her head toward Wade who worked on his laptop filling in forms for the insurance adjuster. "Wade's a wealth of knowledge too. Aren't you, Wade?"

He glanced in Fran's direction. His blue eyes widened like a buck in the headlights. "Whatever you say, boss."

Was Wade distracted counting dollar signs and insurance premium hikes? The poor guy had blood on his cuff after visiting Derek in the emergency room. Today might not have been the best first day on the job, but it surpassed her last day in Ron's office.

Rising from her chair, Fran grabbed her cane and purse. "I'm going to head out. It's almost five and my husband and I have a class at the hospital tonight."

"Don't worry about us. We'll be fine." The least she could do was reassure Fran and Wade that another disaster didn't crouch around the corner. She stood. "We'll be praying for your surgery."

"Thank you, hon." Fran gave her a side-arm hug. "Several prayer chains are at the ready."

"I'll walk you out." Wade rose and grasped his cane.

"Aren't we a pair." Fran laughed. "The hobble twins." She elbowed him. "When I get back. These props are going to be long gone."

"I hope you're right." Wade flashed a slight grin. "Though, I might have to bribe my doctor for a release."

Wade escorted Fran to her car.

Emma's boss might be a grump at times, but she had witnessed a tenderness and a teddy-bear heart under his grouchy exterior.

On the desk, next to the computer, Emma's phone vibrated. She had forgotten to turn it off after texting from the hospital. A message from Sam flashed on the screen.

COLE AND I ARE STAYING UNTIL WEDNESDAY :)

Emma pumped a fist. Having Sam around to sort family drama and rehash the day's events bested a double hot fudge sundae. Hesitation clouded her excitement. Didn't Sam have an interview? She didn't want to inconvenience her friend further.

She texted.

WHAT ABOUT YOUR INTERVIEW?

IT'S THURSDAY. I'M GOOD. PRACTICE MAKES PERMANENT.

Their late Sunday school teacher and greatest neighbor ever—Mr. Ted—used the same phrase. Emma couldn't remember Sam being unprepared for anything. Except for her cancer.

She surveyed the door to the garage. Wade hadn't returned. He didn't need more shocking news.

DOES WADE KNOW YOU'RE STAYING?

COLE IS TEXTING HIM.

Then Wade knew, or he was finding out. That might explain his delay in returning. Would Wade resent his little brother coming to the rescue? The tension between the brothers resembled a string of taffy that never broke. Even if Cole had been absent from the company for a while, he had jumped in to help after Wade's accident. Cole wasn't the first man to make poor decisions because of a woman. The Bible was full of deceived men going all the way back to the first man, Adam. Or was Wade frustrated watching Cole perform tasks easily, ones Wade could have done before his surgery. Either way, she would do her best to assist Wade while she stayed in Nashville. She wasn't some inexperienced teenager. Office management and small business skills were woven into her DNA. Soon, she'd get the hang of the electrical jargon.

Wade's steps echoed in the hallway.

SEE U SOON.

She stuffed her phone in her backpack and thanked God for the blessing of being able to spend more time with Sam.

Wade entered the office, filling the doorway with his height and broad shoulders. She shook her head and ordered herself not to admire his build.

"Ready to go?" He scrubbed a hand over his jaw. She half expected his chin to elongate like silly putty "That is, if you can drive my dad's Suburban. He and Cole are swinging by the hospital to pick up Derek's van." He reached and removed a set of keys hanging under the counter.

Was that a challenge? Or an insult? Or a simple question? She'd cut him some slack after a long day. She'd only activated the brake warning once in route to the emergency room.

"I made it to the hospital and back in a service van. With only a minor scare."

"Minor for whom?" He flashed the briefest hint of a grin before turning out the hall light. "All I know is, I'm ready for some of my mom's cooking."

Her stomach rumbled at the mention of food. She'd eaten a granola bar for lunch and splurged on a sandwich, chips, and brownie for Wade. Her first payday was four days off and her credit card balance was screaming "not again."

She shut down the computer and activated the answering service as Fran had shown. "You'll be fine with me as your driver. Lightning doesn't strike twice." She took the keys from his hand and gave him a saucy grin. "And for your information, I've never had an accident."

He held the front door for her and blew out an exaggerated breath. "Now, you've jinxed us."

Hah! Wade Donoven actually had a sense of humor.

~*~

Upon entering Linda's home, the aroma of tomato sauce and garlic had Emma melting onto the tiled foyer. No other job offered the benefit of scrumptious home cooked meals.

Sam carried a salad bowl to the dining room table and flashed her classic I-know-something eye bulge.

Did Sam text prematurely? Were Sam and Cole leaving tonight as planned? Emma's mind swirled with worst-case scenarios. Would she get fired after only one day?

"Hey Wade. I was sorry to hear about Derek." Sam strolled toward the coat closet. Her voice sounded sincere, but Emma knew it was small talk before big talk.

"Thanks. What a day." Wade hung up their coats looking as animated as a burlap sack.

Emma lifted her backpack. "I'm going to put this in our room."

Sam followed her down the hall and then tugged her toward the bathroom. "Come wash up. Dinner's almost ready. I want to hear all about your day."

"With the way your acting," Emma whispered, "I should be   doing   the   listening." Sam closed the bathroom door and turned on the faucet.

"I don't think this is anything to worry about but—"

"We're doing bathroom reconnaissance, and you're telling me not to worry?" Emma squirted soap on her hands. The smell of lavender scented the air.

"I'm sure it's nothing." Sam grabbed the soap. "When I called Ernie and asked if he could watch my house until Wednesday, he mentioned seeing a black car. Twice."

Emma's stomach sickened as if she had ingested the flowery soap. How many more setbacks could she take? Had she brought trouble to Sam's doorstep? To Ernie and Gretta? Sam's elderly neighbors didn't need any problems. She blinked back tears.

"I should never have come to Tennessee. I don't want to see you get hurt. Not you or anyone else." She dried her hands. She could use a tissue about the size of the plush bath towel. *Lord, can I get a do-over of the last week?*

"Hey, don't worry." Sam used the towel after Emma. "In

Ernie's words, the kid looked like a college dropout admiring himself in the mirror. The guy drove off when Ernie yelled that he was calling the sheriff."

Emma leaned against the cool marble counter. "I'd feel terrible if something happened to your neighbors. And you." She blew out a rambling breath. "Did you tell Ernie not to open the shed?"

Sam laughed. "Your car is still incognito, and the sheriff said he'd patrol more often. As for you, don't you see God's hand in this?"

"God's hand? Not really." Emma slouched. "Maybe His pinkie finger."

"God's perfect timing has you in Nashville, not Whispering Creek. My house is vacant. The trail will get cold. You'll see." Sam wrapped her in a hug that was softer than all of Linda's plush towels. "God has you employed hours away from Whispering Creek and out of the limelight. Ron Runyard and all the scandal he caused will blow over when the next salacious news story hits." Sam eased away and glanced at her watch. "In about thirty minutes."

"What about your safety when you return home?" Emma squeezed Sam's hand. "I know God's in control, but bad stuff still happens." She didn't want to think about all the horrible situations she'd seen on police shows. She stroked her tortoise charm. *Lord, please keep Sam safe and everyone caught up in this trouble.*

"I'm not bubbly you, and I don't know anything about Ron's business." Sam's smile buoyed Emma's spirit. "Besides, Cole and Ernie are pretty scary. They'll run any trespassers off of the property."

"Do you think we should tell Mike and Linda?" Would they send her packing if they knew her former boss was tabloid fodder?

Emma opened the bathroom door. No one stood guard outside. She almost expected to see Wade waiting with a grim face. But then, he hadn't been complaining to anyone about her. At least, not yet.

Sam stepped into the hall. "The guy was in Whispering Creek. Nashville is almost two hours away. We're good."

Wade rounded the corner and stood at the end of the hall. "Dinner will be ready in five."

"Thanks." Emma beamed at her boss. They'd worked well as a team. Neither of them panicked while they handled Derek's emergency. It helped her sense of safety that Wade resembled a bodybuilder.

Her boss returned to the kitchen.

Sam linked her arm. "Jesus is our rock. He'll give us wisdom and protection."

"I know." Emma forced a smile. "It's just that with this scandal, it seems there are a few pebbles between my feet and the rock. I get an unsteady feeling. Like I'm reaching for God and He's backing away."

"Those pebbles are in your imagination. God knows every detail of what is happening in your life. Satan might be pitching fast balls, but God's got an enormous glove and perfect reflexes."

Emma laughed. "Spoken by a teacher who pulled recess duty."

"Remember when Mr. Ted would put a dime in his hand and let our Sunday school class try to get it out of his fist?" Sam tilted her head and gave a you-know-this eyebrow raise.

"We never got the dime out of his hand, and no one can snatch us out of Jesus' hand. Mr. Ted made sure we knew that truth." She halted near the end of the hallway. "It's just living that truth is harder than hearing it."

"Tell me about it." Sam displayed a lopsided grin.

Her friend would know after surviving breast cancer. "You always make me feel better." Emma gently pushed Sam toward the kitchen. "Now, let's go get some garlic bread. No one's going to snatch that out of my hand."

~*~

After Mike said grace, Emma lifted a piece of bread from the basket and passed it to Sam. Wade and Cole sat across from them at the dining table while Mike and Linda sat at the ends. Linda had pre-plated the lasagna. The waft of the meat sauce made Emma light as a feather. Or had her blood sugar nosedived? She wasn't taking any chances. She set her fork on repeat.

"Hey." Cole's table talk came out muffled from his full mouth. "I checked the notes on my phone from some of my last service calls before leaving. I found one call with a vicious dog. The area was the same as Derek's customer."

She told herself to keep on chewing as silence befell the table. If Cole thought he was making light conversation, he had failed with an enormous F-minus.

Wade pushed back from the table. A feat that would take all her strength because the marinara was calling her name.

"And how in the—" Wade glanced at his dad. "How is that supposed to help us? Derek's already been bitten."

Mike raised his fork. The tines pointed toward Cole. "Wade said he checked the card file. Nothing came up in the system either."

Wade chucked his napkin on the table with his right hand. His left one rested stiffly at the edge. "Did you think to tell us about the dog back then or were you high tailing it out the door?" The heat emanating from Wade's body sent an El Niño blast across the tablecloth. At least she wasn't the cause of this fight.

"Wait." Sam stopped passing the vegetable bowl. "You don't have software to track incidents?"

"The card file has worked fine." Mike's elbows-on-the-table lean would have sent Emma running, but Sam met her future father-in-law's stare head on.

Where was a brake warning when you needed one? Sam glanced at Emma with her proud teacher face.

Uh oh. Sam was in problem-solver mode. And she knew about People Peeps. Emma pressed her lips together and willed herself to stay silent about her program. She tried to send a mental message to Sam to keep quiet.

"Emma created customer service software for her last employer, but it can be used anywhere. Maybe it would work here." Sam glowed like a lantern. She obviously wasn't listening to the subliminal messaging.

All her life, Emma had prayed to make five foot-seven, but missed it by two inches. Now, with every set of Donoven eyes piercing her with curiosity, and one set with disbelief, Emma wished she was five foot even and could slip underneath the tablecloth and disappear.

She shoved a fork full of lasagna in her mouth and nodded. No one spoke. Everyone watched her eat. Bad idea to force feed oneself during family tension because her mouth kept chewing. "Um." That was professional. She swallowed. "I created People Peeps to keep track of resident's birthdays and hobbies at the senior community. There are fields that can be customized. It's never been used." Obviously, since the retirement center was all a scam.

"Sounds stalkerish." Wade lounged back in his chair. "We have a system that works. Maybe if those notes—" He air quoted awkwardly in Cole's direction—"had made it into the card file, Derek would be okay. Besides, I'm not implementing a new software program while Fran's out."

Ouch. She wasn't a stalker, but Wade had a good point about updating procedures when Fran wasn't in the office.

Cole grabbed another slice of bread. "I'm sharing what works for me. There's no pressure to change the system, bro."

Then why bring it up? Was Cole oblivious to how his brother and father might view the mention of his method. Her job required her to work closely with Wade. They were working as a team, and she wasn't going to add any more stress to the situation.

"Wade's right." Her bold statement commanded the table. "I wouldn't want to hurt Fran or hit her with new software on the day she returns. Fran asks customers to put their pets away. I'll make sure I ask the same question and follow up."

Wade scooted his chair closer to his plate. His gaze met hers as he cut a square of lasagna with his fork. His eyes were as blue as a fiery topaz. And they looked...alive. If he kept staring at her, the Italian feast on her plate would go up in flames as would her resolve to keep her boss in the friend zone.

She cleared her throat. "Maybe we could brainstorm a better name for my software because People Peeps does sound weird."

"How about Purely People?" Leave it to Sam to always want to help.

Linda held the lasagna pan. "Who wants seconds?"

Saved by the pasta. How did that woman survive living with three strong-willed men? Was it teamwork? Emma had survived a tumultuous day at her new job by teaming with Wade to solve a crisis. Working with her boss was better than working against him. She'd follow Wade's lead. Emma didn't want to be the subject of a family argument again.

She raised her water glass and silently toasted her first day at Donoven and Sons Electric. Her career could only soar upward from dog bites and family fights and strangers in black SUVs.

10

If the throbbing in Wade's left hand had been an instrument, it would have mimicked a tuba. Sitting in the office, at a desk by the printer, he could hardly hold the paper steady while he signed checks. His brother's revelation last night about having a personal note system which indicated an incident similar to Derek's attack coiled Wade's nerves tighter than a rattler ready to strike. A little forewarning about a vicious animal would have been nice. It could have avoided another insurance claim.

Emma chatted on the phone with a customer as if they were lifelong buds. The woman could talk to drying paint and get a chuckle. She and Fran were like office twins always chatting with people as if they were long lost relatives. Whatever customer relations class they had taken, he must have skipped.

Wade flexed his hand. He had to get back to being one hundred percent and able to drive and perform service calls. Burdening his father with a heavier workload gnawed at his frayed nerves. His dad had slimmed down his service call schedule until Wade's accident had catapulted the elder Donoven back into the field. Why was God making Wade wait for a full recovery? His family needed him to be healthy now.

"I noticed your hand was a bit stiff at dinner last night." Emma rolled closer in her office chair. "How about some help?"

She'd make a great spy since her senses remained consistently on high alert, or she was plain nosy. At least she cared. Although, he didn't think massage therapy was listed on the day's schedule.

"Do you have a doctor's release in your pocket? That would really help." A release to drive had been his goal for weeks.

"Wish I did along with a criminal GPS tracker." She held out her arm clothed in an official Donoven and Sons navy oxford. His mom insisted Emma wear one of hers since Emma hadn't packed for a long stay.

Emma tilted her head with emphasis. "You're doing more of a light tissue massage than applying actual pressure."

Her arm hung in the air as she beckoned him to give her his claw. Should he cave? His hand movements had improved after her pizza night acupressure. But was this appropriate? She was a female employee. "What if someone sees you touching the boss?"

She slouched dramatically. "The mail guy's come and gone, and Mike is going straight home after he finishes his call. No one is going to be scandalized if I touch your palm."

This girl was one determined Yankee. Could he refuse the blessing of being pain-free? She was on company time and healing the boss would help the company. He straightened his fingers and searched for the clock. One hour until close. Could he weather another cramping episode?

"What does the Bible say about seeing someone in need and not offering help?" She shifted her chair a few inches closer.

First, prying and now a mini sermon? He pushed away from the desk. He'd lost this battle. Since he was pinned in the back of the office by a zealous new hire, there was no way he could escape her acupressure session. And if he was honest, he wanted to be able to control his hand. He extended his arm. One plus, she did smell better than the last guy who performed therapy on his hand. The sooner healing arrived, the better. Maybe she'd leave him alone and go back to work.

"So now you're not only the office lady but the Good Samaritan?"

"Exactly." Her voice sounded like she was on a sugar high. "Helping a friend who happens to be my boss."

At least she had the boss part right. Did he consider her a friend? She had helped his family out of a jam and had been supportive during Derek's incident. A competent acquaintance was more like it. This was business after all.

She supported his hand and pushed her middle finger into the same spot she used previously. "This finger is best used with a ninety-degree angle."

Whatever she was doing left his poor attempts at massage in the dust. He stared at her dark nail polish while his bones turned to marshmallow in the chair. He forced himself to remember that she was the temporary office lady. For the pain relief following her sessions, she deserved a bonus. He hated to admit it, but Derek was right. Emma embodied nice.

"When you press that spot, it's like all the stress leaves my body. Cole could walk in and repeat his stupid remarks about the dog bite, and I wouldn't even care. If he hadn't taken off with his last girlfriend, he could have warned us about the animal." Wade blinked. He could fall asleep any moment. "And if Cole had stayed around, he'd have been on the service call when I had the accident. I wouldn't be waiting on a doctor's release." He babbled as she did her nerve hypnotism. Good thing his recovery was on the horizon because he could get accustomed to having her touch his hand.

Emma shifted her finger to his wrist. Her mouth pulled to the side. "You're not blaming Cole for your accident, are you? He may have driven faster or slower or taken a different route that night. Seems to me, you were in the wrong place at the wrong time."

Was she sticking up for Cole? His slumbering heart kicked into high gear while his arm relaxed, warming like a sauna. Miss Nice had stabbed at a sore spot when it came to his brother.

"I mean, if you believe in God's providence, you were in the intersection at the correct time."

"Oh, that's rich. Make the accident my fault or blame it on God." His employee better be careful. She was flunking her probationary period. He attempted to tug his hand free. "Let go of my arm."

She pressed harder. "I'm not done."

Deep breathing, he broadened his chest. "I think you are." He'd rip his arm free from her nimble-fingered grasp if he didn't think that he may harm her and cause another workman's comp claim.

"Your point needs more pressure and time." Her determined gaze narrowed. "I'd like to help you. I also know about going through hard times. My whole life imploded in twenty-four hours. I lost my job, no, my career." Her tone became definite, filled with a defiance he hadn't heard in the chaos of Derek's injury. "My last paycheck never arrived, and I lost the inheritance money my grandmother left me. I'd say I had a bit of a crash, too."

Is this why Cole and Sam brought Emma to Nashville? For a job and a paycheck? Did his dad know her entire sob story? Her experiences made the aftermath of an auto accident seem tame.

The tension eased on his wrist, but his hand remained cradled in Emma's.

"All I know is that I'd never want to hurt my brother. If I had a brother. It's not a stroll in the park being an only child."

"I've never hurt Cole." He formed a fist and withdrew his hand. He wasn't going to share his life story with a woman he barely knew. Words didn't flow freely from his mouth for good reason. This wasn't a counseling session.

She scooted her chair toward the main computer. "*Never* is a strong word. If you blame him for any part of your injuries, then you've already hurt the relationship." She waggled a finger at him. "Don't squeeze that hand after we got the blood flowing."

Her reprimand held one truth. She certainly got his blood cruising through his veins. How dare she act like she knew his history. She might as well have decked him because his jaw ached, and a metallic taste soured his mouth.

"We're done here." He jumped to his feet and grabbed his cane. He'd stomp out of the office even if it meant going back into formal physical therapy.

Her eyes glistened as she studied him. Either she was going to cry or preach another sermonette.

Man, Cole! What did his lovesick brother get him involved with this time? He hurried into the hallway wondering if he could field a workman's comp claim for making an employee cry.

~*~

Emma willed her tears to stay hidden. Her behemoth of a boss hobbled through the doorway to his luxury office. His tight-lipped expression advertised that she'd said too much. She remained at Fran's computer replaying her advice in her head. Her parents had said to speak the truth in love. Even Mr. Ted had been a proponent of speaking what God laid on your mind if it would benefit a friend. She'd challenged Wade on his latent anger, and now her backside might be booted to the curb.

Okay God, I need wisdom from the Holy Spirit here. Do I beg to keep my job or let the truth sink into my boss's thick skull?

The office phone rang.

God Almighty, You are too good. You sure know how to cut the tension.

She reached for the phone. "Donoven and Sons Electric. Emma speaking." For an hour longer.

The caller hung up.

Thank You, Lord. She didn't need a wavering voice and the sniffles dealing with a customer.

The empty doorway greeted her like a porchlight. How would she recap her day when they arrived at Mike and Linda's home for dinner? "Hey, I'm getting the hang of the office, but I insulted Wade. Told him not to blame his brother for his accident. Whoopsie. Too much truth telling with my boss." Yeah, right. She stared at tomorrow's schedule on the screen. Starting over somewhere else would be a big bummer.

Should she apologize? Some people were uptight and closed off as a personality. Wade could have misspoken about Cole taking the service call. She hadn't prayed before speaking her mind either. Being a straight shooter had its benefits until you met a ricochet bullet.

Spying Fran's mason jar pen holder, she emptied the pens onto the desk. She rummaged in her backpack for a quarter and dropped it into the glass container. The plink sounded freeing. Apologizing may not smooth a ruffled ego, but it would save future troubles. If Sam and Cole married, Emma couldn't imagine the maid of honor and the best man shooting eye darts at each other. Although, it could make for interesting wedding party photographs.

Carrying her makeshift sorry jar, she strolled like an attendant carrying a cup to the king. She knocked on the threshold to Wade's office and entered.

Wade sat at a desk with his back to the door. He stared out the window into the parking lot. So much for working.

She placed the jar on his desk. "Truce. I don't want there to be hard feelings between us. I'm sorry, so sorry, if I accused you. I'm not an expert on your family or your car crash."

He swiveled his chair and acknowledged her presence.

Stepping toward the hall, she laced her fingers and swallowed through a desert. Why did she have to open her mouth earlier?

"Sam is my oldest and dearest friend. She and Cole were trying to help me out. You don't have to keep me on staff if it's awkward." Forcing a smile didn't work when her mouth rebelled and fought the curve.

"I'm not firing you, Emma." He said those four words as if he'd just come from pulling a twenty-four-hour shift. He eyed the jar and his lips flatlined. "You were a big help yesterday when Derek got hurt. And today, you handled the phones like a pro. You've got a job here until Fran returns. We've suffered enough changes."

"I can relate." She grasped her silver necklace and shifted her tortoise charm side to side. "But then you know that since I blurted out my changes earlier."

Wade opened the desk drawer and ruffled some papers. He pulled out a quarter and dropped it in her sorry jar. The coin made a muted thud as it hit her contribution.

The sound may not have been as stark as her metal clanging against the glass, but it rallied her spirit that coming to Tennessee wasn't a mistake. She and Wade could work as a team, and she could be a blessing to him and his family while her woes back home settled down.

She leaned against the door frame relieved that her job and dignity were intact. "Sam will be the first to tell you that sometimes my filter gets clogged."

A glimmer of life spread across Wade's face like a tiny flame on a newly lit tealight. "Then I think we might need to keep this around. I'm sorry is a popular phrase at Donoven and Sons." He rotated the mason jar and grinned as if the jar was an autographed football jersey.

Broad shoulders. Bluer than blue eyes. A determined smile. She hightailed it to the main computer. If she didn't get the fleeting vision of her attractive boss vanquished from her mind, she'd have to spring for another quarter.

11

Tuesday night, the local burger joint brimmed with patrons. Every booth was taken. Guys watched football replays while a few women chatted under the ice-skating competition. Wade perched on a tall black bar stool at a corner table. His large frame craved a padded back rest and flooring under both of his boots. The steel rung of the stool caused an ache in his calf while the aroma of fry grease and grilled meat made his stomach growl.

Cole approached with a plate of wings. His expression rivaled a kid at their first stock car race. This outing should be a fun time between brothers, and it could be if only Emma's words hadn't been playing on a loop inside of his brain. Had he held Cole somewhat responsible for all the recent challenges in his life? He didn't want to reveal his past anger toward his little brother, but God wrestled with his conscience. He felt compelled to fess up about the misplaced blame and start with a clean slate. Cole was active in the family business again, and Wade needed to clear the air. He prayed Cole would accept his apology and forgive his big brother's abysmal attitude.

His brother set the plate of wings in the center of the round table. Two smaller dishes sat near the edge with a pile of napkins. The harried waitress had dropped them off when she brought their drinks.

Wade breathed in the aroma of peppers and brown sugar. At least he and Cole agreed on wing sauces. Honey Sriracha and Buffalo.

"I won't tell mom you ordered a full plate of wings after eating her casserole."

Cole plopped on his stool. He looked as amped as the kids in the sports team pictures hanging on the wooden planked wall. "Hey, it's not every day my brother invites me out and pays the bill." Cole rubbed his hands together. "I've been waiting for an invite for twenty-seven years."

"Oh, come on." His brother liked to exaggerate. Though, a quick mind scan couldn't recall a time he and Cole went out socially of late. Was it an exaggeration? Had to be. "I included you."

"Since when did the Homecoming King want his eighth-grade brother around?" Cole shoveled three wings onto his plate and licked his fingers. "I'll take it now, though. But I can't help being a little suspicious about the reason."

"Do I need a reason?" Wade sipped his cola and had to work to get the liquid through his straw-thin throat. "I wanted to clear the air before you left tomorrow."

"The air's clear where I'm sitting." Cole prayed over their food and dove right into his second dinner.

Why did Cole have to be so glib? Couldn't he stop stuffing his face long enough to consider there may be something Wade needed to get off of his chest. They were both part of the family business again, and Wade still needed a doctor's note to participate fully. Not to mention, Cole had unleashed a tornado named Emma who played psychologist for the office while improving Wade's physical therapy.

He grabbed another wing before Cole inhaled the whole order.

"It's...well...Emma mentioned—"

"Hah! I knew it." Sauce seeped into the corners of Cole's mouth. "I knew Emma would grow on you."

What was his brother babbling about? Donoven and Sons

was an electrical company, not a greenhouse or dating service.

"She's not growing on me." He bit off a hunk of chicken and let the sauce sizzle on his tongue. "Emma blurts out what she's thinking about life and work. Something about not having a filter."

"Sounds like Emma." Cole's stupid grin returned. "It can be annoying until you get used to it. Then, it's no big deal."

"No big deal unless you're accused of harboring anger in your heart and hurting the relationship with your only brother." He regurgitated Emma's accusation and waited for Cole's reaction. Would Cole be curious about his confession or keep stuffing his mouth? His brother was a sharp guy, but sometimes he stalled and acted oblivious.

"You like her." Cole held a half-eaten wing across the table. "Admit it."

"What? No." Hadn't Cole listened? His brother needed to open his ears and respond. A little chewing might help. This was one of the worst mistakes of Wade's life. He should never have listened to Emma. Note to self. Her psychotherapy was best nipped in the bud. "I'm stuck in the office with her. Someone has to train her in day-to-day stuff. We were talking, and something I said made her accuse me of holding onto anger."

"About your accident?" Cole's mouth gaped and not for another bite of chicken. Finally, his brother had focused.

Man, he hoped honesty was the best insurance policy because he didn't want to be at odds with his brother again.

"She suggested that I was angry toward you." He wiped his hands on his napkin and waited for the reaction or retaliation.

"Me?" Restaurant noise accompanied Cole's shock. "I wasn't in Nashville or even working for dad when you had the accident."

"I know." He curled his toes in his boot and prayed his words would bring healing. "I was mad about the way you left the company. When I had the accident, it was easier to lump all my anger together and blame you. Thinking you might have taken the Sunday service call. If you had, then I wouldn't be injured." Voicing the thought made him realize how heartless he'd been.

"So, I'd have had the crash instead of you." Cole leaned against the back of the stool. His expression emptied as his gaze studied a replay of last weekend's game.

"Maybe." He gave his brother credit for sitting calmly and not lashing out. "I'm sorry for even thinking it." Truly, he never wanted to see his brother harmed.

A vision of Emma and her mason jar flashed through his memory. He'd apologized more in the last few days than he had in the last few years. "I'd never wish my injuries, pain, and recovery on you. Or anyone." How could he have been so petty? His stomach ached and not from the Nashville Hot appetizer. "I love you, bro." Eyes tingling, he swiped his cheek. "When you left the business because of your old girlfriend, I got mad and never let go of the bitterness. I want it gone, now. You've really stepped up in a big way. Can you forgive me?"

Cole slumped as if Wade's baggage weighed on his spirit. "Wow. All this from one conversation with Emma?" Cole scrubbed a hand over his jaw. "I had the anger thing going, too, when I left the business for my ex. It took Sam to show me how far I had traveled from God and how important my family was in my life. When you asked me to pitch your bid in Sperry's Crossing, I looked at it as an olive branch. So yeah." Cole's eyes grew misty. "Of course, I forgive you. You'll always be my big brother."

"Thanks, little bro." Wade's whole body became light and

carefree like he felt after one of Emma's hand therapy sessions. For the first time in a while, he was on the same page with Cole, with God, and with the person he had been before the collision. Resentment didn't distort his thoughts. Why couldn't he have seen this before? He'd have to thank God for using Emma to open his eyes.

Cole cleared his throat. "I hope we can do more nights like this."

"Sure, we can go out again." Wade tempered a huge smile. "But next time, you're paying."

Holding up his almost sauce-free hands, his brother flashed a satisfied grin. "No problem. I'll pull an extra shift here in Nashville to pay for it." Cole pushed the plate of wings toward him. "Last one is for you. I left a big tip on your card."

Wade laughed. *Thank You, Lord, for little brothers.*

He hadn't always been appreciative of having his younger brother tagging along. He'd left Cole to fend for himself numerous times, but now he readied to embrace the blessing of having a closer relationship.

He bit into the gift of the last wing determined to be a better brother and a better man. A spit-fire stranger had spoken her mind and upended his world. How on earth was he going to deal with Emma and her words of wisdom for several more weeks? His new hire may be nosy, but she was also intuitive, intriguing, and if he wasn't careful, she'd break free from the friend zone.

~*~

Emma glanced at the clock. The time glowed ten minutes later than the last time she had checked—10:57 PM.

Sam snored softly. Sleep came easily when you didn't harbor regrets.

Emma didn't wish insomnia on her friend. Sam had

survived breast cancer, a breakup, and the death of their mutual friend Mr. Ted. The relocation from Wisconsin to Tennessee was a speed bump in the road, but it had yielded Sam a new house and a new boyfriend. Now all Sam needed was a teaching position. Emma prayed Sam's job interview on Thursday would be fruitful.

Tomorrow, Sam and Cole would return to Whispering Creek, leaving Emma at Donoven and Sons Electric as the new office lady. Too bad she had insulted her new boss. Why did she have to accuse Wade of being angry at his brother? She should have kept that under wraps like she did her People Peeps software. Was Wade venting to Cole about her on their brotherly outing?

Rolling onto her side, she faced the bedroom door. She closed her eyes and willed herself to fall asleep. Wade had accepted her apology, so why wouldn't her brain shut off? She remembered a song from Sunday school about counting one's blessings. Hopefully listing her blessings would calm her imagination.

She liked helping the Donoven family. Her salary filled her bank account. Tennessee had milder winters.

A scraping sound drew her attention to the door.

Her eyes flew open. Did Linda have mice? An adrenaline streak spiked her insomnia.

She squinted at the thin line of light coming from the hallway. Something was shoved under the door and rested on the carpeting. Was it moving? Thankfully, no.

Curious, she slipped from the comforter to retrieve the object. Bending to get a better look; she knew what it was. A quarter.

Her heart kicked up a notch. *Thank You, Jesus!* She envisioned dancing around the room, but that might wake Sam.

She gripped the quarter in her fist and punched her arm in the air. Wade's rough exterior had suffered a few cracks. She had to remind herself that Wade was her boss because when he was honest, and open, and confident, the gauge rose on her attraction meter.

The fact that Wade had valued her advice boosted her beleaguered confidence. The evening with Cole must have gone well, or instead of a quarter, she'd be getting a pink slip.

12

Emma hung up the phone and stretched her arms toward the ceiling. Thursday and Friday were booked solid, and she had avoided overtime for her accommodating employer. Not an easy task with Derek out until Monday and Cole leaving this afternoon. At the end of work, she'd have logged in three days of pay. With Sam heading to Whispering Creek, she was losing her sounding board and sanity keeper. Thank God the Donoven family was supportive. Even she and Wade had slipped into a routine.

The customer waiting room door opened. Sam entered as if summoned, her arms overloaded with a large brown sack and drink tray.

Emma raced to help her friend. She opened the hallway door and grabbed the cardboard cupholder. "Let me help." Her stomach rumbled as the waft of coffee beans and a hint of orange zest enlivened her senses. The stale office air could use a strategically placed rosemary infused vanilla candle.

"I come bearing lunch and good news." Sam set the large bag on top of the mini fridge. "Fran's husband called, and Fran is out of surgery, in a hospital room, and doing well. She's going home tomorrow."

"That's wonderful. I've been praying for her." The sooner Fran recovered, the sooner the Donoven family could do business as usual. Emma could find a permanent job with a glowing recommendation and not have any gaps on her resume. She wouldn't complain about spending the month with an attractive boss who wore humility and denim well.

That combination was difficult to find in the workplace.

Sam handed her a drink. "They didn't have chamomile tea, but I thought you might need a mid-day pick-me-up. Enjoy your Orange Blossom Brigadoon."

"Do you know me or what?" Emma sipped the succulent scented liquid. The warmth helped ease the loneliness seeping into her spirit at losing her bestie to Whispering Creek. "I didn't sleep much last night and keeping track of technicians is jumbling my brain."

Plopping into Wade's office chair, Sam removed her coat and used her boot heels to scooch closer. "Where's Wade?" She scanned the office as if Wade might appear in the hallway.

"One of the guys got back early and drove him to the bank." Emma sat in front of the main computer. With the caffeinated tea entering her blood stream, she could don a cape with a lightning rod insignia and twirl around the waiting room.

"I'm serious, Em. If this job gets to be too much, I will come and get you. With as fast as news cycles turn, Ron will be forgotten by the weekend. I even cleaned out space in Cole's truck before I came over in case you changed your mind."

"Cole let you drive his truck? Now, that's love." She squinted at the schedule on the screen. "Loverboy should be here in about fifteen minutes."

"Then grab your choice of sandwich before the carnivores arrive." Sam handed her the brown sack.

"Hope you're right about the media." Emma opened the bag and chose a veggie wrap before returning the food to Sam. "I feel like I'm living in an alternate reality. I made the newspaper for high school plays and the Dean's List, but never white-collar crime. I keep asking God why this happened to me. I liked the idea of making people's lives special. Especially in their golden years. I even prayed about accepting the position with Ron and felt a sense of peace. Now, look at me."

"Oh, Em. I don't know why this is happening either, but I know that you are a blessing to me and the Donovens. God will work all this out. Just wait and see." Sam held her sub sandwich high and came in for a side-armed hug.

Having someone in her life who truly cared and shared her faith in Jesus rallied Emma's resolve. A few more weeks in Tennessee was no big deal. She liked the mild winter and making new friends. Mike, Linda, and Wade had stepped up in a big way by giving her employment and opening their home. Wade's initial doubts about her abilities had waned, and he was fast becoming someone who brightened her day. She hoped she'd be around to see his last triumph and celebrate a driving release.

Sam pulled away and began unwrapping her lunch. "The Lord is my rock, my fortress and my —"

"Deliverer. Psalm 18:2." The delight of remembering her old Sunday school project had Emma smiling. "How did you remember Herbie's verse?"

"Come on." Sam sputtered her lips. "We made those in fifth grade. I don't think Herbie swamped that stone until our freshman year in high school. I think my cactus died after a month. I can't even remember my verse, so I adopted yours."

"I've been remembering the beginning of that psalm every time I get the creepy feeling that someone is watching me." A shiver pimpled her skin. She bit into her sandwich and leaned against the counter desk grateful for the buffer and the anonymity that Nashville offered.

"That's your overactive imagination. No one in Tennessee has heard of Ron Runyard." Sam piled potato chip bags on the counter. She extracted her phone from the back pocket of her jeans. "Before I leave, why don't you call your mom. I know you haven't been using your phone much. Your mom is probably worried."

The hospital was the only place she had used her phone in Tennessee. Could phone records be hacked? Ron and Annette stole money. They weren't private investigators, were they? She was curious if reporters had been by Home ScentSations. Her parents worked hard and didn't need to be devoured by the media. Neither did she, but she had been the duped participant in a fraud.

"Thanks for the offer." Emma bit her lip. "I'll give my mom a quick call before Wade returns." She swept breadcrumbs from her hands and tapped Sam's phone.

"Sam?" Hearing her mother's voice cinched Emma's heart. She couldn't pop over after work for dinner or stop by the store and inventory candles. She even missed seeing a few snowflakes.

"It's me, Mom. Sam's heading back to Whispering Creek, so she's letting me use her phone."

"How long are you staying?" Her mom's voice held an ethereal tone like it had when her dad was in ICU, and her mom couldn't remember the simplest to-do list for their business. The weight of being an only child grew heavier in times of crisis. She wished she could be in two places at one time. In her parent's stockroom and in the office with Wade.

"For a month. My job will last about that long. Long enough for the press to forget about me. Has the mayor's niece been bothering you and dad?" Her neck muscles tightened at the thought of someone harassing her parents.

"She came by the store last weekend. Mall security was called. I haven't seen anyone, but one of the gals thought she saw her again. Wearing a wig, no less. It's obvious you're not here. What do they think? We're hiding you among the boxes of candles."

Emma grinned. The thought had crossed her mind. She relaxed in the office chair and praised God that her parents' store operated as usual.

"The way time is flying, I'll be home before you know it." Home. Her throat grew thick. "I love you. I'm praying for you and Dad." Even though her parents thought prayer was useless and that God was only a word written in black ink on wispy paper.

"We love you, too. You're in our thoughts daily." No prayers. Only impotent thoughts or moody vibes.

The waiting room door opened. Wade and Cole entered.

"My boss is here. I've got to go. I'll try to call soon. Love you." She ended the call and already missed the familiar and easy banter with her mom. The newness of Tennessee and all the changes in her life had her feeling like a loose, untied balloon swerving through the air. She tapped her shoes on the office floor. Her fingers instinctively went to grasp her silver charm. Her work oxford prohibited a single caress with its high buttons. She bit her sandwich and willed herself to forge ahead for twenty-one more days, maybe less.

Sam stood and waved. "We've got food."

Best male attention getter ever.

Wade shuffled into the office. His cane hung from his arm. He balanced well without assistance. She'd whoop at his accomplishment if she wasn't on duty.

He brushed hair out of his eye and cleared his throat. "Did everything go okay while I was gone?"

Was he expecting another disaster? Her gaze settled on his blue eyes, and the world stopped for half a heartbeat.

"It went perfect." She tamped down a blush or an exuberant smile. Sam would be searching for any dimple or the slightest mouth movement. Emma stayed stoic.

He held out a white paper sack. "I brought you some local fare. Candy with peanuts, marshmallow, and milk chocolate. It's a Nashville favorite."

Was Wade thinking about her on his bank run? Her body temperature spiked to tropical. She took a deep breath and tried to calm her traitor of a hot flash. She'd be leaving in a few weeks when Ron Runyard was a ghost of a memory.

"Sounds yummy. Thank you." She smiled a professional smile as if the boss bringing her chocolate was an everyday occurrence. He knew she wouldn't be here long and probably hoped to boost her spirits.

She kept repeating the platonic reasoning because Wade was her boss and the reason she received an envelope of cash as a paycheck. She couldn't allow him to become her Nashville favorite.

~*~

"Slow down!" Wade squeezed the door handle of the service van and clutched the sack with their chicken dinner. The van slowed.

Emma cast a glance in his direction. She reminded him of his strict third-grade teacher or how Cole looked when Wade dunked a basketball over his head. Her strict and sassy expression suited her too well. His insides felt funny, and it wasn't from the threat of another crash. He had to keep their relationship professional. The last thing he needed was a harassment lawsuit after the accident and dog bite.

"I was slowing down. I know this is an unmarked intersection." Her hair flipped side to side as she checked the cross street. "Your dad drove this the other day."

"Sorry." The moment after he said the word, he laughed and relaxed his death grip on their chicken tenders.

"Tomorrow is bring a quarter to work day." Her face

swept into a teasing grin.

"I'll be quiet and let the GPS guide you to my house." Almost two months ago, his life had taken a nosedive. Going back to living on his own was like opening an old yearbook. He hoped his mom and dad had tidied up the place when they dropped off his stuff. He couldn't remember doing much the last time he stopped by.

His parents were going out to eat after visiting Derek and dropping off some food. Were they celebrating one less house guest? His mom was probably texting her book club. Emma wasn't around during the day, but in the evenings, they could talk recipes and royal drama. Or books. He didn't read much except for appliance manuals or blueprints.

"Must be nice living close to your parents." Emma turned down his street and kept her speed to a minimum.

Okay, so she was a competent driver.

"It has its positives and negatives." Right now, he had Emma close by to chauffeur him to work. The positive column was winning.

"It's on the right." He pointed to the tan house with the navy shutters. "God gave me two of the best parents. I don't know what I would have done without their help. Probably gone to some rehab place." He shivered at the vision of blood, hospital beds, and blinding pain. He didn't want to dwell on the days of lying in bed unable to comprehend what day it was.

After parking in his driveway, Emma pointed to the red and white sack warming his thigh through his jeans. "Shall we divvy up dinner?"

Should they? He'd lived in the Donoven household long enough to know it wasn't polite to send someone off to eat alone. His house sat empty, ready to be used again. He scrubbed a hand over his jaw. Was that a metaphor for his life?

He had sat on the sidelines with an injury, and now he was ready to get back into the game and quarterback a new set of downs. Why not invite Emma in. They'd eaten meals together since she arrived. This meal was nothing special. Poor girl was too scared to use her phone to call in an order.

"We can eat here. Food will be cold by the time you drive to my folks." He flapped his hand toward the front door. "Place hasn't been condemned in my absence." He prayed the waft of peppery chicken batter masked the smell of a closed up, vacant house.

Emma hopped out of the van and came around to his side of the vehicle lugging her backpack. "I'll take the food since you have the cane." Her nose scrunched. "You didn't use your cane when you and Cole arrived at the office earlier."

Did she think he was faking? No, not Emma. She'd seen him in pain. A caring attitude filled her bone marrow. She showed compassion when Derek was injured and her patience with customers was heaven sent. "Cole dared me to try and walk without it." The grandpa reference would not be named. "He also said he'd catch me if I fell." Wade closed the van door and headed toward the front porch with his cane ready but not supporting his weight. He fumbled in his pocket for his house key. "I don't want to think what would happen if I fell on you. We've got enough employees injured."

"Yeah. I never was a good catcher." Emma followed him inside. "I tried the position in fourth grade and a softball took a wicked bounce off the plate. I think I still have a scar under my chin."

He led her into the family room which sat to the left of the entry.

"We can eat in here. I'd like to watch TV and hear what they're saying about the upcoming AFC Championship Game. Nashville is so close to winning it all." Wade hung his cane on the back of the couch. He had done two short walks today unassisted. Making it into the kitchen shouldn't be a problem. It was walkin' Wednesday. "I'll get some plates."

"This is awesome." Emma ran her hand over the back of his L-shaped leather couch.

No one had ever praised his couch before. His mom called it man-cave brown. He didn't know why, but Emma's few words of encouragement bolstered his ego. Her praise was like a scoop of tin roof ice cream in root beer.

"Having the sofas in a U-shape makes it easier to see the flat screen." He leaned over the arm of the couch and turned on the television.

"That, and you can use the angles for physical therapy." She strolled around his furniture. "You have the backs of the couches to steady you and this big open space in the front to practice your balance. It's perfect." Her smile lit the room brighter than the overhead lighting. "You'll be cruising around without your cane in no time."

Only Emma could turn his living space into a rehab center. She did seem to care about his health, diving right in to help his recovery. Was that what he needed? What his family needed? A fresh set of eyes to get him over the last hurdles. Emma had enough energy to deal with his nagging ailments and occasionally depressed spirit.

Emma perched on the couch, rocking back and forth as if to get comfortable. Memories of their first pizza night flashed in his brain. "I get dibs on the first tenders since you critiqued my driving. Hurry up, but don't fall, boss." Her sassy smile surfaced.

He hid his smirk. What had Cole and Sam unleashed on him? She had only been around a few days, and she was ordering him about in his own home. Worst part about it, he liked her spunk. She was a quick learner in the office, and her pushiness had helped with pain relief in his arm and strength in his leg. He shook his head as he returned with plates. Time would tell if she made employee of the month.

Cartons of chicken, ranch fries, and corn were opened and arranged in a line on the coffee table. His stark living room felt alive with her lounging on a cushion and organizing dinner. She even had the wrapping stripped from the plastic silverware. He embraced the calm after a busy day at work. Emma seemed to be settling into a routine, too.

He sat next to Emma and prayed over their chicken and sides. Grabbing the remote, he turned to the news station. Sports was in the "coming up" box in the corner of the screen.

"Mm, mm. What did people do in the days before ranch dressing." She chewed her chicken tender chipmunk fast.

"We prefer a little more fire with our meat here in Tennessee." He swept the tip of his chicken in hot sauce. "And a little more winning with our football team."

"Oh, please." She rolled her eyes and plopped the last of her chicken into her mouth.

Her easy-going nature had him choreographing a touchdown dance in the end zone. With the progress he had made in the last few days, he could envision himself moving without a curved hunk of metal.

Staccato music blared from the television as a special alert banner flashed across the screen. He hoped it didn't shorten the sportscaster's time.

"This just in from Wisconsin," the newswoman reported.

Emma's attention bounced to the screen.

Underneath the woman's picture read, "charred remains identified as white-collar criminal Ron Runyard."

Was that the same Ron that Emma worked for? Had to be. How many criminals named Ron were there in Wisconsin?

Emma hurried toward the screen hunching to read the

wording. Wade's dinner sat like a cracked engine in his gut. So much for a relaxing evening.

"Neighbors said a woman stayed at the remote Northwoods cabin with Runyard." The newswoman's composed demeanor contrasted with his houseguest who jabbed a finger at the television and flailed her hands like a game of charades. Emma's mouth fell open as if she consumed the reporter's words. He expected a high-pitched scream from her lips. Not silence. Her silence had him searching for a living room bomb shelter for when her voice awakened. His only shelter was a leather cushion and a too-short coffee table. Neither would protect him from Emma's potential blast.

"Identification of the body was delayed due to its charred state. Witnesses say the fire began on Sunday night. Investigators haven't said if this will hamper the retrieval of stolen funds. Anyone with more information is asked to call..."

"That's him," Emma squealed. "That's my former boss." She hugged her waist with one arm as the other hand pushed her bangs up to her scalp. Her eyes widened in horror, and he became the recipient of her contorted stare. "I wonder if Annette killed Ron. She was so...so normal. Was I working next to a murderer? And an arsonist?"

"Now, onto the big game," the newswoman said. The image on the screen changed to the sports desk. So much for football news. His new employee was having a meltdown. How did one calm a frantic woman? This was one of the few times in his life that he wished he had grown up with a sister.

Emma began pacing back and forth in front of the screen. "You don't think they'll assume I had anything to do with this?"

Lord, You better help me here because this sounds like a locked and loaded question. He knew enough not to answer questions about women's fashions and waistlines, but potential murder? He needed to think like a businessman. Rational. Factual. Unaffected by a stranger's dead body.

"Do you look like the other woman?" He shoved a fry in his mouth hoping he didn't have to keep talking about Emma's former boss, and even though it pained him, he turned off the television.

A wind gust escaped from Emma's mouth. She traipsed back to the couch and imploded on the cushion. "Annette has like five inches on me, and she's older. Like forty. But I don't remember her and Ron ever traveling together. Sometimes their trips did overlap. Both of them ran away at the end. When they left me with an empty office."

And holding the tattered bag.

She covered her face with her hands. "Why is this happening to me? The story was supposed to die down. Why would Annette or anyone kill Ron? I didn't like him after he stole people's money, but I didn't want him to be murdered. Now how will anyone find the money trail?"

Her eyes glistened while red streaks marred her cheeks from where her hands had face-planted. "Why is God allowing this to happen? I try to do what God wants me to do. I follow Jesus and pray. I even prayed about accepting the job with Ron."

Theology on a full stomach? How could he answer her when no one could possibly know the mind of God? Or the future. He needed to say something comforting. His brain scraped the bottom of the barrel making him lightheaded.

"What do they say about no honor among thieves?" He nodded like he had spoken helpful wisdom, but it was the first thing that had popped into his brain. "Look on the bright side. God gave you an alibi for Sunday night. We were having pizza in Nashville. We weren't even in the same state." How lame was that comfort? Where was his sermon, Scripture, and old Sunday school smarts?

She wadded a napkin in her hand and dried a tear snaking down her face.

Oh no, he didn't do well with emotional women. He hardly cried when he was in the hospital. *Way to tank a perfectly good evening, Ron.* Or should he say, Annette.

"And," he forced a smile to encourage his wet-cheeked office lady, "you can start using your phone again. I bet the killer has fled the country."

She pulled her phone from her backpack and started to cry. A no-holds-barred sobbing cry. One of those cries that has to work itself out. He'd learned about those from his mom when Cole went AWOL and when his mom tried to encourage him after his body became broken and bloodied.

Why did this have to happen when he was beginning to feel like a new man, like his old self. Life was getting back to semi-normal. Emma had been the spark he needed to put his life in order. She made him feel in control again. Now, her life was falling apart.

Lord, I need some wisdom here.

Taking a swig of his sports drink, he leaned against the couch cushion and waited for Emma to compose herself. She'd speak soon enough. Emma never remained speechless for long. He, however, could go the rest of the night without talking about Ron, the swindler. His fraud had caused Emma undue pain. Wade's teeth clenched while he envisioned punching Ron in the face.

He liked Emma. He was starting to like her a little too much. Right now, his position as her boss kept him seated at the opposite end of the couch, arms loosely folded, attempting to uphold professional boundaries.

A small part of his brain cheered for him to wrap Emma

in a comforting hug. His mom was a hugger. Hugging one's mom was different than bear-hugging an employee who wept on the boss's couch after dark.

Their fast-food meal had turned into a lingering, emotional dinner. A few weeks ago, he would have raced from the house to avoid a crying woman. At the moment, he didn't find Emma's tears all that frightening. He could relate. He'd shed enough tears in the quiet places of his life. So many that he was willing to forego football highlights to help a new friend.

~*~

She had to pull it together. Losing it in front of her boss was not acceptable. A meltdown almost dawned after her first day at Donoven and Sons, but she had managed to learn a brand-new computer system and find a hospital in a foreign city. She swiped wetness from her cheeks and cleared her throat. Ron's murder would put him on the front pages of Milwaukee's news. Mayor Van Wenkle's blood pressure would skyrocket. She prayed the mayor and his niece stayed away from the mall and her parents. Another investigator sitting outside of Sam's house wouldn't be good either. Sam had job interviews and a life to live. The media didn't need to stake out her friend's home. Emma plucked a waffle fry from the cardboard container and didn't even raise a fuss about the overabundance of salt burning her tongue.

Wade leaned forward on the couch, so much so that she could envision him rolling into a three-point stance. He clutched the remote. She gave him credit for turning off the television and not changing the station to an all-sports network.

"I'm sorry." He rotated, mouth gaping as if he had uttered a curse word. "I'm not making fun of your situation.

Honest. It's just—"

"You're fine." A sputter rumbled from her lips. "I'll spot you a roll of quarters because I don't think this murder story is going to vanish before midnight." She made one last tear sweep and forced a stiff-upper-lip smile. "I should be relieved. Ron can't scam any more people. According to one of the detectives who interrogated me, this wasn't Ron's first rodeo. Or whatever Ron's name is. I was hoping the authorities could at least retrieve some of the stolen money." She'd like the inheritance she had invested to be returned.

Wade rested his left arm along the top of the couch. He hadn't had any spasms in his hand at work. Her gaze traveled from Wade's hand to his chest and for a brief moment, her professionalism fled the room. What would it be like to be snuggled into Wade's large frame and surrounded by his strength and his subtle clean-scented cologne? Don't go there. She banished her wayward boss thoughts. She brushed bangs behind her ear and prayed her cheeks didn't match the red striping on the takeout bag.

"If you don't mind me asking," Wade swigged his sports drink, "how'd you start working for Ron? Seems like you read people pretty well."

She always thought she knew who was fake and who was the real deal, but now she wasn't so sure. Wade's praise bolstered her battered self-esteem.

"I was thinking about that the other night." She fingered the bump of her tortoise necklace underneath her work shirt. Too bad she didn't wear more jewelry to fidget with. "I remember meeting him at a chamber of commerce gathering. My parents have run their candle shop in the mall for years. They're long-time business owners in the community. We know our fair share of council members and civic leaders." If only an upstanding business had offered her a job, she wouldn't be in this mess.

"That's a great place to look legit." Wade consumed nearly a whole tender in one bite.

"Or to hire someone with a recognizable name." Not that she was a super star, but she had interacted with the chamber when her dad was recovering from his heart attack. Had she blipped onto Ron's radar then? Her muscles tensed as she sat higher on the cushion. "The last thing I want to do is hurt my parents or their business."

"Tell me about it." Wade cracked a smile that had her wanting to snuggle into his strong arms. "I think we're on the same page there."

Where was the grumpy, inconsiderate guy she had met on her first night in town? She might have tried a little harder to get to know him if he had been half this welcoming. Now his understanding attitude acted like a magnet. As his employee, she resisted the pull. She grabbed her soda and let the fizz eliminate the drainage in her throat and the fantasies in her head.

"Problem is, I liked the idea of being part of a retirement community where people could have fun and live out their last years in a nice place. I even put time into that human resource software so we could keep track of birthdays, anniversaries, and hobbies."

"The peeps software." His lips pressed thin. Was he fighting a laugh?

"Names can always be changed. Just ask Ron." She poked a fry in Wade's direction. "Oops. Guess we can't." She swallowed her salty potato mash while Wade shook his head. "I shouldn't be joking. My parents store might be swamped with reporters. Even though I'm mad at Ron, I never wished him dead. In jail, yes. But not murdered by his senior office lady."

Wade raised his plastic sports drink bottle like a toast. "Why do you think I keep saying sorry to my office lady?"

Now that was funny. Where had this humorous side of Wade been hiding?

"Don't worry. I won't invite you to a remote cabin after swindling millions of dollars." She would not let her mind wander to Wade in jeans and a tight lumberjack shirt.

"What a sad ending for someone." Wade tidied up the dinner wrappings.

"Yeah, it is." She finished off her last cold fry and flattened the cardboard box. "People lost a lot of money in his scam. Including me." Her confession didn't deter Wade's clean-up. Maybe he assumed she meant her paycheck and not an inheritance. "I keep asking God why this happened. My life was going so well, and then it turned upside down. I know God's not going to light up the sky with a warning sign, but I had peace about working for Ron and Annette. Couldn't the Spirit have made me feel ill at ease. Sometimes, I get frustrated at God for allowing this upheaval." She was also frustrated with herself for being blind to the workings of criminals.

"I hear you." Wade nudged the cane hanging from the armrest. "I shared a few words with God after my accident. Some of those exchanges were intense and heated."

Should she have mentioned second-guessing God? Wade had suffered physically from his accident. What were a few sleepless nights, dwindling bank account, and upset stomach? She hadn't experienced pain and surgeries or the loss of mobility. She chastised herself for oversharing and shoved her garbage in the fast-food bag.

She readied an apology without using the word sorry.

"I shouldn't have complained about my situation. You've been through much worse." She pulled her legs beneath her and settled into the warmth of the couch. "When I met your mom at Christmas, she was a nervous wreck leaving you for a few hours. Sam was worried about you. Cole was worried. I didn't know you, but even I was uneasy about your parents being in Whispering Creek."

Wade rubbed his jawline. His head bobbed like he was agreeing with her.

"That's the thing." He stilled his nod. "I wouldn't want to go through a crash again, but the accident brought my brother back into my life and back into our electrical business. My family is hanging out again. Like we did when I was growing up. I'm not sure I'd be talking with Cole if I didn't end up in the hospital and unable to work. I was forced to reach out to my brother for help."

His head tilted toward the ceiling. "Not that I want another life changing accident like that, Lord."

She prayed toward the ceiling as well. "Likewise, Jesus. I'm not finished with my first one."

Thumping his cane against the rug, Wade glanced at her, not as a down-on-her-luck-stranger, but as a friend and confidant. A cool stream awakened every nerve in her belly.

"You noticed the bitterness I kept locked away toward Cole. I was glad you...encouraged me to talk with him the other night."

"I like Cole. If he hadn't met Sam, I wouldn't be sitting on your couch telling you about my problems." She flashed a carefree smile. The shocking news about Ron's death didn't seem as haunting after she confided in Wade. He knew about being a business owner. Not all business owners were created equal. Some were crooks using their connections to target another victim. Wade made her realize that Ron had targeted her because of her good reputation and business relationships. A pebble of shame tumbled from her shoulders.

Wade set his cane aside and scrunched the paper sack,

rolling the top tight. He rested the bag on his thigh.

"There aren't any secrets at Donoven and Sons that I know about. My life is pretty simple. How your former boss kept his multiple lives straight, I have no idea. I'm glad you're here filling in for Fran and are away from that mess. And I don't intend to tell you any lies."

Wade's honesty was better than a pay raise. He'd seen her unravel, but he knew how to put the threads back together. He'd lived through a personal trauma and worked to get his life back. She was trying to figure out how she could get her life on track again. Too bad she wasn't staying here long term because Wade understood what she was going through, and for the first time in a long time, she didn't feel like crying.

~*~

Later, she pulled the work van into Mike and Linda's driveway. Her phone pinged with a message. She reached to see who had heard the scandalous news about Ron and was the first to reach out.

Sam won.

WHAT A SHOCK ABOUT RON! I'M SO SORRY.

Emma laughed at the message. Sam owed her a quarter.

13

The office at Donoven and Sons was fast becoming Emma's second home. She updated accounts with information from the infamous card file while fielding remodeling inquiries. Her electrical vocabulary had blossomed. In the back corner of the office, Wade handled accounts payable from his laptop. She took note of Wade's typing skills. Both hands participated in the key clicks. His claw had thawed. She sat taller in her office chair knowing she had contributed to his healing by coaching and nagging him to do his hand massages and unassisted walking. At least she had one recent win in the life column. Her career at the retirement community was a total loss.

She hoped Wade didn't see her as a charity case, or worse, someone who could be duped easily. The idea that Ron may have seen her as a mark made her bristle. If she stood out at chamber of commerce meetings in Milwaukee it was because running a business had been woven into her life. In her defense, she had been scammed by the best. People twice her age had lost large sums of money. She wasn't going to let Ron's fraud ruin her reputation.

Her phone flashed a message from Sam.

INTERVIEW WENT WELL. NOW I WAIT.

Emma texted a quick reply. Inwardly, she happy-danced around the office.

She rotated her chair toward Wade.

"Sam texted that her interview in Whispering Creek went well." The small Tennessee town agreed with her friend.

Securing a teaching job close to home would be a big answer to prayer.

Wade glanced away from the laptop screen. "Hope she gets it." He cracked a brief smile. "Cole's been wanting her to find a job here."

"So, she won't fly the coop back to Wisconsin?"

"Something like that." Wade cleared his throat. "I like having Cole around again. Sam's the one that made him turn a one-eighty. She's all right."

"Yes, she is."

"And you helped clear the air between me and my brother, so thanks." Wade pulled at his collar. He looked as comfortable as a soaked kitten.

Her heart grew soft and snuggly. Partly because God had used her to heal Wade and Cole's relationship. Only an outsider could have picked up on Wade's resentment of his brother. And partly because Wade's dark lashes blinking with a look of sincere vulnerability was the best cozy blanket to her spirit. She didn't like being away from home, broke, and second-guessing herself, but if God used her to help brothers reconcile, then some of her struggles had been a blessing.

Wade stared at her with an is-anyone-home expression.

She had daydreamed and dropped the conversation. Did he think she was ignoring him?

"We all need a Sam in our life." Truth fled from her lips. "Sam did the heavy lifting. I blurted out an observation. My mouth does that sometimes." She released a quick smile at Wade and then focused on her computer. Work shouldn't get too personal. Once Fran returned, there wouldn't be a position to fill. This was a short-term fix not a career. She needed a reminder post-it note stuck to Fran's dancing flower.

The phone interrupted their conversation. Saved by a ring. When Wade opened up about his past hardships, her heart grew in size and threatened to pop the official blue buttons on her work shirt. She knew Wade didn't open up to everyone, and she felt privileged that he shared his struggles with her.

"Whoops. Got to get back to work." She answered the phone. "Donoven and Sons Electric."

No one greeted her with a request.

"Hello. Is anybody there?" Probably a spam call.

"Do you check appliances?" Every syllable trembled from an aged voice.

Emma stayed upbeat with an ounce of caregiver calm. "I'm sure we could help. What seems to be the problem?"

Wade rolled his chair closer. Could he hear the elderly woman?

"I think something's burning." The customer sounded uneasy. Did she have dementia?

Electrical fires were not her expertise, but smoldering wires would definitely smell. Her scandalous boss had been killed in a fire. She didn't need a customer to die that way, too.

"Maybe you should call the fire department and have them check it out. We wouldn't want your house to burn. Or you to be harmed." She tapped her shoe on the floor. Why couldn't this be a routine inquiry? Was this how a 9-1-1 operator felt?

"Do they charge? The ambulance company sent me a bill."

Emma's skin tingled. She needed to go in a different direction.

"Where do you live?" Hopefully, close to the office.

As the lady recited her address, Emma typed it into the computer. An invoice popped onto the screen. Gertrude Johnson lived a couple blocks from the office.

"Ms. Johnson?"

"Yes."

Praise God for technology and loyal customers.

"I don't have any technicians available right now, but I'll drive our owner over. You're not that far away. Do me a favor and stand by the front door for an easy getaway if something should ignite." Emma's brain had already started the frantic journey to Gertrude's house.

Wade flailed his arms. His no-go signal was done with perfectly flat hands. Her physical therapy had worked wonders, but where was his compassion? Wade acted like a stingy boss stamping out sympathy with his heavy work boots.

She pointed to his coat with a no-nonsense jab. She was going to help Ms. Johnson with or without him. Preferably with him as she knew nothing about wiring.

"Oh, that would be lovely. I will see you soon." Ms. Johnson repeated her address before hanging up.

Emma ended the call and leapt to her feet. She would not be reprimanded sitting down. Wade was too tall, too broad, too muscular. She ended that unnerving line of thinking. Presently, he was one big grump even if he was a handsome grump.

"Wade." She jammed a hand into her hip. "We're going to save an old lady. We need to be a Sam in somebody's life." They could provide excellent customer service and help a neighbor in one call. "You can argue with me in the van and call for back up when we get there."

His blue eyes widened pushing his dark eyebrows higher on his forehead. If she was a mouse, she would be scurrying for the nearest crevice.

He leaned toward her, and every ounce of righteous piety puddled at her feet. He grunted, hit the answering machine button, and grabbed his coat.

"Just don't drive like a maniac." He wedged his cane under his arm.

She'd pump a fist if he wasn't her boss.

Slinging her backpack over her shoulder, she followed him out of the office. He'd soon discover that she was right. Jesus said to love thy neighbor, and Ms. Johnson was a neighbor in need. The elderly lady was also a former customer. Repeat business was the best.

She raced to the service van and opened the driver's door. "Speedy granny driving coming up."

~*~

What just happened? He was the co-owner of a company that had rules for engaging customers and for service calls. He had deferred too quickly to Emma's judgment without thinking this situation through. She was a new hire and northern transplant. A temporary transplant. He should have called the authorities. Though, Emma would have them there before the police or fire department arrived. Sirens might scare the old lady. His muscles were as stiff as the plastic dash. *Lord, please go before us to Ms. Johnson's home. I can't take any more stress in my life.*

Emma eased the van to a stop at an intersection. She tilted her head and cast a glance in his direction. She smiled like this was a normal day at work. Well, it wasn't. He rolled his eyes at her cheerful bossiness.

"She's a damsel in distress and a former customer. Your dad installed a streetlight two years ago and there have been some updates since. We have the office covered. Our answering machine is on in case someone calls. Besides, you'll have a customer for life when Gertrude sees you looking all handsome in your dark blue electric shirt." Emma's face blanched. She leaned into the steering wheel like a nearsighted senior driver and hit the gas.

An attractive woman thought he was handsome. He stretched his back, easing the tension. Too bad Emma was an employee. Knowing her, it was a slip of the tongue. Words flew out of her mouth without a second or third thought. He played ignorant of her compliment and stifled his grin.

"The address is about a block away. On the right." The coordinates flew from Emma's lips. Was she babbling to cover up her assessment of his good looks?

"You're right. Ms. Johnson doesn't live far from the office." He could give Emma some encouragement. She had picked up the office duties without peppering him with questions, and she also treated every customer like a long-lost cousin. A few people had mentioned her helpfulness when he went over the cost of fixtures. In the electrical market, he needed as much repeat business as possible. Fran was good with people, but Emma had a gift.

Emma turned into a curved driveway angling toward a ranch home. The house sat back from the busy street with its front stoop shaded by two maple trees. Thankfully, no flames or smoke rose from the roof.

As soon as the service van parked in front of the house, the front door opened, and a woman peered through the screen. He assumed it was the elderly lady because no man he knew would wear a bright yellow top. The color put his lightning bolt insignia to shame.

He opened the van door and waved to the woman. She didn't look familiar. Dad must have handled the calls. Emma hurried around the back of the van. She appeared carrying a toolbox with his cane hanging from her arm.

"I don't need that." He pointed to the cane. "I've lapped my couch this morning, and I'm feeling steady on my leg." *Thanks to you.* Emma had pushed him harder than any of his former therapists. Her pushiness was one reason he was here on this crazy call.

"No problem. I'll carry it just in case." She sounded breathless as she beelined it to the front porch. He followed her whirlwind dash to the door.

The screen door opened.

"Hey, Ms. Johnson." Emma waved with the cane wedged into the crook of her elbow. "I'm Emma and this is Wade Donoven. We're here to check out your smell." Laughter bubbled from Emma. "That's probably the strangest greeting I've ever given. I hope you're doing okay?"

An elderly woman with wiry gray hair and wearing glasses upside down on her head shuffled outside. She kept the screen door open so they could enter. "I'm glad you came."

"Thank you, ma'am." He entered the home and went into diagnostic mode. "Where did you smell the burning?"

Sniffing sounds interrupted his thoughts. Emma was breathing in and out audibly. "Do you use those plug-in waxes? I'm detecting a faint aroma of bold lemons. Summertime Lemonade maybe? That's a bestseller."

Why was Emma mentioning air freshener? Time was of the essence.

"Ma'am, the burning—"

"The pluggable wax is in the kitchen where the smell was coming from." The elderly woman shuffled through the tiny foyer into the kitchen. She tugged her cardigan tight over her floral housedress. "You don't think the smell has anything to do with my air freshener, do you? I've used them for years."

"Probably not. Unless there's something wrong with the outlet." He stopped in the middle of the rectangular kitchen and inhaled the air. "Yep. Something is going on in here."

Emma set his toolbox near the refrigerator. "There's a

burnt toast smell mixing with your lemons, Ms. Johnson." She pointed to an outlet with a small plastic insert. "My money's on this outlet."

"Just a minute." He was the only certified technician in the room. Many households plugged in scented oils or warming wax holders. That didn't mean the outlet was burning. "Before we do anything, I need to shut off the breakers to the kitchen. Where's your fuse box located?"

"The woman pointed toward the front door. "It's in the first bedroom on the left. In the closet."

"I'll shut off the electricity to the kitchen." He flexed his hand. The claw hadn't overtaken his muscles in a few days. At this rate, he'd be making these service calls alone without the professional sniffer.

"Do you need my help?" Emma's upbeat tone didn't grate on his nerves like it might have weeks ago. He was so close to jumping into his old life again where he didn't need to ask for his parents, brother, or employees to assist him. He hadn't been on a call diagnosing problems in months. Being in this kitchen, making a difference, had him grateful to Emma for dragging him out of his office cocoon.

"I'm good." A grin threatened to explode. He was good. Good enough to do his job.

When he returned from flipping breakers, he stood in the entrance to the kitchen. Emma had coaxed Ms. Johnson into a chair and was rearranging her eyeglasses.

He scanned the set up. Sunshine from the window over the sink brightened the room, and helped him figure out the cause of the smoldering scent. The house was older, but it was clean and well maintained. Judging from the cat food bowl on the side of the counter, there shouldn't be a mouse problem. Every corner of the flooring was swept clean.

He studied the outlet with the plug-in again. A

coffeemaker, toaster, and bean grinder sat beneath the power source on the counter. A single black plug occupied the lower terminal. Did Ms. Johnson pull out the cords when she used each appliance?

"Will you be able to fix it?" Ms. Johnson's raspy voice shook as she grasped the top of a dinette chair. He imagined she was fearful of being here alone if a fire started. At her age, he would be too.

"Don't worry." Emma patted the older woman's hand. "Wade will figure it out. He's not only an electrician, he also owns the company. I'm sure we'll get to the bottom of this. It's like finding the last puzzle piece. Sometimes you need to look on the floor."

The floor wasn't a problem. He pulled the appliances away from the main outlet. All three cords snaked over the counter edge. Not one was plugged into the lower outlet terminal. He opened his toolbox and grabbed a flashlight. Shining the beam between the counter edge and the refrigerator, he noticed a power strip. Lowering his head, he did his best impersonation of an Emma sniff. Something was definitely caustic.

"Where'd you get the power strip for your appliances?" The flashlight revealed cheap plastic and a nonexistent surge protector.

Furrowing her brow, Ms. Johnson faced Emma. "My grandson, I think. It was packed with some boxes in the closet. From his time in college."

"Did he graduate recently?" Emma made it seem like they were having a chat over tea and cookies.

"Oh no. My grandson's almost forty."

Emma's brown eyes bugged his direction. "I think we're gonna need a new strip."

His thoughts exactly. Emma's shocked expression made

him want to laugh, but he kept a professional demeanor.

He pulled the strip onto the counter, the plastic overly warm to his touch. "I think I found our puzzle piece. I wouldn't trust this strip much longer. It's cheaply made, hot to the touch, and there's no certification stamp." He unplugged the power strip from the wall and wrapped the cord around it. "I may have a strip in the van to replace it."

Stepping away from Ms. Johnson, Emma reached for the power strip. "I can go get the new one out of the van."

"I've got it." And he did. His leg felt strong. His fingers were nimble. And he had helped a customer solve a problem. He flipped on the breaker before heading out to the van. The light that illuminated the kitchen mirrored his future. He grinned. It felt good to be in charge again. All he needed was a driving release, and he could get on with his life.

When he returned, Emma had opened a window. She talked non-stop to Ms. Johnson about winter weather in Wisconsin. How could people enjoy a frozen tundra? Her quirks were cute. Ms. Johnson hung on to Emma's every detail.

"I've got a white strip to match your counters." He held the new one so Ms. Johnson could see it. "I'll plug in your appliances, and we should be good to go."

"Let me give it one more sniff test." Emma rose and did her deep breathing. "Wade solved your problem. No more burning lemons."

"Oh, thank you." Ms. Johnson stood, squinted through her glasses, and grasped his good hand.

His hand swallowed hers as if he held a newly hatched bird in his palm. An image of Grandma Donoven flashed through his mind.

"What do I owe you? You came so fast." The elderly woman glanced between him and Emma. "I was getting scared."

He knew the answer before he spoke it. "No charge. We were happy to come by. We appreciate your past business and want to help. Keep us in mind for the future."

"Are you sure?" The surprise in the woman's eyes made his heart swell.

"We're sure." Emma's gaze met his, and he would have sworn she swiped a tear away. She looked at him as if he was wearing a cape and had superpowers. If he was forced to admit it, Emma was the one with a superpower. She might have a big mouth, but she had a super-sized heart. His heart did a funny dip as she smiled in his direction.

"How about some cookies? I made a batch yesterday." Ms. Johnson reached for a set of jars near the sink.

"Well, we can't turn down cookies." Emma opened the plastic baggie Ms. Johnson had handed her as their customer filled it. If anyone walked in, they would swear Emma was a relative or neighbor.

An ever-growing part of him wished Emma lived nearby.

He grabbed the toolbox while Emma took his cane and the cookies out to the van.

They were about to get into their seats when a sedan stopped abruptly behind their vehicle.

A middle-aged woman sprinted from her car.

"Is everything okay?" Her words came out as frantic as she appeared. "A neighbor called me about the electric truck being here. My mom has been forgetting things."

"Nothing forgotten here." Wade set the toolbox down and rubbed his hands together. An odd yet welcomed sensation. "Your mom smelled something burning and called the office. We've done some work here before. We came out to check on her. She smelled an old power strip going bad."

The woman breathed out and pressed a hand to her chest.

"I'm so glad you came. Thank you. She doesn't tell me everything." The woman cast a glance at Emma who stood on the opposite side of the van. "Did she say where she got the strip? I don't remember one being here."

"Supposedly from a box her grandson left in the closet," Emma said.

"That's so scary. I don't even know what's stored in some of those closets." The woman shook her head and briefly closed her eyes. "Thanks again for helping her."

"You're welcome. Call us anytime. Everything worked out for the best." Wade turned to get in the passenger seat.

"Hey, do you mind if I take a picture of you two and your van? That way I can remember who to call if I need work done." The woman must have assumed they'd be agreeable since she fished a phone from her coat pocket.

What could it hurt to have a photo with Emma. She instigated the drive over instead of phoning the fire department.

"Sure." Emma scooched beside him all smiles as usual. "We're happy to troubleshoot."

He grimaced at the camera. Good thing they wore their official jackets for free advertisement.

The woman checked the picture. "Thanks so much for coming out. You two were my mom's guardian angels today." She flashed a brief smile before rushing toward the front door.

"You're welcome," Emma called, rounding the front of the van.

He didn't feel like an angel as he slid into the passenger seat. A grumpy one, maybe. Emma had a huge heart for people. If he had fielded the call, Ms. Johnson's kitchen might have gone up in flames.

Emma eased the van down the driveway and stopped at the curb. Her hair whipped back and forth as she waited for the traffic to clear before pulling out onto the street.

He grabbed the wheel. "Wait a minute. Before we leave, I'd like to say something."

"Oh, no, no, no." Emma placed the van in park with a determined look on her face. "I don't have a cup or jar with me, and I don't want quarters on the floor of your work van."

As soon as his brain made sense of her words, he barked out a laugh. A carefree laugh pent up for too long behind bitterness and anger and whatever else came from being sidelined from life for weeks on end. He turned as far as the seatbelt would allow and tried to wipe the grin off of his face, but his cheeks wouldn't stay flat.

"I wanted to thank you. I'm glad we came. I don't know that I would have driven to Ms. Johnson's house if you hadn't..." He scrambled to find the right word. One that wouldn't insult his employee. "Encouraged me."

"First of all, you didn't drive." Emma's eyes hurled golden-brown beams at him that reminded him of a jovial school lunch monitor. "But I believe you would have come if you could have driven, or you would have sent one of the technicians. The fear coming through the phone was scary. It melted my heart, and I'm sure it would have melted yours."

"You give me too much credit. I've been in a bad state since my accident. I've held onto bitterness toward Cole, the world, even God." He blew out a breath and put on his best linebacker face willing his emotions to stay under control. "I'm glad the anger is leaving. And that call." He hooked a thumb toward the ranch home. "That was fun. I've missed being around customers. Solving problems. I didn't know how much I missed the interactions until today. So thank you for pushing me out of the office."

"You're welcome." She tapped her chin with a sparkly fingernail. "I think you are the first person to praise me for being pushy. So thank you." She elongated the *oo* sound mimicking a local.

He grinned at her imitation southern drawl. "I wouldn't call it pushy."

"Your answer deserves a cookie." She sat taller in the driver's seat. "Open the baggie and hand me one before we head back to the office. Chocolate chip are my favorite."

"Mine too." Gripping the plastic, he unzipped the top with ease. No cramps or clawed fingers hindered his movements. Emma had helped him solve that problem. He handed her a cookie.

She took a bite and moaned. "These are so good." After another swallow, she faced him, all business. "You should do a post on the company's social media about flimsy electrical strips. I never would have thought that could be a problem. They're all the same to me." She popped the last of her cookie into her mouth and grabbed the steering wheel. "Are you ready to get back to work?"

"Yes and yes." It surprised him how much he was looking forward to returning to the office. With Emma. She had only been in his life a short time, but she was what the doctor and therapist ordered. Emma didn't see him as a patient or victim. She saw him as a business owner ready to run his company again and support his family members. She could talk about staffing, customer relations, sales, and inventory without missing a beat.

He leaned his head against the seat while Emma drove toward the office. The sweet, rich taste of chocolate awakened his mouth. Life was looking up. Up. He grinned. *Thank You, Lord for having Ms. Johnson call. I'm so close to being back in charge of my life, I can taste it.*

14

Saturday morning, the brisk fifty-degree air invigorated Emma as she left the bank with cash in her account after a week of work. Her salary made sure she wouldn't overdraft on the rent for her Milwaukee apartment. What a blessing to have a little spending money to start building a wardrobe in Tennessee that didn't involve the color navy blue or a lightning insignia. Life was looking up, and she was growing accustomed to the warmer winter weather in her temporary home. Her heart was also warming to her new boss. If she stayed around, maybe something would grow between them. She didn't have to go back to Wisconsin, did she? Her parents were close to retirement age. Would they move south?

She closed the door of the service van and collapsed in the driver's seat. On the dash, glowed 9:40 AM, January 27. No need to rush back to the Donovens' house and interrupt their morning routine. She could savor a few minutes of peace. *Thank You, Lord.*

With Ron's death and the law looking for Annette, there was no need to stay undercover anymore. Even the news had gone silent on Ron's demise, especially the local Nashville news. The Northwoods of Wisconsin were closer to Canada than Tennessee, and reporters had raced to the next tragedy. She pulled out her phone and dialed Sam.

"You're up early. I thought you'd sleep in after a full week." Sam's voice swept Emma away to playgrounds and happy times.

Emma snuggled into the leather cushion of the seat. "Says

the girl who was out on a date last night."

"Cole and I were just stargazing on the UTV."

"Yeah, I know about your stargazing." When she had visited in December, Sam's neighbor had joked about the stargazing and kissing that went on in the hills above Sam's property. Emma conjured up a vision of Wade and his toolbox in Ms. Johnson's house. When he got all personal while they waited in the van and blinked those dark lashes at her, she had all she could do not to lean over and plant a kiss on those tempting lips. She shook the image out of her head. Wade was her employer and boss. Not a stargazing companion.

"Earth to Em. Are you working today? I can always drive into the city and kill time with you."

"Do the Donovens ever take a break?" Rhetorical question. She knew better with her parents being business owners. "Wade and I are going into the office in a little while. The doctor released Derek for light duty, so we're going to re-work the schedule for Monday." Everyone's life was getting back to normal. Wade was walking without a cane. Derek's hand was healing. When would her life be predictable and boring? Maybe after Fran returned and she scoured the Internet for a job in Milwaukee. Or perhaps here. Would Wade stay in her life if she worked nearby?

"Cole will be happy to hear about Derek's recovery. But I can drive there if you need some company. I feel bad. You came to see me, and I put you to work." Sam's last words sounded muffled. Was she biting a fingernail?

"Don't worry about me. I'm a natural in the office, and now there isn't a gap on my resume." Someone trusted she wasn't a crook. "I'm an interstate office manager. And I have some healing mojo because Wade is doing great. I might have him out boot scootin' or whatever they do down here." With all her early morning energy, she shut down the image of

Wade wearing a cowboy hat.

"That's the girl I know. Though, I'm serious. I can come out to see you anytime. I've been praying this whole thing with Ron goes away. No one should blame you. You're a victim like everyone else."

A dupe like everyone else. Losing the ten grand from her grandmother hurt the most. She could find future employment somewhere. Working at Donoven and Sons had proven her skills. She hadn't robbed them blind and taken off into the sunset like her former employer. "Thanks for the offer, but I'm good. I just wish I knew what God was doing. I know He's in control, I do. It's just nothing has ever happened to me like this before. I'm not a white-collar criminal. Or any type of criminal for that matter."

"It's not your fault. Who would have thought that Ron was a fraud. He seemed nice when I met him. A natural." A breath stormed through the phone. "Don't beat yourself up over it, okay?"

"I won't." She infused her reply with an upbeat tone. She didn't need to bother Sam for advice and encouragement while her friend tried to find her own employment. "I'd better get going and chariot my boss to the office. I'm hoping Linda has some leftovers for me. I smelled sausage cooking when I ran to the bank."

"Linda's cooking is the best."

"And Wade and I received chocolate chip cookies from a customer on Thursday." Were any left for a second breakfast?

"Keep talking and I will be on Linda's doorstep. I'm praying this all works out. I love you, Em."

"Love you, too." Emma's grin rivaled the size of the bulky service van as the call ended.

She tilted her head toward the gray carpeted ceiling. "I needed that, Lord. Thank You for providing the best friend ever and a job that pays the bills. You went over and above giving me a place to live with an excellent chef. I know You care. I'm sort of clueless on why everything is so crazy right now, but I'm trusting You to help me figure it all out."

Emma's stomach rumbled. "Now, that's an honest amen."

She drove to the Donovens' house to eat a quick breakfast before picking up Wade. Hard as it may be, she would keep her thoughts professional at work. Boss man Wade was off limits. She didn't need to complicate her employment. The one part of her life that was on track.

The aroma of sausage surrounded her as she entered the Donovens' foyer.

Linda popped her head from the kitchen all perk and smiles. "How about some egg casserole. It's not every day our company makes the life section."

Egg casserole registered, but why was Linda talking about the newspaper? Did Wade place an advertisement? Maybe Mike and Linda didn't know about the ad since Wade handled most of the marketing.

She walked into the warm kitchen with her stomach more grumbly than rumbly.

Mike turned in his seat at the small kitchenette table and held the newspaper open. "Check it out."

A black and white picture of her, Wade, and the Donoven and Sons van graced the middle of the page with the headline "Good Samaritans Save the Day." Moving closer, she stared at the photograph. Her fingertips tingled. So much for floating under the radar. The reporter simply named her as Emma. Only Emma. Thank the Lord. A last name like Uranova would be easy to track online. Hopefully, most readers would focus on the electrical company and not the employees.

"What a great picture of both of us." Now she had another mental picture of her good-looking, vulnerable boss.

She swallowed the saliva pooling in her mouth. "We had no idea the lady would send it to the paper." Emma scanned the sentences under the photo. The reporter had mentioned that old, cheap power strips were a hazard. Great marketing minds thought alike. Wade had taken her advice and put the warning on the company's social media yesterday morning.

"I couldn't believe my eyes when I saw it. No one contacted the office for a statement that I know of." Mike grinned as if he had won a special trophy.

"That's so cool." She smiled at Mike knowing that free press was a business owner's dream, but she'd have preferred a normal ad with a slogan and a phone number. She prayed being nice and neighborly hadn't brought her a media circus or further questions from law enforcement. She halted her mind from going to a dark place. She had followed her conscience and the Spirit's leading and helped an elderly lady in need. Even if she possessed a time travel device to go backward to Thursday afternoon, she wouldn't have changed her decision, and she definitely wouldn't have missed her special time with Wade.

"Have a seat across from Mike." Linda brought a plate loaded with egg and sausage casserole and the biggest blueberry muffin Emma had ever seen. Not a bad reward for doing the right thing. First cookies and now breakfast casserole.

Her low-key Saturday instantly kicked up a notch. She could imagine the office phone ringing non-stop. Busyness would be a welcomed distraction from thinking about Wade. After a week at Donoven and Sons, which included dog bites and confused callers, she was confident that she could handle just about any disaster. But infatuation with, or dare she say falling in love with, her boss was never in one of her procedure manuals.

~*~

After a text from his dad, Wade scanned the newspaper online and found the picture of their Thursday service call. Emma's smile leapt off the screen like a beacon. No reader could swipe past Emma's exuberance, so the entire Nashville readership would be warned against faulty power strips. He wiped his hands down the front of his hoodie and decided on one more walk around his couch before Emma arrived to take him to the office.

Leaving his laptop on the brown leather cushion, he grasped the edge of his sofa and began to stride like his former self. He never would have guessed that an out-of-state, bold speaking, northerner would be just what the doctor and physical therapist ordered. His gait was improving, and he hardly needed the cane anymore. If a doctor's release came next Wednesday, he could drive and leave the office to Emma. Being with her constantly caused him to view her as more than an employee. His stomach hadn't become a handball court over other new hires, and he didn't stare at other women in the newspaper deciphering their expressions or how well they fit under his arm. He was too busy to think of dating, especially someone in his employ.

He brushed a hand through his hair and chastised himself for letting life get messy when it was beginning to resemble a comfortable broken-in work boot.

Lord, I want to go back to work with no strings attached to a woman. My emotions have cross-trained enough. I need smooth concrete to travel and not a pitted dirt road. Thank You, Jesus. Amen.

The aroma of brewed coffee drew him into the kitchen. He filled his travel mug and decided to rinse off in the shower and be ready for his office manager's arrival. He shouldn't worry about the future. God would handle it. He had only known Emma a week, so these jitters had to be due to the excitement of leaving his trials in the dust. He was thankful Emma had prayed for him since his accident, but so had many others. His church family and friends would still be here when Emma returned to Wisconsin. He had to keep his distance. Isn't that what his company lawyer and insurance agent would advise?

He swigged the warm caffeine and headed to the shower. *Get a grip, Donoven.* He owned a business at thirty-two years of age. A successful business. He had no time to waste on a temporary hire. As a matter of fact, he should text Fran and see how she was coming along after surgery. Maybe she could return to work early?

The next few days, he had to stay busy in the back office away from Emma. Then, on Wednesday, if the doctor agreed to let him drive, he'd schedule himself on service calls to avoid her. For now, he prayed he could focus on business and not his attractive, intuitive, ever-present office manager.

15

Downtown Nashville blinked and flashed like a crayon box of neon colors. Emma scuffed the sidewalk in borrowed western boots and Linda's blingy straw cowboy hat. She and Linda blended in with all the Saturday night cowgirls on the main honky-tonk street.

Wade and Mike walked a few steps ahead in their jeans, boots, and jackets. Brilliant vertical signs silhouetted their bodies. Wade used his cane in the crowd of people. Caution was justified with the selfie-takers and clueless sightseers stopped in the middle of the rush. She would have been a lone clueless sightseer if Linda hadn't invited her at breakfast to a family night out on the town. Emma wasn't family, but the Donovens included her like a long-lost cousin. She wouldn't let her mind wander to thoughts of a date night with her handsome boss, even though Wade had taken her feelings on a tilt-o-whirl ride.

Her feelings of gratitude were morphing into more than a crush. She had to rein in her half-in-love heart. Wade would go back to running the company and making service calls soon. Her life and career were stuck in limbo land. In a few weeks, she would leave Tennessee. That is, if her plans stayed the same. What if they changed? She couldn't dwell on staying. Not with cowboy Wade moseying in front of her.

"Some up-and-comers were discovered here." Linda pointed to the corner restaurant. The twang of an electric guitar and the base beat of drums echoed from the three-story eatery.

Emma breathed in the aroma of grilling meat. Her stomach did a happy dance. She had skipped lunch after Linda's celebration breakfast. The undercurrent of music and microphone noise meant she didn't have to discuss drive times and overlapping appointments with Wade. Crossing too far over the line into his personal life would add to her emerging feelings. She could keep her heart at a distance by chatting with his mom.

Mike opened the door to the lively restaurant. Red neon advertising beckoned them inside. The smell of barbecue sauce had her volunteering to dive into the vat.

"Is downtown like living in a video game every night?" She stepped next to Mike at the hostess stand and unbuttoned her fringed leather jacket. Another gem from Linda's closet that made her a country music loving imposter. The forty-five-degree weather constituted a heat wave to her winter-hardened bones, and she was pretty sure she had never purchased a coat with leather tassels.

"Pretty much." Wade's deep voice cut through the conversations of the patron-filled room. "I don't come down here that often because of the crowds. The wait times get long."

His comment gave her comfort. Part of her didn't like the image of Wade surrounded by flirty cowgirls. Were flashy women his type? Not that she had any claim to him.

"This place has the best ribs." Linda rubbed her hands together and exuded enough excitement for the four of them. "There's a small dance floor in front of the artists. Line dancing gets popular later on."

"We have church tomorrow." Wade scowled at his mom's suggestion. "I'm not sure we'll be here for the dancing."

Linda made a face at her son. "I wasn't talking about you." She rested a hand on her flower-accented western hat and clicked her boots as if she was ready to start the party.

Emma stifled a laugh. After all the caregiving Linda had done, she deserved to let loose. God had restored Wade's health, and that was a huge blessing.

"They have our table." Mike motioned for everyone to follow the hostess who, like a third of the crowd, donned a blue and silver football jersey.

Wade leaned down, his mouth at the rim of Emma's hat. "Saved by a reservation."

Her boss could save her anytime, especially if he used that husky, baritone voice. She grinned at his exasperated expression. Would he even be interacting with her in another week once he received a doctor's release and recaptured his head honcho status? He'd be out on service calls helping customers. Her excitement dimmed. She'd hardly see him.

A singer explained the background to his upcoming song.

Emma sat at their table which was a few feet from the half-moon, faux-wood dance floor. The strum of the singer's guitar did little to quiet the talk of patrons. Conversing with the Donovens would be difficult as long as the musician played. Some distance and a musical diversion would keep her mind off of Wade. Yeah, right. Her eyes were like homing pigeons to his good looks.

She would survive this night and guard her heart. Ribs were one of her favorite foods. The Donovens were one of her favorite families. Nashville was fast becoming a favorite city. She'd enjoy the barbecue and the Nashville experience and tamp down any thoughts of what it would be like to date her boss. If Linda wanted to line dance, then Emma would grab her hand, forget her worries, and leave the Donoven men with their truffle fries.

~*~

Wade knew this was a bad idea. When his mom texted about taking Emma to dinner downtown, he should have texted that his leg hurt, but that would have been a lie. Emma's therapy and constant encouragement had him walking almost as good as new. And she was a quick learner, managing the office well, if not better, than Fran. Emma had a way of guiding customers who couldn't make up their minds, and she was even cheery to those who changed their appointments. The article had increased their Saturday call volume with no complaints from Emma. How could he begrudge her legendary barbecue and some fun?

He tried to keep the evening professional by walking with his dad and taking the seat diagonal from Emma. He didn't need to sit next to her like they were on a real date. If he put his arm on the back of her chair, people would think they were a couple. Nothing romantic was going on. This was only a family meal. He'd keep that excuse on constant replay.

Emma gestured with her hands as she chatted with his mom. The decibel meter on the band erased all hopes of hearing any conversation. A guy in a brown cowboy hat stared at Emma from across the dance floor. He appeared to enjoy her elaborate hand gestures. His grin would make one believe he heard everything Emma said. Why did Emma have to look so darn cute in her borrowed cowgirl get up. That jacket was a bit flashy on his mom but it fit Emma's outgoing personality. He should have insisted Emma wear a Titletown cap. The green and gold would repel locals. He stifled a laugh. Nah. Every single guy would look twice at his office manager even if she donned Green Bay's colors.

He sipped his drink, which went down like dirt, and he clapped when the song ended. His hand hadn't made a claw since Emma showed him her pressure techniques. If his dad and Cole had listened to him and let Emma find a job elsewhere, he wouldn't have to fight these confusing feelings. Feelings that were probably more gratitude and thankfulness for helping his family out in a pinch than they were genuine interest. Would the doctor be able to see him before Wednesday? The sooner he got back in a service van the better. He bit into the last pork rib on his plate and let the peppery sauce burn a hole in his tongue.

The band began playing a popular country slow song.

His mom stood. "Come on, Mike. This is one of my favorites."

Dad tossed his napkin onto the table and rose. "It's better than line dancing." He grasped mom's hand and led her out onto the tiny dance floor.

"That's so cute." Emma beamed at him.

Her smile was like a blow to his Adam's apple. He could barely breathe and almost choked on his pork. Her cheerleading made him want to burn up the dance floor.

"They don't get out much." He cleared his throat. "Work and all." And an injured son. The joke was on him. He hadn't been out in months either. He couldn't even remember when he'd been on his last date.

Emma swiveled to watch his parents and two other couples on the intimate dance floor. Brown hat strode to the edge of the flooring, his hat tilting and swaying as he tried to stare at Emma through the gaps in the couples. Was the guy going to make a move? Why not? Wade had a cane hanging from his chair and his distance from Emma relegated him to brother status. It didn't help that Emma kept time to the beat with her torso. Her swaying fringe was a duck call to every hunter in the restaurant. A grim idea crept into his thoughts. It would only take one whack behind the knees with his cane to put Brown Hat out of commission. Okay. Now he was losing it.

Brown Hat dodged a couple and swaggered toward their table. He sported a cringe worthy leer.

Sweat dampened Wade's forehead. Could he let that guy sweep Emma away? What if she liked the rugged cowboy type? Fran would be out for a few more weeks, but could he place a hold on a relationship until then?

"Wanna dance?" Wade leapt to his feet and motioned toward the floor with an arm that suddenly felt as if it had broken out in hives.

Emma popped out of her seat and scooted toward him. Her nose crinkled. For once she looked shy.

"I don't know that song or how to dance country. I only know a few polka steps or what we did in high school. Hold on and barely move."

"Works for me." He grasped her hand and stifled a smirk as Brown Hat did an about face. Blocking the warning signals going off in his brain and ignoring any inquisitive gazes from his parents, he drew Emma in close and started the slowest three-hundred-and-sixty-degree turn of his life. The brim of Emma's hat tickled his chin and whatever floral perfume she was wearing had him rocketing to Mars. He liked the feel of her curves in his arms. He tightened his hold around her lower back, and when she snuggled closer, he almost sang with the band. Yep, he'd better call the doctor straightaway for a medical release and create a few degrees of separation from Emma. Holding her in his arms felt too real and too right. Why hadn't he learned how to polka?

~*~

Emma reached for her phone on the nightstand. The hum and strum of a night in downtown Nashville had her too charged to sleep. When she closed her eyes, she transported into the circle of Wade's embrace. Why had her boss asked her to dance? Was it because of his mom's encouragement? To be a gracious host? To prove he had recovered? Or did he enjoy her company? Because if possible, she'd continue going round and round and round with Wade until the flooring wore out. Part of her was still trying to hold onto the tingle of his touch. Her insides were jumbled and fluttery like crepe paper caught in a ceiling fan.

She flopped on the bed and texted Sam.

STILL STARGAZING?

A few minutes passed while she checked her social media.

CHANGE OF PLANS. WE HAD DINNER AT GRETTA AND ERNIE'S. THEIR SON JEDEDIAH IS IN TOWN. SHE BRIBED US WITH BRISKET AND CHEESY POTATOES. WE PLAYED HEARTS AFTERWARD.

Hearts. An applicable subject.

I WON AT HEARTS TONIGHT. WADE AND I DANCED TOGETHER DOWNTOWN.

SLOW OR FAST?

PAINSTAKINGLY SLOW.

Emma could almost hear the squeals coming from Whispering Creek.

I KNEW IT. YOU'RE JUST WHAT THE DOCTOR ORDERED. LOL.

FUNNY. HE'S MY BOSS. OFF LIMITS.

Would Sam agree?

FRAN WILL RETURN IN A FEW WEEKS. THEN YOU'LL BE FREE TO DATE EACH OTHER.

A heart emoji followed Sam's text.

Would Wade want to start a relationship? He wasn't forced to hug her for three point nine minutes tonight. And he did. He even held her hand and led her back to the table. At one point during their dance, he grinned, and she thought he might kiss her. Silly dream. Her chest housed a bass drum when she thought about Wade's take-charge attitude, business skills, and sparkly eyes.

She scrunched a pillow under her head. Dating was not on her radar when she fled south.

IF HE'S INTERESTED. That was a big IF. MAYBE IT'S A REBOUND THING.

WADE HAD A LEG INJURY. NOT A HEAD WOUND. IF HE ASKED YOU TO DANCE, HE'S INTERESTED. REBOUNDS COME AFTER BROKEN RELATIONSHIPS NOT BROKEN BONES.

Sam had a point. BUT HE LIVES IN TN.

SO DO I. ENJOY YOUR TIME AT D&S AND PRAY TO GOD FOR WISDOM.

Great advice spoken by her bestie.

She texted Sam until her brain decompressed enough to sleep. Gazing at the ceiling, she asked God to sort out her future.

What was that verse about not worrying about tomorrow? She did a web search on her phone.

The screen showed Matthew 6:34.

THEREFORE, DO NOT WORRY ABOUT TOMORROW, FOR TOMORROW WILL WORRY ABOUT ITSELF. EACH DAY HAS ENOUGH TROUBLE OF ITS OWN.

She laughed in the darkness of the bedroom. "You've got that right, God."

16

By Monday afternoon, Emma didn't have time to dwell on her slow dance with Wade. The phone rang non-stop. The weekly schedule was full, and the next week was filling fast. Many customers mentioned the picture in the newspaper. The word was spreading about the hazards of cheap electrical strips. Wade hummed a joyful tune. She assumed it was the increased business, but Derek had returned, and Tennessee had won the AFC Championship yesterday, so Wade had a few reasons to celebrate. Super Bowl fever was blazing throughout Nashville. February would be an exciting month.

She stretched her legs by pulling papers off the printer for her boss. One sheet was from a doctor's office. Had Wade received his driving release? Surely, he would have mentioned being sprung from driving prison. She set the papers on his desk.

Wade glanced from his laptop. Little blue sparks brightened his eyes. Handsome boss on aisle three. She forced any romantic thoughts from her head and reminded herself that this was a professional relationship.

"Thanks." His not-a-care-in-the-world-smile whip-started her heart. "The claims department needed a copy of Derek's work release. Figured I should have a copy on file, too."

"Pretty soon that will be yours." Then she'd hardly see him in the office. Their friendship would stall. Lunch settled heavy in her stomach.

"I certainly hope so. It's been a long time coming." He placed the paperwork in a file holder atop the small corner desk.

She returned to her computer, dreading the silence that would befall the office when everyone was out on service calls. She'd also miss Wade's presence. They made a good team inside the office and outside of it. Dwelling on that fact would only frazzle her focus.

"Hey, Emma." Wade called her name as if they were the best of friends.

Had their dance buffed some of his hard edges? She swiveled in her chair and flashed her best customer service smile.

"Talking about these medical reports had me thinking about your human resource software."

"People Peeps?" She said the name with glee even though it had been ridiculed.

"Yeah that." He rubbed his jaw. "It won't hurt anything if I open it on my laptop. Would you mind if I took a look?"

Was he serious? Adrenaline surged through her body as she grabbed her backpack. Her skills with callers must have made an impression. She fumbled the zipper on the small compartment on her backpack where she kept her flash drive. Her heart rallied a joyous beat as she prepared to explain the software to her boss.

"I'd be happy to answer any questions. I tried to make the interface as user friendly as possible." She handed him the drive. "Click on customers and you can see the data fields." She refrained from line dancing down the hallway. Had she found her first customer? Did Wade recognize her love for helping people.

Wade inserted the drive into his laptop.

Too hyped to sit, she leaned against the counter. She resisted the urge to hover over Wade and treat him like a student. Her self-confidence rebounded a notch after all the bruises it had taken from being scammed by Ron. When she had shown her former boss the software, his interest seemed miles away, and they had been interrupted before she had finished showing all the capabilities.

Nothing familiar appeared on the screen. Where were the happy geriatric faces? Had Wade decided to check accounts receivable?

"What on earth?" Her boss didn't sound dazzled by her creation. Wade squinted at the screen and then jolted like he'd been electrified. "Emma, this isn't your software."

"Yes, it is." She had created it on her own. "Did you hit the customer tab?"

Wade stared at her as if she had burned through a red traffic light. "There are no customer tabs. This is an electronic wallet." His deep voice spiked to a soprano.

"A what?" Her heart thudded in her ears creating a booming warning.

"Cash. Funds. Crypto currency."

Any money she owned was in her backpack or in the bank, not on a flash drive. She gripped the counter so she wouldn't collapse onto the floor. This had to be a mistake. "I don't own any crypto currency."

"You do now." Wade leapt to his feet and pulled the drive from his laptop. "I think we just peeped into where Ron stashed his money."

~*~

"I'm locking the front door for safety." Wade was in the hallway before he realized that he had left his cane in the office. "I don't want any visitors while we try to figure this out." He shivered and felt his skin chill with bumps. His leg felt solid, but not his wits. How could such a small device hold so much money? The plastic and metal felt odd in his palm.

Emma followed his movements with huge eyes like she was concentrating on a hypnotist's charm. Hand at her throat she fingered a silver chain and stood like a pillar against the counter.

They possessed evidence and a substantial sum of stolen funds that Emma had been carrying in her backpack since she arrived. Was she truly clueless about the drive? She had to be innocent, or why would she hand it to him? The poor thing looked like she was going to faint. Emma was an emotional, energetic woman, but he didn't see her being this good of an actress.

He threw the bolt on the front door and rushed back to his desk, closing the blinds to nefarious eyes. The shaded room mirrored his mood. Emma might be in danger. He might be too since he knew how to access the money. Every healthy nerve in his body screamed to protect her, but only she could solve this problem. She knew details about Ron's business. He didn't have a clue. Gently, yet firmly, he placed the drive in her hand.

She clutched the culprit. "What do I do with this? Call the police?" She picked up the office phone. The receiver trembled in her hand. "I have a detective's card from Wisconsin."

"Wait." His heart drummed a driving rhythm. The police might think Emma had knowledge of the heist. At the moment, a large sum of money inhabited her fist. He pointed at her hand. "Put that in your backpack. It's business as usual until I call…" Who? He didn't want to involve his family. Not now anyway. Emma needed a lawyer. Would the company's attorney be able to help? Perhaps he knew someone who specialized in white-collar crime. It was worth a try.

"Let me call our attorney and get some advice. I don't want you to get into any more trouble." Trouble where they would place her in jail.

"More trouble?" Her breath hitched. "Like this isn't... bad enough?"

"New trouble." He tried to sound in control, but his mind whirled with worst-case scenarios. "Why don't you sit down?" He grasped her shoulders and settled her into her office chair. He rubbed her shoulders until they didn't feel like wood. Totally unprofessional, but he didn't remember reading anything about this situation in the executive training manual.

"I'm scared. Will you pray for me? For us?" Tears glistened in Emma's eyes. "I don't want anyone to get hurt on my account. I don't know how—" Her chest heaved. "How I have this money?"

His throat ached seeing her so undone. Where was his cute, confident, office manager? He resisted the urge to wrap her in his arms and rock her slowly. "I believe you, Emma." His whole being was at peace with that statement. He had worked and lived beside Emma and never seen anything to suggest she had millions hidden in her backpack.

A breath shuddered from her lips. Another, calmer, breath followed. When she raised her glistening gaze upon him, he nearly swept her off her feet and booked a flight to the Caribbean.

"Thank you, Wade. It means a lot that you support me."

He took her tiny, fragile fingers in his, and cleared his throat. "I'll pray." And he would send a silent prayer to the Lord to restrain Wade from bending and kissing his office manager. How could life be cruel to someone with a big heart like Emma? Someone who had helped his family and someone who had encouraged him to get better. To be his healthy best.

"Lord, we need You more than ever." He squeezed Emma's hand. "Please watch over Emma and protect her from any more harm. Protect those we love. Give us wisdom on how to proceed. We need a lot of guidance here, Lord. Light the path ahead for both of us." *Especially Emma.* "May You right all the wrongs that Ron has caused. In Jesus' name. Amen." He let go of her hand. Instantly, he missed her touch.

"Thank you." She sniffled. "That was beautiful." Turning toward her desk, she reached for a tissue.

He hooked a thumb toward the hallway. He wished he could do or say more, but he was Emma's boss, a friend, nothing more. "I'll call the attorney from my back office."

On cue, the phone rang.

"Duty calls." She forced a quivering smile and answered. Only the slightest strain sounded in her voice.

Why Lord? Why does Emma have to go through this trial? Somehow that word held a whole new meaning. Would the police get involved? Would he be an accomplice since he knew about the funds? He hadn't gotten his life one hundred percent in order and this scandal dropped. He should never have asked to see her software. But if everything is done in God's timing, he would have seen it sooner or later. Wouldn't he? The beginning of a headache pulsed in his temples.

He collapsed in his black leather office chair and called Brent's direct line.

"Wade. I haven't heard from you in a while. How's the recovery going?" Brent was always cordial, but he kept a professional distance in his voice.

"I'm doing well. I should have my full doctor's release this week." Euphoria eluded him. "I have an unusual question to run by you."

"Anytime. I'm here to help."

Wade visualized the client meter ticking off dollars per minute.

"We have a new hire. Temporary help to replace Fran since she's out for surgery. A friend of Cole's." *Way to distance yourself Donoven.* "Anyway, she worked for a guy in Wisconsin that scammed people out of money. A phony real estate investment scheme."

"Would this be the guy on the news a few days back. He's dead, isn't he?"

"One and the same." Wade swiveled in his chair.

A long whistle came through the receiver.

"Today, the girl discovered a flash drive with some information on where the money might be located. I advised her to get an attorney before calling the police." He hated being so general. Emma was more to him than a generic temp worker who came and went without much interaction. "Would you know anyone who handles that type of law?" *Please, God.* His good leg jiggled underneath his desk. His healed one could have jiggled alongside thanks to Emma.

"Smart move to call, Wade. I do know someone. My college roommate is an attorney here in Nashville. He handles high-profile cases. Some for our government and some for foreign countries. If he can't help you, he'll know someone who can."

"Great. I'm at a loss here. And since she's a friend of a friend, I'd like to help her out." Emma was becoming more than a friend, but Brent didn't need to know that information.

"I'll text you his name and contact information. But let me call and give him a heads up. See what he advises." Brent's breathing whooshed through the phone. "Here comes the straight talk as your company lawyer. How well do you know this girl? Could she be an accomplice?"

"Accomplice. Emma. No, no way." Emma had a big heart. She wouldn't be capable of hurting people.

"Did anything show up in the background check?" Brent was asking about basic precautions that should be done when running a business, but somehow the questions danced on Wade's last nerve.

"I didn't run one because ..." Everything happened so fast. Emma was Sam's friend. The company needed help. Wade picked at the stitching on the leather armrest. None of those answers made good business sense or negated the seriousness of possessing stolen funds. "No, I didn't check her past history."

"I'm sorry, Wade, but in my judgment, this girl shouldn't work for Donoven and Sons anymore. You and your company could possibly get embroiled in some bad press. Now that she has evidence of a crime in her possession, you have to cut her loose. We don't know where that evidence will lead."

Wade sat stunned. Brent suspected Emma wasn't above board. His mouth parched as he tried to form a response to Brent's advice. Emma shined as his office manager. Shined in his heart. Losing this job would crush her. The thought of her reaction bruised his being.

"You mean I have to fire her today? Could it wait until the end of the week?" He couldn't get Emma's captivating eyes and their well of tears out of his mind.

"Since we've talked. You have to fire her within the hour. I'm sorry to be the bearer of bad news, but we don't have anything to show a work history or her innocence. Hopefully, my buddy can help you out and clear her name."

Slumping in his chair, Wade switched his phone to his other ear and into his right hand. He couldn't trust the damp fingers on his former claw to grip the phone.

"I appreciate your help and guidance." Like a mixed martial artist's punch to the gut. "I'll wait for your text. Thanks for the straight talk." A total lie. He'd prefer some lawyer fluff or legalese.

Wade ended the call and stared at the beige wall of his office. He scrubbed a hand over his face. A sour aroma filled his nostrils. How was he going to break the news to Emma?

He reclined his head against the cushioned leather of the chair. "Why Lord? Why did You bring Emma into my life? Didn't I have enough stress going on? I like her. I really like her. She gets me and this whole business responsibility stuff. Now I'm supposed to take her job away and erase her financial support. I don't get this at all."

His eyes burned, but he willed the emotion away. Bosses didn't cry. He'd fired people before, but not his employee of the month, and a woman who he'd like to court as a girlfriend. He could kiss any relationship with Emma good-bye after he fired her.

A brief remembrance of holding her in his arms and her sexy smile shining up at his face threatened his composure.

He pounded the desk with his healthy fist. Reinjuring his thawed claw wasn't an option. Emma wouldn't be around for pressure point massages. Curse words filtered through his brain. *Forgive me, Lord.*

Buzzing broke into his thoughts. How long had he been lost in his regret?

Attorney Zach West's name and address flashed onto his phone screen. Zach would meet Emma at five thirty this evening. He doubted that he would receive an invitation to join her after her termination, but at almost 3:00 p.m., he could pay Emma for the full day of work. He texted his thanks to Brent. A thank you for blowing up Wade's life.

The odd burn behind his eyes turned into a strange tingle. Dismissing Emma hurt worse than all his physical injuries. She had erased the cramping in his hand. Her encouragement to walk had him confident in his leg holding his weight. She made him believe a driving release was eminent. His physical setbacks were on the road to recovery. The hurt he was about to cause Emma made him relive the stitches and blood and casting he had endured in a hospital bed.

For the first time in his career, he more than hated, no he loathed, being the boss.

17

Emma's head whipped toward the blinds at the front of the main office. Was that a shadow? Her nerve endings readied to fight or flee.

"Do you have a trip charge?" the customer asked, her voice muffled through the receiver.

"Yes, we do." Emma tore her gaze from the window and back to the computer. "But it's waived if we perform the work." She gripped the phone tighter. How was she answering mundane questions when she was stuck in a horror movie. "I could squeeze you in on Friday afternoon." Office manager mode kicked in to seal the appointment. She recited times and procedures through her life fog, ever the professional, swallowing the fear numbing her brain.

Hanging up the phone, she crossed her arms on the counter and rested her head on the fleshy cushion. *God, how could You let this happen to me? I didn't steal anyone's money. You know the truth. I know the truth. How do I convince the world I'm not a criminal?*

She prayed Wade's attorney knew someone to take her case, or take the money, and let her disappear into anonymity. If she left the Nashville area, she'd have to leave Wade. Her stomach hollowed at the thought. What would she do without the man who gave her heart flutters and made her feel like Superwoman battling bad guys and soaring into the sky? *Thank You, Lord, for the man who restored my confidence and became a friend.* Sam was still her best friend. Wade was fast becoming her best more-than-a-friend. Just thinking about

Wade gave her encouragement to get out of bed in the morning. Even electrical quotes became interesting when he spent time with her explaining the system. Did he share the same attraction? She hoped so or she'd be back doubting her worth and intuition.

"Emma."

Wade stood in the doorway to the office. The off-white counter contained more color than his features. Had he struck out on attorneys?

"I have a name of a lawyer in the city. A friend of a friend." Not one ounce of enthusiasm buoyed Wade's message. Was he still in shock? "He can see you tonight."

An audible sigh whooshed past her lips. Finally, some good news. "Thank You, Jesus." And thank you, Wade. Her handsome protector. A millstone of worry lifted from her shoulders. "I didn't know who to call next if you came up empty. Sam has an attorney who handled Ted's estate. I think white-collar crime might be out of his league." She rubbed her forehead feeling that spark of hope that God would have this problem solved by midnight.

"I have something else I need to tell you." Wade fidgeted like a toddler with a full bladder.

"Legal advice?" Of course, he'd share any wisdom he had on the matter. Wade had been running the company a while and would want to help. She almost bounded out of the chair to kiss him. "I'll take all the free counsel I can get."

He nodded and braced an arm on the threshold. Leaning into his stance, his face wrinkled. Was he worried for her? God had blessed her with such a kind friend. Friend was an understatement. She knew it, and he knew it. Heat rose in her cheeks.

"You can't work here anymore."

The warmth in her cheeks chilled. Did she hear him right?

Or was he joking—a worst-case to better-case scenario. "Don't tease me."

"I'm not. You have to leave right now." The words were coming from Wade's mouth but not a hint of emotion flashed across his face. He might as well have been reciting an answering service message. Did he not care about her? Appreciate all she had done for him and his business? What about all the time they had spent together? Didn't it mean anything to him?

Her hands clenched, and she rose from her desk, fighting to control the anger surging through her body. "Why? Why do I have to leave?" She had projects to finish and people to help. She'd never left work undone. Ever. Didn't Wade understand her by now? Her life was freefalling and the person she relied on to hold the safety net gave the impression he was ready to bolt through the nearest exit. Traitor!

"It was our attorney's advice. Once he knew about Ron's money..." Wade paused. He held out his hand, but as fast as a glimmer of hope registered in her brain that he might regret this as much as she, Wade cupped a fist with his open hand. A weird guttural sound disturbed the silence in the office. She would have gladly filled the stillness, but her mind blanked. If he was fighting for some resemblance of sanity, or decency, or a future, he had forfeited the match. And sacrificed their relationship. A weird stinging settled behind her eyes. The kind of feeling you get when something good has been lost for eternity.

"I should never have handed you that drive. I had no idea..." How could something that she was so proud of torpedo her happiness. *Lord, why did he have to ask for my software?* Why now? Ron had victimized her again.

Wade avoided her gaze. His shoes were more interesting than his office mate. Mate. That was a mirage. "The attorney also texted that you probably shouldn't wear our business shirts." Wade's hand fell from a scrub of his jaw and hung lifeless at his side. "I'm so sorry."

Who was this man standing before her? She thought he was someone special that God had brought into her life. Men who cared about you didn't fire you on the spot and demand you dispose of their shirt? If she had a change of clothes, she would throw this one in his heartless face. He knew she wasn't a threat, didn't he? At least, deep down. Her future with him was going through her internal shredding machine. She had been scammed again. She squared her shoulders and lifted her chin as if this was a performance review. In a way, it was. Her new beginning was over. Dead. Wade had sprayed weed killer on any budding romantic dreams.

"Don't worry. I think I can solve the association problem right now." She yanked open the desk drawer and removed a roll of thick gray tape. She tore a strip with her teeth and slapped it over the Donoven and Sons name and their emblem. "This will work temporarily."

"I don't want to do this, but I've worked hard to build this business. People count on me." He shuffled closer, staying out of reach. The sparks of personality that she had coaxed out of Wade had vanished, leaving an unrecognizable husk of a man. "I can't unhear my attorney. I'm really sorry."

"Don't." She held up a hand to stop him from coming any closer. "If you apologize one more time, I will throw whatever quarter container is around, against that wall." She jabbed a finger at the wall closest to his body. "It's not a funny joke anymore." The truth in that statement was almost laughable.

Remembering time spent with Wade driving in the van, at Ms. Johnson's home, and dancing round and round threatened to crack the levy behind her eyes. She couldn't cry. Not in front of him. If he was going into business mode then so would she.

"Text me where I need to go. I will drive you home and leave the van at your parents' house. I can call a shared ride to the attorney's office. Before we leave, I'll send an invoice for time served." She'd pat herself on the back for the pun, but in reality, she'd need every penny to pay for legal expenses.

"Em—"

She knew he was fighting another apology. Fighting to say something to bridge the harshness of being a boss. Simply fighting an impossible situation. But her heart and ears couldn't listen.

Even filled with remorse he looked good. Too good. She'd sort that out later when her heart had scabbed and healed.

"Don't worry. My family owns a business." For the first time in her life, she disliked that statement. Oh, to simply be naïve and clueless. "I came to Tennessee so their livelihood wouldn't be impacted by my scandal. I like your family." She fought the shed of a tear with all her fortitude. "I don't want them impacted by my negative press." She finger quoted her negativity.

Her boss mirrored the glum oaf she met on their first pizza night. "It's not like that."

"Yeah, Wade. It kind of is." She forced a smile, but even she knew her mouth resembled a dead catfish. "I'll be in the waiting room when you're ready." Reading old magazines, guarding millions in stolen cash, and bandaging her barely beating heart.

She brushed by Wade using her backpack as a barrier and strode the hallway until she found an upholstered chair close to an exit. She needed the distance to pull herself together. Ugh, Wade followed her.

"You can't share a ride with strangers." He glanced at the windows and leaned closer, leaving a few feet between them.

"That other woman is still on the loose, and you have information on that drive. Crypto, too. Drive me home in a van but take my truck to the attorney's office."

"You're going to let me drive your truck? Oh, that's right. You have an auto policy for that liability." Was she being too hard on him? She'd process that later because her brain was short circuiting at the moment.

He nodded and returned to the office, shuffling like he had aged two decades.

Finding the flash drive of Ron's accounts had spiraled their Monday into an abyss.

She slipped her phone from her pocket and texted Sam. How did she begin to explain her latest predicament?

NEED PRAYER AND GUIDANCE.

After a few minutes, she received a response.

HANG ON. I'LL CALL.

Her life verse scrolled through her mind. The Lord was her rock, her fortress, and her deliverer.

Somehow her favorite Scripture wasn't cutting it today. Because if her precious cactus, Herbie, was in the chair next to her with the rock etched with the opening to Psalm 18:2, she might just hurl him at the wall.

"Jesus, where are you? My world continues to fall apart, and there's no bottom in sight."

~*~

Wade resisted the urge to grip the hand hold on his side of the service van as Emma barreled toward his house. All his muscles stood on high alert. Not because he feared another car crash, but because he had hurt someone special, and he couldn't apologize without infuriating her.

"Don't worry." Emma's features were as blank as copier paper. "I'm not granny driving, but I won't let anything happen to you. You're burning through office managers like a short wick."

Her snark was pure Emma. He couldn't blame her for being mad. If possible, he'd run away from himself.

"Thank you."

She didn't acknowledge his words. Worse off, she hardly acknowledged him as they tore through town. Even with all his electrician skills, there was no rewiring this relationship.

18

Driving Wade's truck was a huge mistake. She had placed herself in a huge metal keepsake box. Every time she shifted her weight, Wade's cologne wafted into the air. A turquoise football koozie sat in the cup holder and a Donoven and Sons cap rested in the passenger seat where Wade should be sitting if he hadn't kicked her out the company door. She bit her lip and focused on the road. Wavy lines in her vision wouldn't help her navigate traffic.

She blew out a deep breath and tried to calm her jumble of feelings. If she was having mixed emotions over leaving after seven days of working with Wade, what would it be like after six weeks. Wade never mentioned a future or a first date. He'd fired her after a phone call with his attorney. Whatever she thought was blossoming between them had been a hoax. She felt more foolish now than believing in Ron's investment jargon.

Lord, please keep me from making any more mistakes in work or love. A steady, predictable life doesn't hurt quite as much.

Her focus had to be clearing her name and staying out of jail. Forget six days of working with a handsome boss if she was sentenced to six years for aiding a criminal.

The attendant at the special parking entrance ushered her inside and directed her to the fifth floor. Well-placed lighting saved the structure from resembling a cement tomb. She couldn't help but visualize her backpack emanating a homing signal attracting nefarious gangsters. She had second thoughts about refusing Wade's offer to ride along. His presence might ward off thieves, but the silence and regrets would be too awkward.

Snap out of it. She didn't need Wade. Jesus was here with her. She'd pray for a guardian angel and dash down the stairwell to the lobby. Frantic, petite women could do a lot of damage at full speed.

Gold and crystal chandeliers lit the entrance to Zach West's office building. The marble flooring and pristine bronze elevator doors didn't bode well for her attorney bill. Wade didn't mention this being a pro-bono case. A sickly swirl cramped her stomach.

She entered an office with five attorney names, one of the names being West. The leather seats in the waiting area stood empty.

A receptionist slid open the window at the side of her desk. "You must be Emma."

She nodded. How many clients had money on them that exceeded the GDP of Lichtenstein? The receptionist led her to a conference room with a long mahogany table and comfy rolling chairs.

"Mr. West will be in shortly." The woman's smile held the warmth of a fancy plastic doll. She handed Emma a clipboard. "There are a few forms to fill out. The top one is the acceptance of Mr. West's representation. I'll collect them before I leave."

Time to sign her life away. She accepted the clipboard and took a seat at the conference table. On the top form, blaring in bold print, was the notice that she owed Zach four-thousand dollars today for a retainer. Her cheeks prickled. She could have sworn the chair beneath her hovered above the carpet.

Four grand would max her credit card if they accepted plastic payment. What if this case dragged on and she owed Zach more money? Would he drop her as a client? She struggled to hold the pen as she signed her solvency away.

The money she had coming from Wade would pay living expenses for a brief while, but then what? Asking her parents for funding was out of the question. Not until she was desperate. At least more desperate. She didn't need to hear about consultations of star patterns and a denial that God existed.

A bald man entered the conference room clutching two laptops and a black leather portfolio. He kicked the door closed with brown wingtips that accented his blue suit. His hand shot toward her. "Zach West." His smile and meadow green eyes eased some of her worry. Her attorney exuded the charm one needed in front of a jury. His gaze darted to her paperwork as she shook his hand. If she hadn't been a filing queen and paper organizer, she would have missed his instantaneous perusal for a signature.

"Emma Uranova." She introduced herself and pointed at the top paper. "I hope you take credit cards."

"Oh that." He dismissed the amount with a flick of his hand. He placed the hardware and folder on the table and sat. "Retainers are standard at the firm. My assistant will take care of the finances."

One day soon, she hoped she could dismiss four grand so casually.

"Brent mentioned you used to work for Ron Runyard and may be in possession of, or have knowledge of, some of the stolen funds." Zach folded his hands and gave her a look as if they were old friends catching up over coffee.

Inwardly, she grinned. Her attorney was cool under pressure and left a few escape routes in his question.

"Unfortunately, or fortunately, depending on how you see it, yes I do." She could talk in self-preservation speak, too.

"There's something I must discuss before we finalize

representation."

Adrenaline seeped into her bloodstream. She resisted the urge to fan herself with his clipboard. High-powered attorneys weren't abundant in her contact list.

"I represent two other clients who had funds stolen by Mr. Runyard, so I'm familiar with his antics. If..." he accentuated the uncertainty, "you are in possession of some of his monies or know where they are located, we may be able to pull resources and reclaim some of the funds."

A ray of hope sparked on her mental horizon.

"So I may get some of my money back? And lost wages?" Ron owed her a few weeks' pay along with her inheritance money.

"Possibly." Zach clicked his pen. "Ron is deceased. If we can tie the funds to his company, then we can sue for damages in a class action suit."

Sue a company that didn't exist. She laughed. "The Ron Runyard Group was a fraud."

"You'd be surprised how many companies are formed out of thin air or have sketchy financing. I've worked many cases where a company looked legit only to find their balance sheet was a forgery." He rubbed his hands together. "If there are assets, we can go after them. May I see the flash drive to see how we proceed?"

She unzipped the compartment on her backpack and handed the flash drive to Zach.

He opened one of the laptops. "This computer isn't connected to the Internet." He inserted the drive and stared at the screen. Nothing registered on his face. Not happiness, regret, elation, or disappointment. "You believed this drive held software?"

"A customer service software. I designed it to track residents' birthdays and interests for the defunct Greener

Groves facility. I named it People Peeps." Perhaps the name did need to go because Zach's mouth twitched at the mention of peeps.

"And you believe this information came directly from Ron?" Zach cast a calculated glance at her with those perceptive green eyes.

Was this a trick question? Was she under cross examination? Sure, she was. A floating feeling overcame her body. She had to stay grounded in her truth. The truth. God's truth. *Lord, give me wisdom.*

"I did share a desk with Ron's assistant Annette, but she was on top of her game and never left anything lying about. She showed no interest in my software. Ron encouraged the project. I actually showed it to him shortly before he disappeared. We were interrupted by a man, a visitor. I didn't recognize him, but his arrival made Ron nervous. So nervous that Ron dropped my drive." She released her fisted hands and let the blood flow through her fingers. "What's odd, now that I think about it, is that the man must have used the back door to the office. No one came in that way because it was an emergency exit. It's the only scenario that I can think of for why his presence was a shock." Reliving the last days in Ron's office seemed like a lifetime ago. "I told the detective about the man, but I don't know any specifics. I'm not even sure I could identify him."

"You gave a statement to a detective in Wisconsin?" A tic pulsed in Zach's jaw.

"A brief one. I didn't know anything. I didn't know where Ron and Annette had gone. I still don't know where they fled except the news said Ron was killed in the northern part of the state."

"You played dumb?" Zac's expression was as stark as a white, dry erase board. Where was this line of questioning going?

"I am dumb." Her ears flamed. She never thought of herself as stupid and admitting that she had been played was a punch to her belly. "I never took any money, and I certainly don't know where these accounts lead. I barely looked at the computer screen when it popped up on my boss's laptop."

"We know where the money flowed now." Zach removed the flash drive from his computer and gripped it tightly. "This, young lady, holds an extremely large sum of money and tracks deposits in overseas accounts. It's pretty impressive that you have it."

"But I don't want it." She pushed away from the conference table and held up her hands. Her arms trembled. "I'm afraid of it. I wish I didn't know about it. I keep seeing black SUVs and feeling like I'm being watched. I don't want that thing back."

"Duly noted." Zach's voice didn't even rise one octave. Hers screeched like an out-of-tune symphony. "We'll get a safe deposit box downstairs at the bank. In both of our names. I'll text an assistant manager I know to come in and help us. I don't want you carrying this evidence in a backpack."

She had schlepped it across the country. Good thing she hadn't eaten in a while because she was ready to vomit.

"You mentioned a black SUV. Were you followed?" Zach clicked his pen more than once. Was he worried? Should she be more worried?

"After I left Ron's office, and after I gave my statement to the detective, I thought I may have been followed. I lost the tail." Every black car in Tennessee had become a suspect. She wanted her mundane life returned. "Do you think it was Ron or Annette?"

Zach raised an eyebrow. The bushy brow contrasted with his shaved head. "We don't have to worry about Ron, but

Annette, Sandra, Eva…she's had her share of aliases. I'm not so sure. She's never bothered former employees of the defunct LLCs or any investors. When was the last time you saw her?"

"The last day that I saw Ron. The day before they disappeared." Her heartbeat thudded in her ears as she recounted entering the office stripped of all the electronics. An eeriness settled over her spirit. She had worked next to a cold-hearted scam artist without a clue to the truth. "Am I in danger? From her?"

"I don't make promises when I'm ignorant of all the facts. But I do know there are high-level people looking for her." He set the flash drive between them on the table as if it might explode. "Who else knows about the drive? We need to keep this quiet."

She slumped in her chair and rubbed her tortoise charm. Her wrist hit the wide silver tape on her shirt. She had forgotten to remove it before entering Zach's office. No wonder the receptionist gave her a funny look. Her thoughts strayed to Wade. Had she placed him and his family in danger? What about her family and Sam? Never in her lifetime had she ever felt so alone and isolated. Her whole being drowned in dread. Meeting Zach's stare, she tried to formulate a list of people who knew about the money. She also noted that her attorney hadn't said that she was out of trouble.

"The Donoven family probably knows. My boss Wade is the one who discovered the money. He and his dad run the company. My best friend knows about the drive. That's it. And Wade's attorney, Brent." Already, the circle was widening. What was the adage about loose lips torpedoing boats?

How quickly Wade had become a name on a list and not a future boyfriend. Her chest tightened. She missed Wade. She wished he was sitting beside her, holding her hand, but her ex-boss made it clear that was forbidden by his lawyer.

"Well, if you see anything suspicious, don't hesitate to call 9-1-1, and then call me." Zach rested his palms on the table. "Sit tight. I'm going to contact the bank manager to meet us downstairs. Once the money is secured, then we can video your testimony. I'm already in communication with the DOJ and FBI due to my former cases. I'll need to update them on the evidence in our possession."

Her mouth gaped. "Did you say FBI?" With her mind going in every direction, she could barely get out the words. "I didn't know we would be contacting the government." Wade might not be her favorite person this minute, but he had advised her to talk to an attorney before calling the police, and he had done her a solid.

Zach rose and crossed his arms. His no-nonsense-lawyer look was impressive.

"Ron Runyard snagged some politicians in his scams. He also tripped some suspicious bank transfers with all his dealings. Several important people want their money returned and his accomplice brought to justice." His stance softened. "Don't worry. I'll work for the best outcome for you and all the investors who lost their savings." Zach headed for the conference room door. "I'll be right back. We have a lot of work to do."

Burying her face in her hands, she said a quick prayer. "Lord, I am out of my league. I need Your wisdom and clear thinking. This is all new to me and very scary. Thank You for being my rock. I want to feel Your rock beneath my feet, I really do. Help me know for certain that You are with me. Please help me, my family, and friends. Amen."

"I'm right here."

She raised her head and scanned the room. Zach hadn't returned. Was someone talking in the hall? That had to be it.

No way was she telling anyone that she thought she heard the voice of God. She needed all the credibility that she could get.

Glancing at the ceiling, she whispered, "Thank You for reminding me that You are with me, Lord. Whether it was a secretary or You I heard, it was a nice reminder of the Holy Spirit's presence." She grasped her hands tighter. "And Lord, can my life get a little less crazy? It's already late, and I need some chamomile tea and a chocolate chip cookie."

~*~

Wade lounged on his living room couch and pressed the remote, flipping between sports stations. The football analysis and stats weren't his top priority anymore. He wanted to make sure Emma was safe and that fallout from Ron's crimes didn't land her in jail. He felt worse than the flu with no energy, a headache, and a barbell of remorse crushing his pecs. He was beating himself up for not fighting harder to keep Emma as an employee. She was only going to be around for a few weeks. He should have worked out a deal with the insurance company and his lawyer, but white-collar scandals were out of his league.

The doorbell rang.

A rush of adrenaline energized his weary limbs. He rose, eager to hear how Emma's appointment had gone and if her attorney had a strategy to combat any money laundering charges. He doubted she'd be down for a long conversation since he had fired her. It didn't take a genius to figure out that he wasn't her favorite person the way she peeled down the road earlier.

He opened the door and rocked backward. "Sam."

Sam stood on tiptoe and stretched to see into his home. "Hey, Wade. Is Emma here?"

Fat chance.

"She wasn't at your parents' house." Sam sounded deflated. Join the club.

"Emma's not back from the attorney. Come on in." Here came lecture number five after Brent, Dad, Mom, and himself.

"We talked earlier, but I thought she'd be done by…." Sam glanced at her watch as she entered the foyer. "Eight-thirty. I saw the van out front and figured she was filling you in on what the attorney said."

"She took my truck downtown." He wasn't holding his breath that Emma would stay long enough for a meaningful conversation.

"Oh." Sam's eyebrows shot upward. "I didn't know Em was a truck gal."

"She's been driving service vans around town all week." *Driving me around.* "She's been doing a good job." Another stab at his decision. "Have a seat."

Sam wedged herself in the corner of the couch like Emma had done the night she had opened up to him about her life. The weight of his actions made him feel as lively as the stuffed cushions.

"I wasn't planning to come until tomorrow morning, but I thought Em might need a friend tonight. After the attorney visit and stuff."

The word *stuff* brimmed with hidden meaning. If he had any hope of restoring his friendship with Emma, he needed to explain himself to her best friend.

"I'm sorry I had to fire Emma." Short and to the point, except a jar of quarters filled his mind and did little to alleviate his guilt. "She did a great job managing the office." *And managing me.* "She even beats Fran with her customer service skills."

He had never been so glad to hear a lighthearted giggle from his brother's girlfriend.

"That's my Em. She could sell candles to the sun. I knew she'd work out. Well, until today." She frowned and shook her head. "I wish Emma had never worked for Ron Runyard. I met the man, and he seemed genuine to me."

He'd only known Emma for over a week, but Sam was her lifelong friend. He needed some advice if he had a shot at a future with Emma. That was if Emma stayed in Tennessee, and if she would forgive him for placing his company before their friendship. He also prayed that being in possession of millions of stolen funds didn't place her in legal jeopardy.

"I never wanted to hurt Emma's feelings. I'm kicking myself that I asked to see her software. All I wanted to do was encourage her, help her out." He shifted forward on the couch and turned to meet Sam eye-to-eye. "Do you think when this blows over, she would want to be friends. Go out sometime. She's been a big help to the company and to me."

"It's not your fault. Em would have worked on People Peeps eventually and discovered the error. And I can see that she's been a big help to you." Sam had a funny expression on her face as if she knew a joke and didn't want to laugh before the punch line. "You aren't even using your cane to walk."

As Sam glanced around the room, he did, too. Where had he left his cane?

Chalk up another reason why he felt awful about firing Emma. "She pushed...uh...suggested I walk around my couch and balance using the back of the sofa. I'm pretty much back to normal."

Sam bestowed a carefree smile. "Practice makes permanent."

Was that a teacher motto?

"So, do you think she'll forgive me?" He rubbed his hands together relishing how well and flat they fit together. Emma had defrosted his claw. What part of his life hadn't been affected by Emma?

"I know she'll forgive you. And deep down she knows you have to do what is best for your family's company. She grew up in retail sales and knows what it's like to be the boss." Sam grew serious. "I'm going to take Emma to Whispering Creek. She can stay with me for a while until she gets the all-clear from her attorney. I'm not sure if she's planning to stay in Tennessee long-term. But when things settle down, if you want to be more than friends, look for an opening and take it."

Women. Sam's advice was as clear as barbecue sauce.

19

Bracing her arms on the steering wheel, Emma stared at the red light wishing it would turn green. She didn't expect to be at her attorney's office for over three hours. *Her attorney.* The word pairing sounded odd. Life had sure handed her lemons. She could forget about making lemonade, these lemons were old, hard, and crusty. All she wanted to do was to fall into bed and spend as little time talking with Mike and Linda as possible. Her brain was a ball of dust bunnies. Sam better arrive early in the morning.

She dreaded handing the truck keys to Wade. Purplish bruises encased her heart where he was concerned. She'd be leaving Nashville for Whispering Creek and probably wouldn't see him for a while, if ever. If Cole popped the question, she'd see Wade across the aisle at the wedding. Her spirit free-fell at the thought.

In her gut, she knew a doctor's release was in Wade's future. He could get on with service calls and running the business like he did before the crash. Her life was stuck in quicksand.

A peppy honk jarred her into reality. Green light. She hit the accelerator.

"Lord, get me through this hand off to Wade. I need Your strength right now because I am running on fumes."

She took a deep breath to increase her oxygen levels. The truth of the situation poked her conscience. Wade really didn't do anything wrong. If their roles were reversed, and an employee was a threat to her parents' candle business, she'd have fired the employee. Thriving businesses weren't built in a day, but over years of sacrifice, ingenuity, and grit. What she regretted most was not being able to spend her days with Wade. All her troubles began with an R, not a W. Still, it was hard getting over what resembled a betrayal from a man she was beginning to lo...like.

A white SUV was parked in front of Wade's house. A geyser of energy streaked through her veins. Sam had arrived a day early like the Calvary.

"Thanks for sending reinforcements, Jesus."

She wished she had placed a microphone under Wade's couch, not that it mattered. Her legal woes had taken center stage. She didn't have plans to return to Nashville unless it was to see her attorney or reclaim her stolen inheritance. She was shutting the truck door on everything that could have been with Wade, and she might as well have slammed her hand in it.

The front door opened, and Sam wrapped her in a big hug.

Emma needed those warm, loving arms to make her body feel real. She wasn't even going to imagine what an embrace from Wade would feel like. Slow dancing with him rated eleven out of ten.

"I'm so glad you're here." Smashed against Sam's shoulder, her words came out muffled. Why did she have to be shorter than all her friends?

"Someone had to whisk you away to Whispering Creek." Sam stepped backward and blocked the glare of the porch light. "Herbie misses you, and Ernie keeps asking about the scents wafting from the shed."

"Those candle scents have been discontinued just like my last two jobs." She tried to smile, but her mouth was stuck between a grimace and a grin.

Wade hovered a few feet from Sam in the foyer. He looked contrite with puppy eyes and his hands in his jean pockets. Her mind couldn't process the what-ifs. She threw the keys to Wade. They sailed more forcibly than she had planned.

"Thanks for letting me use your truck. There's only one new ding." Ask my heart. "I'm only kidding." The nerves in her lips started to tap dance. She had to leave before she blubbered, for this day ranked as one of the worst in her life.

"Emma, I'm—"

"Don't." Please don't make me cry. She waved as a fire ignited in her chest. She tugged Sam toward the SUV. Back lit by the foyer lighting, Wade stole her heart once more. One last time. *I'm sorry, too.*

~*~

After Emma left with Sam, Wade plopped on his leather couch, exhausted as if he had lapped it two hundred times. Even the room reminded him of Emma. His dislike for Ron Runyard bordered on hate, and he hadn't met the man. *Forgive me, Lord.* From the grave, Ron was trashing people's lives.

His phone buzzed, and he glanced at the screen. Great. Cole was calling. No doubt Sam had filled him in on the firing. His muscles tensed as he swiped to answer.

"Hey." He spoke casually, hiding the implosion of his life.

A gust of breath filled Wade's ear. "Heard you let Emma go. That must have been tough on you since you two seemed to work well together."

His brother made him feel lower than a worm snake, but Wade didn't like an armchair quarterback. Especially one that had never been in charge of the team. He didn't need his brother's approval, or any handholding. Wade had worked alongside his father for years and owned fifty-one percent of the business.

"I didn't want to fire her. It was a direct order from Brent. I wasn't going to pull Dad off a service call to do the deed. Even though he hired her, and you did your best to encourage it." He didn't want to alienate his brother again. Cole had only recently stepped back into the business after Wade's accident, but truth was truth. Wade's jaw ached from tamping down his frustration. "Hey, I'm sorry." Another reminder of Emma.

"Maybe we could have come up with another solution." Cole sounded discouraged. After Emma stormed out of his life, Wade was drinking from the same glass of discouragement.

"I don't know." He'd hoped for a possible long-term relationship with Emma, and it had exploded at work. Wade had shoveled enough blame on himself. Should he have pushed back on the attorney? Hindsight had perfect vision. He didn't trust his decision-making capabilities right now. "Brent kept asking questions. We didn't hire Emma the right way, and with her association with Runyard, it all blew up when she had access to his money. I didn't want any blowback on the company. People count on me for their paychecks."

"They count on us. Dad and I would have been there for you if anything went south. I'm sorry you had to deal with this because it couldn't have been easy for you or Emma. I heard you made a good team." Cole's words brought Emma front and center into Wade's brain and showcased how they had learned to complement each other. They'd even become friends. Started going deeper in a relationship. He shared Emma's anger at the whole situation.

Should he have contacted his dad before firing Emma? His dad had enough on his plate since Wade's accident. Wade doubted Brent's advice would have changed even if Dad had reached out. This situation was way beyond his and his dad's expertise. And it was a galaxy beyond Cole's.

"Sam mentioned you hired her a lawyer."

"Brent knew a guy, but I didn't hire him." Another thing he would have considered in the office if he hadn't been blindsided. "Apparently an old roommate handles these types of cases. The guy met with Emma tonight. He works for a big firm downtown." At least he could steer Emma in the right direction after he dried up her source of income.

"You let her go downtown alone?"

Watch the tone, little brother. He didn't need another serving of guilt.

"She drove here from Wisconsin all by herself, and she's driven me all over the city. Sam was here and took her to Mom and Dad's. I'm Emma's least favorite person at the moment, except for Runyard, and he's dead. She made it clear that she didn't want me around." He gripped the armrest of the couch. Should he have insisted on going along? The flash drive held millions. "What was I supposed to do? Brent sent a clear message that the company needed to distance itself from Emma. I run the company. Emma is a smart woman, and she made it clear that I should get lost." He wanted to fire himself over this situation. Oh man, had he messed up.

Cole didn't reply. Silence settled like humidity before a thunderstorm. He could feel Cole being pulled between the stickiness of family and the concerns of a future fiancé.

"I get it." Finally, some understanding. "I guess I'm overly cautious because Sam worries about her. But when Emma sets her mind on something, there's no stopping her. You were in a tough spot."

He had Emma to thank for the newly filled relationship potholes with Cole. She had helped him release some misplaced animosity toward his brother over the accident. Another reason he should have thought about pushing back against his boss brain and kept super cute, super-organized, superhero-manager Emma.

"I mean, this whole scam fallout is surreal." Cole's voice rose like it always did when he was trying to smooth things over. "Did Emma say if she needed anything?"

"Not to me." He wished he did know what Emma needed. He wished he knew if she thought of him as more than just a friend before the flash drive hit the fan. "I doubt Emma will open up to me anymore." The statement sent a stab to his heart. *Lord, what have I done?*

"Anymore? Were you two starting something?" A hint of disbelief made his brother sound as if he had been the one to find a flash drive full of money. "Sam thought you might be."

"Emma was an employee." Evasive truth. He wasn't going to admit anything to Cole. Why bother? Emma would disappear to Whispering Creek or Wisconsin as soon as the attorney got her out of this mess. If the attorney got her out of this mess. *Please, Lord, please get Emma out of this mess.*

"Well, if I hear any updates from Sam on your former employee, I'll text you." Smug Cole had returned. "These problems with Runyard are bound to blow over. I'm praying for you and Emma. Don't count her out."

"Thanks." He was pretty sure he was down for the count with Emma. He should have placed a night drop box on his front door because seeing her distraught and emotional earlier brought a hurricane of hurt and regret. "Text me with news."

Just when his life was almost back to normal, whirlwind Emma had found an unlocked door to his feelings, ripped it open, and blew off the hinges. All he needed to do was locate the door and try and install it again. If that was even possible.

20

"Stop sign." Wade flinched as his dad raced toward the red octagon without slowing down. When the doctor released Wade to drive, he was definitely taking command of the wheel.

His dad smirked. "I've driven this route to work hundreds of times. I had plenty of room to break."

"Sorry." Wade needed to ban that word because Emma's face appeared every time he said it. At least Emma smiled at him when he backseat drove. He missed her pep this Tuesday morning. His dad needed another cup of coffee. Or maybe his dad didn't like being back on chauffeur duty.

A few minutes later, his dad pulled into the company parking lot.

"I'm going to drop you and head to my first call. I'll try to beat traffic."

"Got it." Wade exited the van. He grabbed his cane almost as an afterthought. In the last week, he had overcome his final hurdles toward recovery. His leg had gotten stronger, and his hand flexed as good as new. Thank You, Lord. Thank you, Emma. He had to stop thinking about her and manage the business. He doubted that she'd ever settle in Nashville. Whispering Creek and Wisconsin were her homes.

Before he shut the van door, he said, "I'll call the temp service we used last time we needed help. I'm praying I get a driving release tomorrow." Handling the office work was easy. He needed to get back out on service calls and add to the bottom line.

His dad rested an arm over the steering wheel. "I don't think we're going to get as quick a study as Emma. I hated to see her leave with Sam this morning."

No wonder his dad seemed off. Saying good-bye to Emma had to weigh on his old man since he practically escorted her into the office.

Every time he thought of the collateral damage from Runyard's scam, he wanted to punch the creep.

"How is Emma doing?" He didn't want to know, yet he needed to find out as her former boss and friend.

"Pretty good." Which meant there was some 'not good' in his dad's answer. Dad scratched his jaw. "I'm glad Sam came last night. Those girls are like two peas in a pod. When I left for work, they were talking about recipes with your mom."

Wade's throat thickened. "Good." He nodded like everything was back to normal. Normalcy reflected in his windshield, but not in Emma's. "I'll call the temp agency right away. See ya later." He shut the van door and strode toward the office entrance, making a mental note on what to tackle first.

He unlocked the main door and headed straight to the coffeemaker. He rinsed the carafe and set it on the counter. After filling the water compartment, he added coffee grounds and hit the power switch. The beloved scent of dark roasted beans bolstered his energy level.

A delivery guy hustled through the front door.

"Can I get a signature." The guy set three boxes on the floor below the acrylic-glass opening and pushed his clipboard through.

Wade grabbed a pen and signed the paperwork.

The guy grabbed his clipboard, tore a receipt for Wade, and backstepped toward the door. "Your coffee is leaking."

Wade turned to see the carafe on the counter and coffee

dripping onto the heating element and onto the floor. Great. The last thing he needed was another slip and fall. He pushed the carafe underneath the coffee stream and grabbed a roll of paper towels.

The phone rang.

"Really?" He slapped paper towels on the floor and lunged for the phone, answering it on the fourth ring. "Donoven and Sons Electric." He calmed his voice as his heart galloped in his chest.

"This is Donna Clay. Is Emma there?"

"Not at the moment." Who was he kidding? She wasn't coming back, but he wasn't going to confess that he had fired her to a customer.

"Do you know when she'll return? You're coming on Friday to install some ceiling fixtures, and I wanted to get the paint colors she recommended. I can call again later."

Calling in the afternoon wouldn't solve his problem. He rolled his shoulder trying to release the tension in his muscles from ten minutes of work. Should he tell her that Emma was history? Would the woman be upset? Would she still want to keep her appointment? Maybe so, but what if he couldn't find the colors? Did Emma note the name of the paint in the customer file? Too many questions circulated in his brain before his second cup of coffee.

"Hang on. Let me get into our computer system and see if Emma made any notes on your conversation. It's C-l-a-y?"

"Yes. On Sutterfield Road."

He typed in the woman's name.

Come on, Emma. If I find one color listed, I will be forever grateful. He mentally kicked himself for asking to see Emma's flash drive. All he wanted to do was support her after seeing how well she interacted with customers, and everything blew up in his face. He'd lost the best thing that had happened to his business in months. His chest sank. The best thing that had happened to him in months. Now he knew why people didn't like attorneys.

Donna's name and address appeared on the screen. Below the phone number were a few sentences about the lighting fixtures and bingo, paint recommendations. If Emma had been sitting beside him, he would have kissed her. If only she was sitting beside him. He wasn't her favorite person with the way she threw his keys at him like a fast pitch.

"Ma'am, it says here that you discussed Elegant Eggshell and Glory Morning."

"Oh, fantastic. I should have written them down." The woman sounded giddy.

He shared in her relief. His decorating tips were non-existent. "There's also a mention of a Lavender and Lacey?"

"The candle scent. Thank you. I had almost forgotten. I wanted to make an impression on my fiancé when he sees the room for the first time. Please thank Emma, and tell her that I owe her one."

"Will do. Glad we could help." His conscience gnawed at him. He didn't want to tell Donna that Emma was gone, but he couldn't lie either. He'd have to text Emma a thank you from Donna later. A text wasn't like an open door that Sam had talked about, but maybe it was a cracked window. He'd even take a doggie door. "Our technician will be there on Friday to get the fixtures swapped out. Have a nice day, Donna."

He hung up the phone and slouched in the chair. Emma's chair.

Lord, I'm not understanding any of this. My accident. Emma's boss and his betrayal. Why You brought her into my life and then took her out of it? I'm confused and need some clarity. Please give me wisdom about the future. Amen.

He stood and trekked over brown-stained paper towels to fill a mug with coffee. Caffeine would definitely help his focus. He doubted he had ever discussed paint colors before eight in the morning. He certainly had never recommended a candle scent. He grinned. Only Emma.

Derek entered the office and plopped a stack of invoices on the counter. "Morning. I've got my paperwork and Antonio's." He glanced around the office. "Where's Emma?"

Wade shuffled over to collect the invoices. On top of the pile sat a newspaper folded to reveal the picture of him and Emma at Ms. Johnson's home. *This isn't funny, Lord.*

The phone rang again.

He wrestled a frustrated roar.

If someone else asked for Emma, he was going to put the answering machine on, fill a travel mug with coffee, put his earbuds in, and power walk around the block. Ah! Even the mention of walking had him mentally thanking Emma. Maybe it was for the best that she had left the city because as her boss, he was getting in way too deep. Just the thought of her sauntering up to the counter with her saucy smile had him envisioning lighting a Lavender and Lacey candle and kissing her lips.

His goal of forgetting about Emma today was an epic failure.

~*~

Emma brushed bangs out of her eyes and slung her head against the headrest in Sam's SUV.

"I have never been so happy to see that wooden Welcome to Whispering Creek sign in my life. After Linda's tears and another two hours with my attorney, my brain is a bowl of oatmeal with soggy berries on top."

Sam glanced in her direction. Static electricity from the

cloth seat splayed her ponytail.

"Your attorney's office is quite impressive. He seems pretty intense, too, from what I could tell seeing him through the reception window."

"I can hear my retainer dollars disappearing by the minute. I sure hope with this new information from the flash drive that Zach can move swiftly and reclaim some money for investors. My bank account could use a windfall." If she still worked for Wade, she would have had a steady income for a few weeks. She thought she had a new friend, but that vanished the minute Ron's funds exploded onto Wade's laptop.

"If you need money, Em, I'll give you some. You don't even have to pay it back. Think of it as a hug from Mr. Ted. The inheritance he left me has bought me some time to look for a teaching position."

"Which you will be getting soon. Whispering Creek ISD should be calling this week to snap you up." Emma admired her friend who had battled breast cancer and won, but the time away from her classroom left Sam without a renewed teaching contract. Sam lived without one breast. What was a little job turbulence compared to cancer? Unless it led to a courtroom battle and possibly jail time. Emma wouldn't let her mind go to that disturbing place. She had hoped to plan activities for seniors and keep track of their most important life events. Her fingers didn't fleece wallets or bank accounts. That crime belonged to Ron and Annette, or whoever the woman claimed to be.

"I'd love to work close to home and teach in my community." Sam flashed a conspiratorial smile. "I also know a local place that will pick up your spirits."

An image of a young boy running around A Brew 4 You and huge cinnamon rolls warming a plate had Emma quirking an eyebrow. "Is Daniel out of school for the day because I could use a blast of that kid's energy." She checked her phone. "Daniel should be roaring around the restaurant." If her time was occupied by the owner's son, then she wouldn't be thinking about Wade. Her short stint at Donoven and Sons had brought her some cash, boosted her self-esteem, and she had gotten to help Wade get over the hump and return to health. She chastised herself for not being grateful for those blessings and only pondering a future relationship with Wade. *I'm sorry, Lord.* She grinned. Even her short prayer brought the handsome electrician to mind.

Sam drove down the main street and parked a few spots away from A Brew 4 You. The black iron clock in the hardware store window next door showed two-thirty.

"Sugar and caffeine coming right up." Sam chewed her lip. "Only if you're up to it. I could make coffee and hot chocolate at home."

Emma hopped out of the SUV and straightened her belt. "Are you kidding? No way am I missing Lucinda's cinnamon rolls. One nice thing about being fired, I don't have any work to do. I get to hang around with my best friend and wait to see if my attorney gets justice for hundreds of victims. I can even do more tweaking on People Peeps now that I have electrical office experience. I have a file saved on my laptop."

"That's the Emma I know. The optimistic entrepreneur." Sam locked her car. "I should have you read and improve my resume. I'd have a position in no time." Sam opened the door to Lucinda's café.

A familiar jingle of bells transported Emma back to her visit over Christmas when her life had been stable and normal. She hadn't realized then that her job in Milwaukee rested on the roof of a tower of trading cards.

The Lord is my rock, my fortress, and my deliverer. God was with her at the top of the teetering structure, and He was with her now at the bottom of the heap of dog-eared cards. Her thoughts needed to be on God, upward, and forward, not on the past. Ron wasn't coming back, and Annette was in the wind. Emma breathed in the cinnamon and coffee aroma and gave all her cares to God. *Help me to remember that You are in control of everything, God.*

"Earth to Emma." Sam nudged her forward. "Why don't we grab a table against the wall."

"Works for me." Emma grasped her backpack and shifted it higher on her shoulder. "We can see who's coming and going."

Sam pulled out a chair, sat, and leaned across the shiny wood table. "Did your attorney say to be careful?" she whispered.

"No." Emma plopped into her chair and let her backpack slide to the floor. "I like to people watch." If only she would stop the replay of Wade chasing her down and wrapping her in his strong arms. She'd have to restrict the small-town romance channel for a while. "It can't hurt though. You know what my mom says about being aware of your surroundings."

Sam laughed. "I remember that talk every time we left your store and went out into the mall to shop." Sam did her conspiratorial lean. "Have you told your mom about…" —her eyes widened—"finding the drive."

Shaking her head, Emma squinted at the chalkboard menu above the bakery counter. "I can't. I'm sworn to silence." She tugged on her jeans. "I did call this morning and let her know I was heading here to Whispering Creek. I may have inferred that Fran was coming back earlier than expected. I am praying for Fran's recovery. Jesus could work a miracle." She slouched and drummed her fingers on the smooth varnish of the table. She couldn't bring herself to utter the word *fired* to her parents. To a retail manager, it was like receiving a bold, red F. "Everything is fine at the mall. The reporters and strange shoppers have subsided. That's a blessing."

"Look who's here." Lucinda rushed toward their table with mugs intertwined in her fingers. "I didn't think we would see you so soon." Lucinda set down the mugs with a small clunk.

Emma rose and gave Lucinda a quick hug trying to avoid the woman's clipped-back hair.

"There's a homing signal on top of Sam's house that pulled me here." Emma winked at Sam. "Plus, you have better winters."

"We'll take you anytime." Lucinda removed a pad from her apron. "Are we doing the usual? Hot chocolate and pecan cinnamon rolls?"

"We must look desperate." Emma grinned and sat down. Her heart warmed at being among friends who supported her. Being with Sam and Lucinda was easy. She didn't have to learn a new business lingo or please a boss. She could laugh and dust off the stress of the past two weeks. Life in Whispering Creek had chocolate sprinkles. "Black coffee for both of us today. Cinnamon rolls sound perfect."

"You've got it. I'll be right back." Lucinda placed rolled-up silverware on their table from her deep-pocketed apron and hurried toward the counter. A few elderly men chatted as they waited at the register.

The front door opened to a jangle of bells. A woman with gray braids held the hand of Lucinda's son Daniel. The boy stood inches taller than Emma remembered. "Daniel's here."

Sam turned in the direction of Emma's smile.

Daniel's dark brown eyes lasered in on Sam. He slipped from the woman's grasp and chugged toward her friend.

Bright lights flashed from his sneakers. That's how he looked taller. Emma would need to find some blinking heels.

"Sam." The boy wiggled into Sam's lap.

"Do you remember my best friend, Emma." Sam's face dipped down to engage with Daniel. Sam had the best kid moves. She mesmerized her students.

Daniel nodded, his eyes becoming like mega-cups of coffee. "We're having a rum sale at school." He held onto the M, sounding like a tiny motor.

"That's one way to raise money for the school." Emma laughed.

Lucinda arrived with a tray of rolls and a carafe of coffee. After she unloaded their food and the much-needed caffeine, she bent to kiss her son.

"The school is having a rummage sale to fund new playground equipment. Daniel and my mom stayed after preschool to help price some of the items. The sale starts on Friday."

A few round fluorescent stickers decorated the sleeve of Daniel's navy dinosaur hoodie. Dark blue favored Daniel like it did Wade. Emma picked a pecan off of her cinnamon roll and almost choked on it.

"You 'K," Daniel asked.

Emma sipped her coffee. "Yes, I am, thank you." Whispering Creek sure did feel like a second home. Could it be a first-place contender?

Sam ducked her head around Daniel to see Lucinda. "I may have a box or two of Ted's things. Ernie didn't take all of the clothes. I'm sure I can round up some books. Ted was a big reader."

Biting into her pastry, Emma thought of a way to help support the school. "Oh, wait." She placed a hand in front of her mouth as she finished chewing. "I have candles in the trunk of my car. Might as well put them to good use. The scents are discontinued, but I have pillars, jars, and votive sets."

"That's a great idea, Em. Ladies love candles." Sam sipped carefully from her mug.

Lucinda clasped her hands, the serving tray lodged under her arm. "This is wonderful. We're expecting a big turnout, and the committee was worried we would run out of items. We'll take it all."

Excitement bubbled inside of Emma. With her free time, she could help the school and find out more about Whispering Creek.

"We can price our things and bring them over by Friday morning. I'm happy to help any way I can." Emma pointed a fork at Sam. "I'm temporarily unemployed, and Sam hasn't put me to work yet.

Sam chuckled. "I think I just did."

Daniel hopped off of Sam's lap and stood next to Emma's chair. He cocked his head and after glancing at his mom, he inched closer with a small hand cupped around his mouth.

"How do candles vote?" he whispered.

Emma bent eye level with Daniel. She stifled a chuckle at his question. She couldn't have ordered better medicine today than a visit with Lucinda and Daniel. She even had a part-time job for the weekend even if it didn't pay.

"A votive is a candle, but it doesn't vote." She noticed Sam's chest heaving as she explained terms to Daniel. "A votive is small and round. You might say it's a Daniel candle." She could play teacher, too. "A pillar candle is larger. It's tall and big like Sam and me. I'll save one of each for you and your mom."

Daniel jumped, his shoes blinking under the pressure. "Yes. I want one."

"You'd like one," Lucinda corrected. "What do you say to Emma?" Now, who was in teacher mode?

"Thank you." Daniel placed a hand on the table and wormed his way into Emma's lap. "I like vote-tives."

Emma's heart swelled. What would the last week have been like if she had stayed in Whispering Creek? She enjoyed the friendly atmosphere and helping meet the needs of others. She'd filled a need in Nashville, but she'd been fired by the boss she'd been assisting and crushing on. The bandage healing her self-esteem needed reinforcements for that catastrophe.

The front door opened, bells jingling.

Heads turned as a black-leather-clad man strode into the café. The clomp of his thick-soled boots echoed through the restaurant. The guys dark hair was longer than Sam's ponytail.

Daniel snuggled into her chest.

The guy scanned the perimeter of the café and waved. Did he need a waitress?

Wait. She had met this guy before. Over Christmas.

Patrons glanced at the man in black as he stomped toward Sam and Lucinda.

"Good afternoon, ladies."

Sam flashed a lazy day smile. "Hey, neighbor. Jedediah, do you remember my best friend, Emma?"

Jedediah crossed his thick arms over his studded leather vest. "Good to see you again, Emma. Glad you didn't bring any snow with you." His gaze was so intense if she had been a steak, she would have been charred. "Are you in town for a while?"

She shrugged. "As long as Sam will have me."

Daniel mimicked her shrug.

"Well, if you need anything, I'm right next door." He

turned his attention to Lucinda. "Dad would like some cinnamon rolls."

"Coming right up. Excuse me." Lucinda hurried toward the front of the café.

"See you around." Jedediah strode after Lucinda.

Emma shivered careful not to dislodge Daniel who was folding her napkin into triangles. "I still can't believe that's Ernie and Gretta's son. On a dark night, if he popped out of the shadows, he'd give you a heart attack."

"On a dark night, you wouldn't even see him in the shadows." Sam quirked an eyebrow.

"Yeah." Daniel giggled oblivious to their conversation. His napkin resembled a small airplane or headless bird.

She ruffled the boy's hair as his giggle vibrations sent a flood of contentment through her body. She understood why Sam liked it here. The simple pleasure of being with her best friend and hearing a child laugh reoriented her on what was important in life. God was her rock, and He had given her a multitude of blessings. She could handle the fallout from the flash drive with friends by her side. Jesus was her best friend, and He taught in the Bible not to worry about tomorrow. Tennessee was growing on her. Her Tennessee tomorrow was looking up.

21

Emma rolled over in bed dragging the comforter with her. She reached for her phone on the nightstand: 11:15 AM. How had she slept so late? She sat and combed through her brain fog. The screen showed that it was Wednesday. That was right. Fired on Monday and then rescued on Tuesday by Sam. Today, she didn't have to rush to work. For her own sanity and heart safety, she wouldn't think about light switches or redecorating or Wade Donoven.

Her forehead ached. Caffeine was overdue. She threw on a green and gold hoodie and traipsed into the living room.

Sam typed on her laptop at the kitchen table. The key clicks reminded Emma of…no, she focused on a flower arrangement of daisies and small purple flowers blocking Sam's keypad from view. No wonder the aroma of coffee beans held a hint of florist. She banished her sleep haze and checked her mental calendar. Sam's birthday wasn't in February, and Valentine's Day was almost two weeks away. She'd ignore that holiday this year.

"Look who finally surfaced." Sam sipped from a mug. "Can I get you some breakfast? We have cereal, cereal, and more cereal."

"You know me so well." Emma swept her arm over the table with a dramatic flair. "My kingdom for a bowl of flakes and raisins." She shuffled toward the refrigerator to grab some milk and a cup of coffee. "Who sent the flowers?" An idea popped into her brain. "Wait. Did you get the teaching position here?" Cole would definitely celebrate that news.

"They're not mine." Sam pushed her chair away from the table and exuded too much perkiness.

Emma set the milk and a mug on the table and headed to the pantry for cereal. "Was Gretta gone when the delivery came?"

Sam shook her head. "They're not for Gretta. Ernie strikes me as more of a blouse or slippers kind of guy."

"Then who are they for?" Emma reached for her raisin cereal. Her life was void of husbands, boyfriends, and romance.

Sam *tsked*. A sound that should be banished before noon.

"You, silly. The flowers are for you."

"Me?" Emma's heart swelled. Sam was such a good friend and so sweet to encourage her with flowers. "Aw, thank you." She hugged her friend being careful not to poke her in the face with the corner of the cereal box. "I feel better just being in your home."

"I wish I could take credit for being a thoughtful friend, but they're not from me." Sam made a face. "Now I have regrets. Open the card. I've been dying to snoop for the past hour."

"And you didn't? Not even a peek or a hold up to the light? You're amazing." Emma grabbed the card. Something round and hard was in the small envelope. Her heartbeat stuttered.

"It's sealed and I didn't have a steamer handy." Sam perched at her computer but eyed the mysterious envelope. "I figured you wouldn't sleep too much longer."

Returning to her bedroom sounded like a great idea. If this was an apology from Wade or dare she believe, a card signed with regret, or love, she'd be more confused than ever.

She opened the glued flap and slipped the card from the envelope.

Donna Clay sends her thanks.

The customer must have called the office again, and Wade talked to her. Was he missing his office mate?

We do, too.

Donoven and Sons Electric

Wade hadn't bothered to attach his name to the thank-you gift. Was this a final good-bye with a hint of good riddance? Her heart bungee jumped off a bridge. A few CPR compressions would be needed to get it back into a normal rhythm.

"Okay, stop stalling." Sam tilted her head and had a bug-eyed look of impatience. "Are they from Wade?"

If only, then she'd be feeling all light and swirly like cotton candy. Instead, she felt like a crumpled and discarded sticky note.

"They're a thank you from Donoven and Sons."

"Really? Not a heart and 'thinking of you' from Wade. Boy, did I read him wrong. I expected more." Sam shook her head and then wrinkled her nose. "What's in your hand?"

Emma displayed the fifty-cent piece. *Double sorry.* Was Wade double sorry that he fired her? Or double sorry that he had been forced to hire her? She was double sorry that she let her emotions get the best of her. Every inch of her face tingled with what mimicked a bad sunburn.

"It's an inside joke from the office." The joke was on her believing Wade saw her as more than a temporary office girl. "The sentiment was nice, but the flowers make my cactus look scruffy."

"Herbie will survive. He has since the fifth grade." Sam popped out of her chair. "I'm going to get more coffee. We need to figure out what we're doing today."

Today? Emma needed to figure out what she was doing with her life. She pocketed the fifty-cent piece in her yoga pants. Out of sight, eventually out of mind. Eventually.

Should she text a thank you for the flowers? Nah. She only had Wade's personal number, and the thought of calling the office made her stomach sink. She had thanked Linda before she left, and that would be enough. Did one even have to thank for a thank you? Especially after they were terminated.

She sat at the table and stared at her cereal. Why had she ever daydreamed about staying in Tennessee? Her roots were in Milwaukee along with her parents, her aging parents who started a family when they were pushing forty, and who owned a successful business. What if her dad had another heart attack or her mom grew ill? Tennessee was too far away from Milwaukee and best left as a temporary destination.

As cereal crunched in her mouth, she beheld the daisies and purple mystery flowers. The arrangement reminded her that she was a professional placeholder to Wade. She needed to put her time and effort into clearing her name so she wouldn't spook future employers. She also needed to help her attorney get the stolen money refunded to Ron's victims.

"You know." She glanced at Sam who was closing her laptop. "We should sell this arrangement at the rummage sale. Fifty percent off."

~*~

The blood pressure cuff around Wade's arm constricted until it loosened in a whoosh of air.

"Your blood pressure is slightly elevated." The nurse removed a stethoscope from her ears. "I'll retake it before you leave. It's nothing to worry about."

"Thank you." He tried to get comfortable in the plastic doctor's office chair. Anyone's blood pressure would escalate if they had to fire a gem like Emma and handle the fallout.

Fight or flight syndrome kicked in every time the office phone rang. He dreaded hearing a customer ask for Emma.

"All your other vitals are perfect." The nurse pushed her mobile cart toward the door. "The doctor should be in shortly."

He nodded and forced a smile. His phone buzzed in his pocket. Even though the sign on the wall said to silence cell phones, he slipped his phone from his jeans. Cole's name filled the screen. Great. His brother better not need any help with the project in Sperry's Crossing because they were slammed in Nashville. And he definitely didn't need any relationship advice from his younger brother. Cole's track record had been shaky before he met Sam.

"Hey, I'm in the doctor's office."

"Is Mom with you?"

Wade squeezed the phone controlling the tension in his fingers. "She's in the waiting room. I'm a grown man. I don't need her holding my hand."

"Just to drive you." Cole's amusement bristled.

Why did God have to make little brothers so annoying?

"Not after today, Coley." His brother hated that name, but Wade's patience was threadbare with all the upheaval at work. And at the moment, he really didn't care what Cole liked or disliked. With Emma, that was another story.

"I'm praying you get a release to drive. We need you to pull your weight again, bro. Good thing you gained a few pounds laying around."

Before Emma arrived, he would have cursed his brother, but she had helped him understand that Cole wasn't responsible for his accident, and that Cole was just being Cole. No animosity, no passive aggression, but not that funny.

"The pounds will come off when I'm on service calls and away from the mini fridge." Wade stifled a grin. He didn't feel like smiling, but being so close to a driving release, his goal for the past months, was dopamine to his brain. "So, you called to see when I would be able to drive around the city and go on a diet."

"I was hoping for some good news, and I also heard that you sent Emma flowers."

The Emma to Sam to Cole message train was on track. His brother sounded as if he enjoyed being included in the gossip.

Wade shifted in the plastic chair hoping to hear his file being removed from the holder outside of the small room. Wouldn't you know with Wade's luck, the doctor was running late.

"The company sent Emma flowers for a thank you." Plain and simple.

"Not you?" Cole sounded as if he was on a fishing expedition.

"Not me." He had asked the florist to enclose a half-dollar. That request came with an explanation that he didn't need a dollar cut in half. He kicked out his legs and tried to avoid gazing at the skeleton poster on the sterile-colored wall. This place could use one of Emma's candles. Not again. He rubbed his forehead hoping to erase Emma's name from his memory.

"Why not you? I thought you were starting to like Emma."

Lord, give me patience.

"Who wouldn't like Emma? She's nice. But I've only known her a little over a week." Nine days in-person and two months as the nebulous friend of Sam's. "She's sorting out all the problems from that Runyard guy and may not stay in Tennessee. I've got a business to run here and can't be driving to Wisconsin for a date." His voice was too loud for the library-quiet corridor outside.

"I guess I read it wrong." At least Cole was conciliatory. "I didn't mean to get you upset."

"I'm not." For sure his blood pressure had soared past the previous 129/85. He needed to be careful. His driving release was his golden ticket. "With my workload, I don't have time for a long-distance relationship." That was sound advice for any business owner.

"Well text me what the doctor says. I've been praying for you for a long time, bro."

Wade's frustration deflated. He leaned forward in the chair and rested his forehead against his palm. Cole meant well and he had taken up the slack in the business after the accident. Wade didn't want to mess up their newly forged brotherly bond.

"I will, but I'm sure Mom will update the family group text right away." Though, the cute girl who pushed him to the finish line wouldn't be on it. And he hadn't received a text from Emma after the flowers arrived. His love life rivaled the dreariness of the medical room. He'd let the Cole to Sam to Emma text train work to relay any good news.

Papers rustled outside the exam room door.

"Got to go." Wade ended the call and returned his phone to his pocket. He took a few deep breaths trying to lower his blood pressure.

His orthopedist, dressed in a crisp white coat and winged tipped shoes, swept into the room. "Wade, good to see you." He held out his hand for a shake. When they were done, he used the other hand to test Wade's claw. Surprise enlivened the doctor's face as Wade squeezed tight enough for an arm wrestle. "That's good. Your grip is excellent. Any pain in the left arm." Doctor McCormick assessed Wade's limb.

"No, not now." Thanks to Emma's pressure points and massage techniques.

"Good. That's what I like to hear." Doctor McCormick scanned the desk area. "No cane today either." He glanced at the chart in his hands. "Why don't I watch you walk down the hall before we discuss a release."

Two Step. Line dance. Quarterback chase. Wade would do them all if he could get cleared to drive. He strolled down the hallway with confidence dodging a discarded wheelchair. He didn't need one of those anymore.

"Looks good, Wade. Why don't you come back into the room. I'm impressed with the progress you have made."

Thank You, Jesus! The praise filled his mind.

You were there every step of the way. And I appreciate You giving me amazing parents, a forgiving brother, and bringing Emma into my life when I needed encouragement and a boost of confidence. Thank You, Lord. In Your name. Amen.

Wade sat down in the stiff chair and cleared his throat. Some of his thankfulness had settled in his windpipe.

The doctor typed on a computer. "You've made a full recovery, Wade. I have to say that the improvement from last time is remarkable. You even seem in a better state of mind." Dr. McCormick smiled as if his own health had been restored. "I'll be issuing a release to drive. I'm sure you're ready to get back on the road and back to a full schedule at work."

"Amen to that. Thank you." Although he wouldn't be getting out of the office until next week thanks to Emma being gone and the temp agency not sending anyone until Friday.

The doctor typed a few more notes and then shook Wade's hand again before mentioning to call if there were any problems. The nurse was being sent back in for another blood pressure check.

Wade relaxed in the chair feeling as if he was floating in a tube down a lazy river. His journey to drive again had ended. He was free to meet customers and solve problems and live the life he enjoyed pre-auto accident. This ending is what he had prayed for since being stuck in a hospital bed. Unfortunately, balloons and confetti didn't drop from the ceiling. His big fireworks extravaganza had ended with a dud.

He pulled out his phone. No text from Emma. In the back of his brain, he wondered if the doctor had a note system like People Peeps.

GOT THE ALL CLEAR, he texted Cole.

Tilting his head, Wade glanced at the mottled grid of ceiling tiles overhead. "Lord, can I get an all clear for my brain, so I don't keep thinking about Emma?"

22

"Whoa. This is sensory overload even for me." Emma backed away from Sam's shed as the door raised.

Today included the routine chore of pricing candles and dropping them off at the school at the end of the day. The big sale began tomorrow, on Friday. She was excited to help the school especially if Sam received a teaching contract. Even if Sam taught elsewhere, Daniel attended preschool, and he was the closest thing she had to a nephew being that she was an only child.

"I haven't opened the shed since we left for Nashville." Sam closed the cover on the pad. "There's more pine scent in your trunk than from all my evergreens combined."

Emma clapped her gloveless hands. A benefit of Tennessee being fifty-six degrees and not the twenty-nine degrees that Milwaukee cheered. She could get accustomed to warmer winters. A perk of the Volunteer State. Her heart hitched. She didn't want to remind herself of one handsome perk of staying in Tennessee. She took a deep breath. "It's a mixture of Conifer Confusion with a hint of Mulberry Moon and Fresh Linens."

"They have a candle smelling like sheets?"

"They have a candle scent for just about anything you can imagine." Emma opened the trunk of her Beetle and dropped the key fob in her coat pocket. "Three boxes? I thought I only had two."

"Lucinda will be thrilled." Sam inspected the first box and removed a dark green pillar. "I think this is our conifer culprit."

Emma perused the second box and held up a plastic bag. "Here's some blueberry *voting* candles for Daniel."

Sam laughed. "I'd better be careful, or he'll like you best." She hefted a box from the trunk. "This is heavy."

"Maybe we should ask Jedediah to help. He could carry all three boxes at once with his big arms." Wade had nice muscular arms. Emma had noticed the definition when he worked by Ms. Johnson's refrigerator. She chastised herself for going down romantic rabbit trails.

Sam peeked into the third box. "I heard Jedediah's motorcycle rumble out of here about ten o'clock."

"That's too late for coffee." Emma brushed some dust off of her black leggings. "And too early for lunch."

The ringtone of Sam's phone interrupted their task. Sam removed the phone from her jacket pocket. "It's Gretta. I'd better see what she needs."

"Yeah, it may be cookies or an invite to dinner." Emma took over cataloguing what was inside the extra box.

Sam shook her head and backstepped toward the house. "Hey, Gretta." Sam's eyes grew wide. "I'll be right over."

Wonderful. Her box-toting buddy was leaving, and there was no mention of cookies.

Sam slipped the phone back into her pocket. "Gretta needs me for something personal. I shouldn't be gone too long."

"Since you're going over, why don't you take her a candle. Here's a cheery pink one. Last of its kind." Emma handed the pillar to Sam.

"Thanks. Gretta will love the color." Sam hurried down the asphalt lane, her hiking boots echoing off the pavement. "Perfect day for a walk."

"Hurry back. We've got to sticker these babies."

Emma sorted through the third box. She unwrapped tissue paper and found some glass votive holders with a reindeer design. She'd save one of the reindeer holders for Daniel.

Footsteps scuffed behind her. Had Sam returned? Gretta must have solved her problem.

Emma turned to show Sam the cute, leaping reindeer. "Check this out." Emma jumped and dropped the glass holder. The votive base shattered on the shed floor as a streak of adrenaline shivered through her body.

"Annette!"

The gun pointed at Emma's nose clicked. "I want my drive."

The nefarious drive Emma didn't have anymore. She swallowed, but saliva stuck in her throat nearly choking her. She coughed and wracked her brain. Stall. No don't. Sam might return, and the thought of what Annette was capable of chilled Emma faster than dry ice.

"You'd better hurry before your friend returns, or she'll end up like Ron." Annette, or whoever she was, waved the gun in the direction of Sam's house. "What Ron saw in you is beyond me."

Emma only had a professional relationship with Ron, but Annette must have thought otherwise when People Peeps ended up in his possession, and the money ended up in Tennessee. *Oh God, help me.*

"I'll get Ron's drive. It's inside." Her heartbeat thudded in her head so loud and ominous, she could barely think. She took a step toward the house on legs as firm as pudding. "I didn't know I had it."

"Yeah, get going, princess. I'm tired of this place. It's duller than when you droned on and on about it after Christmas." Annette pushed Emma in the back and cursed.

Derogatory insults followed Emma across the driveway and up the stairs to the front door.

What was she going to do? She didn't have the drive, but admitting that to Annette would be a death sentence. Or she'd be kidnapped and held in exchange for the drive. Either way ended badly.

She had to concoct a plan. *Oh, Lord. I need You.* She almost vomited as she entered the living area. Her backpack was on a chair. Herbie and the flowers from Wade decorated the center of the table. She had always kept a flash drive in her backpack, so Annette wouldn't think twice about Emma rummaging through the bag. If she could grab Herbie's base and hurl the cactus at Annette, there would be time to wrestle for the gun. But if the gun fired... Emma shuddered.

"Don't do anything stupid. I'm in too deep to shed any tears." Annette slammed the door. She aimed the gun at Emma's chest. "You have fifteen seconds." A smug laugh erupted. "Ten, nine..."

Please God, let my plan work.

With every synapse in her body short circuiting, Emma grasped her backpack and threw it on the tabletop. She scrambled and found a spare drive at the bottom of her pack. The cover was red, but it would have to do. She hid the bright color with her thumb.

"Six, five..."

As she turned, the dummy drive clutched in her left hand, she shifted forward, feigning a step. Her other hand gripped the base of the cactus. A single thorn stuck her wrist. The sting was nothing compared to a gunshot.

"Three, two."

"I've got it." She met Annette's cold stare and mentally petitioned God for more protection.

Annette's grin proclaimed that all her words were lies.

Her gaze flickered to Emma's fingers.

Murderer. Liar. Thief! With outrage flowing through her body, Emma harnessed all her animosity and hurled Herbie at Annette's nose. Score! Herbie stuck to his mark.

Annette screamed.

Emma leapt to seize the gun. A roar, guttural and raw, fled from her lips. This woman had spun Emma's average life into chaos and heartache. The scam and betrayal ended here.

She clamped onto Annette's hand and wrist attempting to dislodge the gun. The woman had muscle, but Emma had more. More fury. More indignation. More compassion to right a swindle.

Annette assailed Emma's hair with her free hand. Tears sizzled in Emma's eyes. Fair enough. If the woman was going to attack Emma's head, she could have all of it. Emma whacked the side of her skull into Annette's face.

"Uh! Let go." Annette muttered, one eye closed and watering. "I'll leave."

Emma wasn't buying anymore of her lies. She grasped the barrel of the gun and tugged with fervor.

The front door banged open.

"FBI. Don't move. Hands where I can see them," a man shouted.

Annette's arm slackened.

Emma ripped at the gun. The barrel budged. A shot erupted as the gun slipped out of her and Annette's hands and sailed toward the floor.

Blazing fire seared Emma's thigh.

The gun clattered until it stopped under Sam's kitchen table.

People dressed in black raced into the living room from the back bedrooms of Sam's house. Long guns resembling stiff elephant trunks took aim at Annette. One of the strangers retrieved the handgun.

Something was burning. Emma looked down. Her legging smoldered and the skin below looked like strawberry jam. She collapsed onto the floor. Touching the frayed cloth, her fingers became awash in blood. Tears filled her eyes as intense pain throbbed through her thigh. Leaning against a kitchen chair, she caught a glimpse of the FBI agent who had crashed through the front door.

"Jedediah?" Sam's neighbor turned his head briefly after securing Annette's last handcuff. Was she hallucinating? Her brain processed the sight in fuzzy, slow motion.

Annette thrashed against Jedediah's grip. "She threw a cactus at my face. Look at it. I need a doctor."

Jedediah pushed Annette outside.

Someone knelt next to Emma.

"Don't get up," the nice voice cautioned. "It'll be okay. An ambulance is coming."

A familiar voice shrieked her name from outside. Sam. She was at Sam's house.

Emma rolled her head to the side. Her body was numb except where her skin sizzled. Ron and Annette had ruined her life and left her crumpled on her best friend's floor, bleeding.

All the hurt of being abandoned by Wade engulfed her heart. She should have been answering phones in Nashville, but instead she was alone, penniless, and in pain. A flood of tears streamed down her cheeks.

Lord, I need You. I need Your refuge right now.

23

Wade parked his truck in front of the office. He should have been soaring like he was drag racing down a deserted highway. Driving again had been his final goal to achieve post-accident.

Until now.

He strode into the silence of the office. Emma and her gorgeous smile were gone. He missed her presence and her friendly greetings. He even missed her reminders for physical therapy. Hourly, he kicked himself for firing her and then sending generic good-bye flowers. Man, he'd been scared, confused, and out of the dating scene too long. Sam had told him to look for an opening with Emma, but he had sealed any cracks with sticky silver tape. What a jerk he'd been. Panic set in after talking to his attorney. All he could think about were the years of sweat and strife his family had gone through to finally meet success. Why couldn't he have focused on protecting the company and the beautiful woman God had placed in his life? His laser focus on the business had hurt Emma and cost him a future with a woman that was camping out in his thoughts.

He sat and stretched his arms in front of the main computer.

Clasping his hands, he began to pray. "Lord, I messed up. Please help me make things right with Emma. Give me wisdom on how to fix the mess I made by firing her. Help me reach out to her and ask forgiveness. Amen."

As he placed his phone on the counter desk, it rang.

Cole's name flashed on the screen.

He didn't feel like talking to his little brother, but Cole was a link to Emma. He swiped to answer.

"Hey, Cole."

"Are you driving?" Cole wasted no time with his inquisition.

"Not now. I just got back from the bank."

"Good." Except Cole sounded nervous like he was using the word and didn't mean it. "I don't know how to say this, so I'm going to spit it out."

"Okay, but you're taking a long time to spit." Wade didn't have much time before the office phone started ringing.

"I'm on my way to Whispering Creek. Sam's hysterical."

That didn't sound like got-it-all-together Sam. Wade's heart rate quickened.

"That woman." Cole cleared his throat. "Ron's assistant. She showed up at Sam's place."

Wade leapt to his feet. He paced in front of the computer feeling as if he had been doused with a cooler full of ice.

"There was a struggle." Cole's recounting of the incident raced through the phone. "Emma threw a cactus at the woman and fought to get the gun. She got shot."

Bracing a hand on the counter, Wade shivered at the mental image of Emma fighting off a killer. "Where did Emma get shot? How bad is it?"

"In the leg, I think. Sam was rambling." News flash. Cole was rambling. "I'm on my way to Memorial Hospital."

"In Whispering Creek?"

"Yeah."

Wade grabbed his jacket and keys. "I'm on my way." Would Emma even want to see him? He had to take the chance because if he didn't go now, the door to a relationship would disappear.

"You're coming? It's a weekday?"

Wade didn't have the energy to explain his reasons, or his feelings, to Cole. A thunderous pounding boomed in his head. His blood pressure boiled at the thought of someone hurting his sweet Emma.

"Yes, I'm coming, and I'm staying at your place."

Before his little brother could say another word, Wade ended the call. He wished he could fly straight to Whispering Creek or snap his fingers and be in the same room as Emma.

Okay, Lord, I'm diving in, and I'd really appreciate my presence at the hospital to be rewarded with a smile and not a slap. And I'll go ahead and say it, selfishly. I would like our reunion to end in a kiss, or two, or three...

Wade had to end that line of thinking.

I need You, Lord, 'cause I'm worried about Emma, and I won't be granny driving.

~*~

Emma lay in her hospital bed staring at her exposed leg. The emergency room doctor had cut off her legging at the upper thigh exposing the wreckage of Annette's bullet. The round had evaporated the cloth and seared Emma's skin, removing the flesh on contact. The doctor tried to clean her wound as gently as possible before wrapping it with loose gauze, but even with deadening medication, every movement of the doctor's fingers unearthed the sizzle of a flaming piece of coal. When her scream split the sound barrier, they gave her a dose of a giddy, floaty-feeling narcotic to calm her tremors.

She stroked her silver tortoise charm. Why couldn't everything in her life be solid and secure and comforting? Replaying the appearance of Annette sent a steady trickle of fright through her veins. So many things could have gone wrong. What if Annette discovered the flash drive was different? What if Sam had returned and been murdered? What if the bullet had struck Emma's knee or worse, an artery, or her heart? Hadn't her heart suffered enough damage?

The green line detecting her heart rate sped across the screen. Great. If her vitals continued to be elevated they may not let her go home. The cozy word pummeled her chest. She and Sam couldn't go to her place tonight because it was a designated crime scene. Either the government or Zach was paying for a motel in town. Correction, if Zach was paying, she was paying. Good thing she had no place to be in the morning like a job. Her eyes stung while the sensation of hovering a few inches above the mattress enveloped her body.

The nurse entered by pulling the privacy curtain open. "Where's your friend? I thought the poor thing would have a breakdown."

Sam had held her hand and shared childhood stories while the doctor initiated the flamethrower cleaning session. Sam had been her rock. No, Jesus had been her rock. *The Lord is my rock, my fortress and my deliverer.* God had protected her from Annette and even though there would be a scar on her thigh, Emma would be walking around in no time. If only she had some job where she felt worthwhile. If only Herbie had survived to be placed on her desk. If only a handsome electrician cared. If only....

The nurse widened her eyes. Oh, right. She had asked a question.

"Sam and her boyfriend went to grab something to eat. They're going to bring some food back for me. I think. I can't remember if I gave them my order."

The nurse checked the display. "You shouldn't be here too much longer. The doctor is working on discharge instructions. Your activity will be limited for a few days. Do you need a doctor's note for work? Or do you work from home?"

Why did everyone have to ask about employment? She grabbed the bed sheet and pulled it over her healthy leg. Her annoyance was being sprinkled with drug-induced glitter dust.

"I don't have a job at the moment."

"You do if you want one." Wade stood in the doorway and strode toward the foot of her bed. He held a square white box decorated with a heart sticker. Her own heart kicked up a notch awarding her with a loud beeping from the stat machine. This wasn't a hallucination. Wade was actually in her room looking too good in jeans and a dark green shirt. Did he realize he resembled a Green Bay fan? Best to keep that thought to herself.

She couldn't stop smiling. "Wade. You came." Her smile stuck on exuberant. "Wade." She turned to the nurse. "He's my um…" How did she explain her relationship with Wade to a stranger?

"I'll let you two have some privacy after I remove your arm wrap and pulse meter. Otherwise, you might have a rush of staff in here." Her eyebrows shot upward as she removed the Velcro sleeve. A knowing smirk strained the nurse's face as she left the room.

Wade stepped closer and held out the white box. "I brought you a peace offering. And I wanted to see how you were doing. I was worried about you. Driving the speed limit was almost impossible knowing that you got shot."

"You drove all the way out here for me?" Her heart softened like marshmallow cream.

"I care about you, Em."

She would have cried, but the meds were messing with her reactions. "Is that why there's a heart sticker on the box?"

His grin was way too sexy. "Yes."

That one word had her shifting in her bed and patting the mattress. "Come sit by me. I want to see my gift."

He handed her the box. "I think I remember how to take down the side rail. He bent and in an instant there wasn't any barricade between them.

"Are you sure you want me next to you?" He cast a glance at her bandaged thigh.

"Positive." Her brain shouted *sit, sit, sit* as she followed his every move.

Wade rested his left arm over her shoulders and nestled beside her on the bed. She had to resist the urge to burrow into his chest and stay there forever.

She opened the box, breaking the pink heart sticker into two pieces. Inside was a chocolate cactus with pecan and caramel flower pods on its limbs. "Oh, it's an edible Herbie."

"Do you like it? I was warned to avoid flowers. The gift shop woman looked at me funny when I said I needed a cactus made out of fudge and pecan clusters. But then you're the only woman I know who can apprehend a criminal with a cactus."

"I love it." She snapped off a piece of the chocolate and popped it into her mouth. The smooth, sweet, cocoa taste made her groan. She offered Wade a piece of his chocolate creation, and he obliged.

Her heart was flipping and flopping in Wade's strong, yet gentle embrace. He'd driven all the way to Whispering Creek after recently getting his medical release, and he brought her a chocolate Herbie. This guy was a keeper. How could she show him his presence meant the world to her? He meant the world to her.

She absorbed his affectionate gaze. "You have something on your lip."

"I do?" He shifted ever so slightly. "What?"

"Me." She pressed her lips into his. Wowza! Lip sparklers were lighting up the room. She broke for air. "If I was out of line, I'm blaming the drugs."

"Girl, you couldn't have fit more perfectly into those lines if you had tried." His smile was bigger than she had ever seen. This wasn't boss man Wade, or Cole's brother Wade, or the Wade she had prayed for. This was simply the Wade she knew with broad shoulders that supported the company and his family, and he was holding the door open for her to come inside his world. "Now, it's my turn. May I reciprocate?"

Yikes! "Yes, Sir."

His kiss was sweeter the second time around even without chocolate and caramel.

Voices filtered in through the doorway.

Sam and Cole entered with drinks and sandwiches.

"We brought your dinner." Sam's mouth gaped. "Oh, Wade. You made it."

The look of shock on Sam's face was endearing.

Emma inwardly laughed at her friend. "We were in the middle of dessert." She displayed the chocolate cactus.

"Well, you know, practice makes permanent." Sam bit her lip attempting to stifle a laugh. "We'll come back in a few minutes."

"Wait, what?" Cole held up the tray of drinks.

"Listen to the teacher, little brother." Wade tipped Emma's chin so all she could see was his wonderous smile. "Where were we?"

"Beginning our practice." She was floating, and this time it was real.

She began to make a list of all the ways that Wade was an excellent kisser when someone shuffled into the room and cleared their throat. Really. Was a neon green enter sign posted outside of her room? She broke the kiss and noticed

Jedediah hovering near the door. Too bad Sam hadn't closed the curtain.

Jedediah held up his hands in a defensive posture. "I'm not here to ask you any questions. Your attorney has placed everyone on notice that anything you say with drugs in your system is inadmissible in court. Though, we pretty much have everything on camera." Jedediah lowered his hands and crossed his thick arms over his black bulletproof vest. "I came to see how you were doing. My parents probably won't let me in the door if I don't check on you and Sam."

Wade nuzzled near her ear. "Who is this guy? Want me to make him leave?"

Wade's protectiveness made her want to give him another kiss.

"Jedediah saved my life. He's an FBI agent and the son of Sam's neighbors." Wait. Was that the truth? "You are Gretta and Ernie's son, aren't you?"

"Yes. I'll claim them." Jedediah grinned. "And I am an FBI agent, but I wasn't here to work on the Runyard case. It seems God had me in the right place at the right time."

"You've got my thanks for saving my girl." Wade winked at her and sent a zing to her heart.

"Hold onto that thought," she said to Wade before returning her attention to Jedediah. "You were the first one through the door. How could you not be involved?"

Jedediah motioned to a chair stationed in the corner near the bed. "Do you mind if I sit?" He ambled over and engulfed the chair kicking out his black boots. "I was planning to come to Whispering Creek soon enough since I had just finished a case in Florida. Before I had finalized plans, my dad called and told me about a guy out in front of Sam's place. Dad said you were in town and that you'd been scammed. I put two and two together when Runyard's name came up. My boss knew I was returning to Whispering Creek, and he told me to keep my eyes open. I had an alibi to be in town."

She shifted in the bed to get a better look at Jedediah. "I'm glad you were here. Thank you. I was scared out of my wits."

Wade massaged her shoulder. Bless him.

"The team assigned to the Runyard case had tracked Annette." Jedediah made loose quotations with his hands. "From Wisconsin to Michigan and then to Toronto. They had no idea she was in Tennessee." Jedediah shook his long head of hair. "It must have been a God thing because I left to go into town this morning, and I noticed a Michigan license plate near Main Street. I called it in to my boss, and the car had been rented in the name of an old alias that Annette had used. We scrambled to get a team together ASAP."

Wade broadened his shoulders. "Why'd they let that woman get so close to Emma? I've been praising God that she's not in surgery or worse."

"Annette shouldn't have gotten that close to Emma." Jedediah pressed his hands together almost like saying a prayer. "I'm sorry."

She cast a glance at Wade, and they shared a knowing look.

"I don't understand what went wrong, but we'll find out. Your attorney will make sure of it. That guy's a jackal." Jedediah scratched his short beard. "I owe my mom big time since I had her call Sam to get one asset out of harm's way. I was sure the intercept of Annette would happen before she got to the shed."

Emma closed her eyes and willed all the horrible memories of her encounter with Annette to disappear.

"When I turned around and saw that gun pointed at me, I almost peed my leggings."

"I almost peed mine, too." Jedediah's eyebrows rose.

"Well, my pants when they let the perp get too close to you."
He stood. "Like I said, I'm sorry. We can talk later if you want.
I'll let you two get back to what you were doing." Jedediah's
lips flattened as if he was holding in a laugh.

Her cheeks flamed.

"And don't worry about the fallout." Jedediah shoved his
hands in his pockets. "I have it on good authority that in the
rental car was a flash drive with some type of peeps software
on it. A source says that it belongs to you. How Runyard and
Annette got so sloppy is beyond me."

"It's beyond me too." Emma swept her bangs behind her
ear. "I guess that's another God thing. Although next time, I
am going to petition that God's will won't involve guns and
gangsters."

"When you're feeling better, I'm sure my mom will have
y'all over for pot roast and cheesy potatoes." Jedediah did a
weak salute and exited the room.

Her stomach rumbled at the thought of potatoes, butter,
and melted cheese. Chocolate was nice, but she couldn't fill
her whole belly with it. At least, not at the moment.

She gazed into Wade's eyes and dove into the
mesmerizing sea of blue.

"Praise God that He watched over you, Emma. I would
have missed you." His voice cracked with emotion. "Really,
really missed you." He kissed her all serious, and deep, and
wonderful.

She gasped for air. "Just to be clear. I'm not working for
you, right? Because after that kiss, if I wasn't fired, I'd have to
fire myself."

24

Wade slung his rucksack over his shoulder, closed the door to his truck, and followed Cole into his apartment in Sperry's Crossing. Leaving Emma in Whispering Creek at the motel with Sam had him unsettled and with enough restless energy that he could punch a wall. Reinjuring a hand wouldn't do him any good. He'd made his feelings clear to Emma, and now she had to decide if she wanted to stay in Tennessee or eventually return to Wisconsin. Owning a family business kept him tethered to Nashville.

Cole flipped on the lights. The clock on the oven showed that it was after eleven.

Nine long hours until he would see Emma again. He and Cole had agreed to meet the girls for breakfast and to deliver boxes of candles to the elementary school. Leave it to Emma to help local children after being shot. He missed her spunk and her big heart. He missed her kisses, too.

"I've got a futon in my den." Cole stretched his arms toward the ceiling and let out a short yawn. "I doubt you want to bunk with me."

"You've got that right. I need to get a good night's sleep." Wade dumped his rucksack on the sofa. Since when did his brother have pillows and a quilt on his couch?

"Are you driving back tomorrow?"

Wade collapsed on the couch. "I'm clear through Monday."

"Monday?" Cole's features awakened like he'd downed a double espresso. "How'd you manage that? I can't remember the last time you were gone from the company for four days. Well, except for when you were in the hospital or immobile."

His brother didn't need to know that the news of possibly losing Emma to a gunshot had him calling home and almost losing it on the phone with his mom. Mom had volunteered to cover the office and oversee the temporary help, a rarity since his mom had sworn off working with her husband years ago.

"The temp agency is sending someone for Friday." He glanced at his phone. "In an hour it will be today. Mom is going to cover the weekend with dad's help."

"Mom is?" Cole shuffled to the kitchen and opened a cupboard. He pulled out two glasses and started filling them with water. "That's a shock."

"She wanted me to be here with Emma." Wade drummed his fingers on the soft quilt on top of the couch. Definitely a Sam addition. "Mom also quipped that she'd like grandchildren before age seventy."

Cole handed him a glass of water and sat on the other end of the couch. "Seems like you and Emma are starting something."

Something. "Sam told me to look for an opening. Emma getting attacked and shot is a gaping hole."

"So, she's staying in Tennessee." Cole eyed him over the lip of his glass.

"I don't know." He'd gone all in leaving work, driving to the hospital in Whispering Creek, and buying a gift that was as unique and special as Emma. He prayed it was enough to show her how he felt. His life had been a carnival twisty ride for months. The end of the thrill ride had been the goal of walking without a cane and driving a service van. Now he wanted more. He wanted life to settle down. He wanted to settle down. Settle down with Emma. She made work fun. "I hope so."

Cole ran a hand through his hair, tugging on his scalp. He must be wiped as well. Sam had been leaning on him for support at the hospital.

"Ya know, after my last break up, when I wasn't speaking to you or Dad, I came out to Whispering Creek to see Ted. Only to find out he had passed away."

Wade took a sip of his water. "Is this a pep talk?"

Cole laughed. "Possibly. Mom had given me a devotional and wrote Philippians 4:13 on the cover. I can do everything through Christ who gives me strength."

"She repeated that to me in the hospital." Over and over. *Thank you, Mom.*

"Well, I met Sam right before your accident, and that's working out well." Cole relaxed against the side of the sofa. "I've been praying for you bro, and I'm not going to stop."

"I don't know what else I can do but pray." Wade downed his water. "I just got over rehab from my accident. I don't think I have the energy to rehab my heart." He leaned his head back against the quilt. "Hear that Jesus, I need some help here. How do I get a woman to love me enough to stay? And can I get the answer by Monday night because on Tuesday I have to get back to running a company."

~*~

Emma shimmied higher against the headboard in her hotel room bed. She couldn't sleep. Adrenaline streaked through her veins every time she relived the moment of Annette's arrival. All the what ifs played in a loop in her mind. When she remembered Wade's lips on hers, the drama and trauma disappeared. That man could kiss! Ugh. Sleep was impossible.

"Sam," she whispered.

"What?" Sam rolled her direction in the queen bed

opposite Emma's. "There's a patrol outside. We'll be safe."

"I know. I just can't sleep. Will you come next to me?" By the light from the alarm clock on the nightstand, she could see Sam sit on the edge of her bed.

"Aren't you afraid I'll bump your leg?"

"Nah, I scooched over." Emma flung the sheet and blanket open for Sam to slide in.

Sam settled in beside her. "Are you in pain?"

"Some." A throb reminded Emma of her scorched skin. "I don't want to take any pain pills. I can't think straight afterward."

Giggles erupted from Sam's side of the bed. "Because of Wade?" The laughter morphed into kissing sounds.

"Oh, please. I'll never get any rest." A tear threatened to stain her cheek. Why was she emotional about Wade? Or was her body short circuiting after the stress. She lay flat and snuggled into her pillow. "What am I going to do about Wade?"

"Move to Nashville."

"That's easier said than done." The weight of being an only child pressed down on her chest making breaths difficult. "What about my parents?"

"They'll manage." Sam repositioned herself in the bed. "Mine are adjusting."

Emma could see her friend's silhouette. The psychiatrist was beginning a session.

"You came here to spare your parents any blowback from Ron's fraud. You did that. They don't know about the shooting or Annette's apprehension. They're blissfully happy. Why can't you be?"

Sam understood the weight of being an only child. Parents didn't stay young and healthy forever, but Sam's parents knew Jesus. They went to church and talked openly about their faith. Emma had shared about Jesus with her parents, but the words fell on hard bricks not softened hearts.

"You know why." Emma gripped the thin bed sheet. "Who's going to share the Gospel with my parents and help them if they get sick? Besides, it takes money to break a lease and pay a deposit on a new apartment. A girl's got to eat."

"But I have…"

"I'm not taking any money from you. My pride has taken enough of a beating lately." In a matter of weeks, she had been swindled, fired, and threatened with death.

"I know. When I came to Whispering Creek, I had been through cancer treatments, and Carlton had dumped me. I had lost Mr. Ted. He was one of the most important people in my life. God had a plan that I didn't even know about, and here I am, looking forward to what God has for me in the future. I'm not looking backward." Sam grasped her hand. "Is Wade worth a new beginning?"

A vision of her endearing former boss had a thrill of energy rallying her insomnia. "You know he is. I should be racing toward Nashville, but I have one leg stuck behind the cheddar curtain."

Sam chuckled. "I could go for some fried cheese curds."

"Stop it. After eating chocolate, crackers, hospital gelatin, and a soggy sandwich, I can't wait to get to Lucinda's café for breakfast."

Sam gave Emma's hand a squeeze. "We'll keep praying. God should have opened a direct line for us by now. And trust Him with your parents' salvation. You've planted a garden of seeds. Maybe it's time for someone else to do the watering of their faith."

"Ah." Emma rested her head on Sam's shoulder. "You're the best friend ever. I love you."

"I love you, too. Now, we have to get some sleep. Enjoy

the weekend with Wade, and let your attorney handle all the fallout."

"I'm seeing Zach on Monday. Wade is driving me." Would that be one of their last days together for a while or the beginning of an exciting tomorrow? She had been praying for the Lord's direction. "I never thought I would say this, but perhaps there's a chance my lawyer can help me sort out my future. After Jesus, of course."

Sam laughed again sending Emma's face jiggling.

"That's the first time I have heard the name of Jesus associated with attorneys."

"Well Sam, you and I have had a lot of firsts in the past few months." And just maybe Jesus would give her the strength to embrace one more.

25

Emma grasped Wade's hand as they walked into the opulent lobby of her attorney's building. Only two weeks ago, Wade had been sporting a cane, this afternoon she gripped one. A leopard print cane to steady her in case her wound throbbed.

Eight days ago, she had retained Zach as her attorney, and since their meeting, she had stared down the gun of a murderer, survived being shot, and fallen in love with, dare she say it, her boyfriend, who happened to be her former boss. She had fled to Whispering Creek for the quiet country life. God had other plans for her getaway, and He had orchestrated each twist and turn. Too bad she had let fear and worry tarnish some of her trust in Jesus.

Wade let out a low whistle. "You've got one fancy attorney." Wade looked fancy in his white cotton shirt, gray slacks, and black wingtips. He resembled a high-powered legal mind. She'd take a small business owner any day. She and Wade understood the world of customer service, managing inventory, and paying invoices. The fact that they shared a faith in God was icing on the cookie.

"I'm not so sure fancy is the word I would use to describe Zach. He's more like one of those marble pillars. Unshakable."

"Glad he's on our side." Wade flashed a reassuring smile and kissed her cheek.

Good thing she had a balancing stick to keep her steady. "I've been thinking about how God has been on my side all along. I had a hard time seeing it. I'm sure God could handle one more hurdle, but I'm happy we have Zach to do the paperwork."

"I am too." He snuggled her hand into his crisp, warm shirt. "God's been on double duty taking care of both of us."

"Amen to that." *Amen, Amen, and Amen.*

When they entered Zach's suite, the receptionist opened her acrylic-glass window. Her guarded smile actually seemed genuine.

"Emma. Mr. West will see you in his office."

Office? No conference room. "Great. Thank you."

"I'll wait out here." Wade looked as comfortable as a kitten doused in a kiddy pool.

Should he stay out in the waiting area? He'd seen her giddy and with mottled makeup in the emergency room. He knew about the flash drive because he believed in her customer service skills and had asked to see her software. They had handled dog bites and confused elderly clients together. She'd seen him grumpy and resentful about his injuries. They'd seen each other at their best and at their flustered, grouchy worst, but they made a good team, compensating for the shortfalls.

Peace flooded her. A true peace only given by God. Life wasn't a set of coincidences. God had ordained each part of her journey. The parts with Wade and the parts without him. The parts with Wade by her side were better.

She didn't want her friendship with Wade to end. A future with Wade meant staying in Tennessee. Stating that fact, in this moment, didn't frighten her.

"I'd like you to come with me." She stroked his cotton-clad arm and held onto his impressive bicep. "If it wasn't for you asking to see my software, I would be living with a dangerous stalker, and in fear of what the future held. I'm thankful to be nearing the end of all this chaos."

He bent down and flashed a slightly surprised, kissable grin. "I like this ending. And I'm not sorry for saying it."

Warmth crept into her cheeks while the sparks in her belly turned into an inferno. "We make the best team."

A throat clearing sound came from the doorway. The receptionist stood against the wooden door motioning them into the hallway. "Mr. West's office is at the end of the hall."

"Thank you." Emma released Wade's arm and used her spotted cane to pivot and enter the hallway.

Wade followed, and as they neared the specified door, it opened, and Zach ushered them inside.

Emma introduced Wade to her attorney.

"Donoven. As in Donoven and Sons Electric?" Zach shook Wade's hand. "You were Emma's boss and discovered the contents of the flash drive."

"I'm one and the same." Wade was taller and broader than Zach, but somehow her attorney gave off the aura of being able to win in a cage match.

Should she mention to Zach that Wade was now her boyfriend. She'd wait. She would wager that Zach knew how to read a room and had noticed every nuance.

Zach indicated for them to sit in chairs in front of a sleek black standing desk with a rectangular lower portion. The configuration could pass as command central. The standing desk housed two large computer screens with a third screen lower down and even with a padded office chair.

"And how are you after that gunshot, Emma? I had some heated conversations about the oversight of contacting counsel."

"The wound is healing." As she sat, Emma tugged at her paisley dress to prevent the material from rubbing her bandage. She'd had to shop for some cheap dresses with better air flow and comfort. Another expense she couldn't afford.

"The burning has died down. I'm more in itch mode."

"Good. Good." Zach faced them from behind his flat top desk. His bushy eyebrows rose toward his shaved scalp. "I mean, it's a good thing for the government that you're healing. Pain and suffering is a negotiable amount." Zach nodded like she tracked with his legalese. He opened a monogrammed leather portfolio. "Our class action suit is gaining steam. I believe we'll eventually be successful in making partial refunds to the victims of Ron's fraud. After attorney's fees, of course."

Fees? A throb settled in her temples. She prayed she wouldn't have to pay Zach any more money right now. She needed to find a source of income and save money to rent an apartment in Nashville. She also had to break a lease in Milwaukee.

"The feds are dealing with Annette." Zach threw up his hands. "Or whatever her name is. How they lost her trail is beyond me with all the technology at their disposal. Speaking of." Zach opened a tiny drawer almost invisible to the eye. "I have a copy of your software. The original will be held as evidence, but I negotiated access to your material."

She was sure she had a recent copy of People Peeps in the cloud, but seeing her creation sitting on top of Zach's desk gave her a sense of pride.

Wade laid his hand on top of hers. "I'd like to get a look at that now that all the financials are gone. You are one talented office manager." His thumb caressed the back of her hand. How was she going to concentrate? She melted inside like a chocolate Herbie.

Her heart hitched. Herbie had helped save her life. Good thing Sam had repotted what was left of him in a new container along with his Scripture stone. Herbie had been part of her life for nearly a decade. Now, Wade was becoming part of her life.

"I guess this is as good a time as any for me to put the finishing touches on my software." She smiled even though she had started two jobs recently and was zero for two.

"We'll take a statement today, but you won't need to come downtown much anymore." Zach bounced his pen on his desk. "I was told that most of the perp's movements were caught on camera, and there's even audio of her claiming ownership of the drive. There shouldn't be any legal issues regarding your involvement. Your financials haven't been flagged for large deposits. It's more case work for me from here on out." Zach opened another drawer on his desk and pulled out an envelope.

Was it a bill? Was he expecting her to add to the retainer? She couldn't. Not today. Her pulse quickened. She prayed there were funds remaining.

Zach scribbled on a yellow pad. "I'll need to update any new contact information. I have your phone number and an address for Samantha Williams. Are you staying in Whispering Creek with her?"

"No. I'm moving."

Wade's intimate hand massage halted. He resembled the guarded man who had shuffled into her emergency room cautious, yet hopeful. She should have told him of her plans, but she'd only felt at peace about a decision when they entered Zach's waiting room.

She showered Wade with a hundred-watt smile. "I'm going to find an apartment in Nashville."

"You are?" Wade was holding her hand with both of his now. Two healthy hands. If they weren't in front of a lawyer's desk, she imagined him carefully tugging her into his lap.

Yowza! She needed to get her head back in the law game.

"Wonderful. That makes it easier for me." Zach wrote on

his legal pad.

"I'll be staying with the Donovens until I can save enough money to cover rent. I think you have their address."

"I do." Zach's serious, all-business expression softened for a milli-second. "I also think I can help you out with the apartment hunt." He handed her the envelope.

She hated to reclaim her hand from Wade, but curiosity had her opening the unsealed envelope. Did Zach know someone in real estate? He probably knew the best of the best of realtors. More than likely, it was a bill. She pulled out a piece of paper. A check. No, two checks. The first one was made out to her for twenty-five thousand dollars. The second one was for five thousand dollars." Her mouth gaped. What had she done to deserve this money?

"Do lawyers give advances?"

Zach chuckled at her response. "Not that I know of. Remember when I told you I had other clients that were swindled by Ron Runyard. Well, one of them posted a reward for information leading to the whereabouts of the money. The other is a government reward for help in apprehending his accomplice. You did both. I made sure the wire transfers came as soon as possible." Zach leaned forward on his desk. "This is the beginning of justice. I hope to recapture more of Ron's funds for you and my other clients."

She slouched in her chair, her mind swirling with disbelief. Most of the worries clouding her future dissipated with one glance at a cashier's check. She didn't have to overstay her welcome with Mike and Linda. She could pay off her credit card and buy some clothes, even a pair of western boots. She could pay rent and afford the deposit. Simply, she had time to heal and to decide what to do next. Her eyes grew tingly. *Thank You, Jesus. You truly are my deliverer.*

"I don't know what to say. Thank you, Zach. This is a

huge blessing." She handed the envelope to Wade.

Wade relaxed against the cushy client chair and scanned the contents of the envelope. His initial wide-eyed disbelief turned into a glistening, twinkling joy which embraced her heart. He handed her the reward money and caressed her shoulder with his hand. She was growing accustomed to Wade's affectionate side.

"You deserve this reward, Emma." Wade's voice caught with emotion. "God has placed it in the best hands. Praise the Lord."

She couldn't have said it better or with more gratitude, herself.

~*~

Later, on Monday afternoon, Emma closed the door to her bedroom at Mike and Linda's. The Donoven guest room fit like a comfy old shoe. She took out her phone and called home now that all the drama had died down.

"Hi, honey." The glee in her mother's voice caused a tiny tingle in Emma's eyes. She missed her mom.

"Did I catch you at a good time?" Emma perched on the bedspread trying to get comfortable. She caressed the silver tortoise charm on her necklace. Her grandmother had been right. With God as her rock, Emma had been tough as a tortoise shell surviving Ron and Annette's schemes. "Do you have time to talk?" Emma worried her parents were busy with their business.

"We're at home. The girl we hired for the holidays, Isabel, has been working out well. She's closing the store for us tonight."

"That's great." Emma's heart sank a half-notch, but she kept her voice upbeat. She had always been there to help her parents, but if recent life lessons had taught her anything, it was that she couldn't be there for her parents every second of every day. A support system for her parents was a blessing.

"You know what's so funny. Isabel invited us to church." Her mom sounded happy, not dismayed.

"Really. That's wonderful." *Thank You, Jesus.* All the invitations Emma had given her parents to join her at church had been met with a threadbare excuse until they begrudgingly came at Easter and Christmas. "Which one?"

"The one by our house. On the busy corner."

Emma stood, grabbed her cane, and paced across the rug. "Are you going?" She tempered her enthusiasm as if she asked a mundane question about dinner options. Her heart drummed an ecstatic beat.

"I don't know. We're thinking about it." Optimism, and less hesitation, buoyed her mom's tone.

Emma tamped the angelic choir harmonizing in her brain. She had prayed, and prayed, and prayed for years for her parents to know Jesus. God's timing wasn't her timing. How well she knew that after the last few weeks.

"You seem happy believing in God. You always say He's watching over you."

Emma let out a short laugh. "Yeah, about that. Are you sitting down?"

26

Emma hurried into Wade's kitchen. The aroma of hot cooking oil permeated the air. Her heart did a contented ecstatic dance seeing Wade wearing an apron and slicing jalapeños. She could get accustomed to this image.

"I scheduled the game to record for an hour beforehand and extended it an hour past what should be the end of regulation. I also placed a jar on the living room table. If anyone mentions the opposing team they owe us a quarter."

"I'm feeling a Tennessee win." Wade's exuberance almost had her changing allegiance from Green Bay. Almost. She had changed states to be near Wade, but she clung to her football team.

Wade motioned her over. "Come help me with the bottle caps. You can dip the slices in the batter, and I'll fry them."

As she came closer to wash her hands, he kissed her lips. "Those jalapeños aren't the only thing that's sizzling."

"Hold that thought 'til later." His grin was spicier than the peppers.

The doorbell rang.

"It's us." Cole entered the kitchen holding two square cardboard boxes with a white bag on top. "The pizza guy arrived at the same time as we did. He said to thank you for the tip."

Sam plunked a huge container of ranch dressing on the counter. "We have dipping sauce for the wings and whatever is permeating this kitchen." She displayed a small bottle. "Sriracha is in the house."

"A game day favorite. Something spicier than cheese and sausage." Wade's teasing grin was delicious.

She lightly bumped his arm as she coated her first jalapeño in batter. "There's nothing wrong with cheese and sausage."

"You tell them, Em." Sam removed her coat and revealed an 'I love my teacher' hoodie. First grade would never be the same in Whispering Creek.

"Tell them what? Are my boys behaving?" Linda headed straight toward the refrigerator. "I brought the ice cream. Tin Roof for the host and Fudge Swirl for the rest of us."

"I never got a tub of my favorite flavor." Cole crossed his arms and leaned against the doorway.

"You can host next time." Wade shifted some browned jalapeños onto a paper towel lined plate.

"No one wants to drive out our way." Cole held Sam's hand. "Now that Emma is going to live here, we're outnumbered."

Emma bit back a smile. She loved the banter between the Donoven men and their parents. Sam had been like a sister, and now she and Sam were dating brothers. Their circle of family and friends had expanded. Instinctively, she went to stroke her tortoise charm and thought better of it with battered fingers.

What would make this day perfect was if her parents could enjoy the Super Bowl with her, Sam, and the Donovens. But leave it to God. He had even better plans. Incredible plans. Her mom and dad had suggested coming for Easter and going to church with her and Wade. God worked in mysterious ways, so she would trust Him and enjoy the journey.

"Emma? I'm ready for the last of the jalapeños." Wade

towered over her in his apron-covered football jersey.

He had caught her daydreaming while she soaked in the dynamics of his family. Her jaw ached while she beamed her biggest smile at him. "And I'm ready for a new beginning in Nashville with you."

Wade gave her a sizzling kiss which only stopped when the oil started burning.

~*~

Wade closed the door and leaned his back against the smooth wood after his family finally left. His throat burned from screaming at the referees and celebrating a Super Bowl win. Now was the best part of the night. Better than a franchise championship. He wanted to spend some alone time with Emma. She'd been the perfect hostess organizing the food and helping with the cleanup. After being shot, she'd come into the office to cover the lunch hour for the temporary hire. He'd been out on service calls during the day, but he would wager a quarter that the phone rang non-stop with customers wanting to speak with Emma.

She'd made him a better man. And he had not only opened his heart to her, but to his family and friends, and the world around him. Bitterness did not plague him about his trials.

Emma lounged on the throw pillows that she'd bought to accent his couch cushions. A candle burned on the living room table. Nothing in his life at the moment, except for God, burned brighter than Emma.

He sat next to her on the cushion and gently resettled her onto his lap making sure her dress didn't drag on her wound.

"Do you realize that a few weeks ago, I wouldn't have been able to hold you or hold onto you."

"We definitely don't need any fumbles or dropped

passes." She quirked an eyebrow and smiled that high-energy smile.

He laughed at her quick-witted reply. Emma made him feel as if he chased a kite. Happy, free, and soaring.

She slid her arms around his neck and sent a quiver across his nerve endings. "God held onto both of us. And He taught me to hold on tight."

Wade kissed her, knowing one thing for sure. This time, he wasn't letting go, and he wasn't the least bit sorry.

A Note from Barbara

Thank you for returning to Whispering Creek, Tennessee with me. If this is your first time reading about my quaint town, then welcome to the amazing foursome of Sam, Cole, Emma, and Wade.

My characters have had upheaval in their lives. Cancer, bodily injury, breakups, and even white-collar crime have brought turmoil into their daily living. Thankfully, getting back into a right relationship with God, or clinging to Him with gusto, has gotten my characters through tough, emotional times. I hope you have Jesus as your rock, too.

I am a breast cancer survivor, and Jesus was my rock through challenging times. Battling cancer makes you realize that every day is a gift from God. I've learned to cherish waking up in the morning. Even though Emma didn't understand God's plan for her life, He was there with her, guiding her steps.

Wisconsin has been my home for over twenty years, and yes, I am a Green Bay fan. I may follow Tennessee closely over the next few years. My trips to Nashville have been memorable, and I wish we had some of their weather in the heart of winter. I hope you enjoyed the nods to my home state and to Tennessee.

With all the books on the market today, I am humbled and ecstatic that you chose to read mine. Thank you. If you have time to review, recommend, or tell others about this book on social media, I appreciate that, too.

May the Lord bless you and keep you.

ACKNOWLEDGEMENTS

This book would not have been possible without the help of so many people. My family has been the best cheering section throughout my publishing career. I am blessed to have their love, encouragement, and support.

A big thank you goes to my editor, Fay Lamb, who helped improve Emma and Wade's story, and to Nicola Martinez who has made my books a reality for readers.

My critique partners cheered me on while writing this story. Without their input, these pages would not shine as bright. Thank you, Sandy Goldsworthy, Olivia Rae, and Kathy Zdanowski.

The author communities of ACFW, RWA, SCBWI, and my publisher Pelican Book Group, have been a huge support in my writing career. The original Barnes & Noble Brainstormers continue to encourage my spirit. Thank you Jill Bevers, Karen Miller, Betsy Norman, and Sandra Turriff.

My church family has kept me going during good times and challenging times.

I want to thank Gale Pearson for the wise counsel of practice makes permanent. Both my boys learned this saying in Ms. Pearson's third grade class. I'm grateful to Burki Electric for answering my electrical questions, again.

And last, but not least, praise to The Lord God Almighty, for giving me the gift of creativity and breath each day to write these stories. To God be the glory.

THANK YOU

We appreciate you reading this White Rose Publishing title.
For other inspirational stories, please visit our on-line
bookstore at www.pelicanbookgroup.com.

For questions or more information, contact us at
customer@pelicanbookgroup.com.

White Rose Publishing
Where Faith is the Cornerstone of Love™
an imprint of Pelican Book Group
www.PelicanBookGroup.com

Connect with Us
www.facebook.com/Pelicanbookgroup
www.twitter.com/pelicanbookgrp

To receive news and specials, subscribe to our bulletin
http://pelink.us/bulletin

May God's glory shine through
this inspirational work of fiction.

AMDG

You Can Help!

Pelican Book Group's mission is to entertain readers with fiction that uplifts the Gospel. It is our privilege to spend time with you as you read our stories.

We believe you can help us to bring Christ into the lives of people across the globe. And you don't have to open your wallet or even leave your house!

Here are 3 simple things you can do to help us bring illuminating fiction™ to people everywhere.

1) If you enjoyed this book, write a positive review. Post it at online retailers and websites where readers gather. And share your review with us at reviews@pelicanbookgroup.com (this does give us permission to reprint your review in whole or in part.)

2) If you enjoyed this book, recommend it to a friend in person, at a book club or on social media.

3) If you have suggestions on how we can improve or expand our selection, let us know. We value your opinion. Use the contact form on our web site or e-mail us at customer@pelicanbookgroup.com

GOD CAN HELP!

Are you in need? The Almighty can do great things for you. Holy is His Name! He has mercy in every generation. He can lift up the lowly and accomplish all things. Reach out today.

Do not fear: I am with you; do not be anxious: I am your God. I will strengthen you, I will help you, I will uphold you with my victorious right hand.

~Isaiah 41:10 (NAB)

We pray daily, and we especially pray for everyone connected to Pelican Book Group—that includes you! If you have a specific need, we welcome the opportunity to pray for you. Share your needs or praise reports at http://pelink.us/pray4us

FREE eBook Offer

We're looking for booklovers like you to partner with us! Join our team of influencers today and periodically receive free eBooks!

For more information
Visit http://pelicanbookgroup.com/booklovers